THE BLOOD MOON PROPHECY

The Prophecy To End All Prophecies

Lauren J. Brown

For all the sons and daughters of God
who shall prophesy

TABLE OF CONTENTS

The Blood Moon Prophecy

Peter stood up with the Eleven, raised his voice, and proclaimed to them, "Fellow Jews and all you residents of Jerusalem, let this be known to you and pay attention to my words. For these people are not drunk, as you suppose, since it's only nine in the morning. On the contrary, this is what was spoken through the prophet Joel:

And it will be
in the last days, says God,
That I will pour out my Spirit on all people;
then your sons and your daughters
will prophesy,
your young men will
see visions,
and your old men will
dream dreams.
I will even pour out
my Spirit
on my servants
in those days, both men
and women
And they will prophesy.
I will display wonders
in the heaven above
and signs
on the earth below:
blood and fire and a cloud
of smoke.
The sun will be turned
to darkness
and the moon to blood
before the great and
glorious day of the Lord comes.
Then everyone who calls on the name of the Lord will be saved."

Acts 2:14-21 (HCSB, emphasis and italics added)

Preface

Before we begin this journey through the starry night of *The Blood Moon Prophecy*, I want to preface this book with a word from my heart. As a minister unto Jesus, I want his heart to shine through every piece of this prophecy. It is his perfect light that exposes darkness and it is incredible love that pierces the hearts of men with a perfect, undeniable holiness. It is my goal as a believer to reveal the Holy Trinity in this work. These revelations and findings came about by the power of The Holy Spirit, by the Father anointing His word, and by the great Rabbi Jesus teaching me. Proverbs 25:2 reads, "It is the glory of God to conceal a matter; to search out a matter is the glory of kings," so while the scriptures may not explicitly state all of the facts I am going to discuss in the book, the mysteries of the stories and the characters in them are there, waiting to be sought out and revealed to us by The Holy Spirit. I do not by any means claim myself an expert in the field of eschatology, end time prophecy, or ancient history but I do write as a humble human under the hand of a holy, omniscient, loving, everlasting God.

It is in this position as daughter of the King that I write from a place of servitude, gratitude, and joy. Though parts of this book will contain hard truths and unsettling information, the goal of this writing is to edify, equip, and *encourage*. This is a story woven by God of redemption, restoration, and a future hope for his beloved. This is not a book to glorify Satan, fallen angels, or demons. The aim of this book is not to make more conspiracy theorists, or instill a fear theology, or broadcast doom and gloom. However, it is a book to inform people of the enemy's evil schemes, his wicked agenda, and his ultimate defeat. This is essentially a source to help the bride of Christ prepare for her bridegroom, to seek God while He may be found, and to bring the light of the Gospel to all nations.

I have done my due diligence in prayer, schooling, research and analysis and have made it a point to notate any postulations, conjectures, or speculative information as well as any areas with scant research. While I strive for excellence, I am not perfect so I ask that you read with grace as well as humility, and I encourage you to use your own God-given set of lenses, letting the discernment of God be your guide.

The blood of Jesus is able to save to the uttermost and so if you are reading this book and feel at any time guilt, shame, or condemnation in any way, please know that Satan is the voice behind such thoughts. Jesus' voice is one of forgiveness, mercy, justice, and hope. His love covers a multitude of sins. Additionally, if along this journey you feel inadequate, disappointed, or afraid, please know that God's perfect love casts out all fear and peace *is* your portion.

My prayer as you read this book is that your spiritual eyes and ears would be open to the Lion and the Lamb's voice, your heart would be tender to explore the hidden places of God, your soul would desire to jump into the deep water of knowledge; that you would receive a renewed mind of greater understanding, a ready and willing spirit for the days ahead, and an incredible revelation of the love of Jesus for you and your household.

If there is anything you take from this book, I pray you take the simplicity of the Gospel: Jesus died for you, he rose again for you, he empowers you, and he is coming back for you because *He loves you.*

In His Hands and with His love,
Lauren

INTRODUCTION
The Blood Battle

A wisp of earthen smoke weaved in and out of the mens' whispers. Broken voices crackled with the fires. Murmurs of prophecy mingled with smoke and dust, floating up to the sky like incense. But the smoky dust that night wasn't brown from the kickup of horses' hooves nor was it gray from the scattered campfires surrounded by exhausted soldiers. No. The smoke blanketing the camps was neither of those colors; rather, it was crimson in hue with a hint of orange like fresh oxygenated blood.

As the soldiers watched the firey red smoke lift from the piled branches, their muddied and bloodied faces met the moon's gaze. The moon, to their sheer unbelief, was *crimson*, a red moon, an omenic *blood moon* as the diviners and stargazers had taught them in their homelands. The moon's sanguine reflection tinted the air and their murmurs. Could this be an omen? Was this a sign sent from the heavens? How would this affect their leaders' military strategy in the coming hours of the night? Would they be eclipsed by their enemy, fighting again to a bloody death or would they be covered by prophecy, reigning victoriously in the starlight? The suspicious chatter united the fighting armies for a moment. Their interpretations divided them forever.

On the night of September 20, 331 B.C., Alexander III of Macedon, also known as Alexander the Great, and Emperor Darius III of Persia locked eyes on a common denominator– the moon. They, along with their tired and waning armies, pondered its meaning. The Battle of Gaugamela was hours away and so were the spirits of Alexander's men. The Macedonians had astoundingly won four previous battles and acquired territories under the young, iconic military leader in just three years but they had also felt the incredible loss of friends and brothers, of familiar culture and comfort. Not only was homesickness and physical exhaustion weighing down Alexander's army, but so was the immeasurable weight of worry surrounding the unknown outcome of the impending battle.

Per Greek spies, the persistent Persian emperor was concocting a military medicine for his troops. He reached to the outskirts of the Persian kingdom, which at the time was the largest empire in the world, and summoned a great number of men along with the finest calvary and scythed chariots from Eastern satrapies. His cure for his kingdom's loss was to crush the young Alexander by number, and Alexander's army knew it. So while the soon-to-be famous battle of Gaugamela hinged on the rising sun, the mens' morales were fixed on the blood moon that shone throughout the land. It was the boost Alexanders' men needed. The moon, according to the Greek astrologers, foretold Darius' defeat; meanwhile in the Persian camp, the moon did not predict the same future. Time would only tell if the prophecy was true, and as it would turn out, Alexander the Great and his men defeated the Persians at Gaugamela. Darius escaped for a moment but would soon die from a traitor in his own court following the battle.

Though the moon itself is not a source of divine power, the orchestrator of divine events is. True prophecy is power and it always serves to illuminate the sovereign power of the creator God and to testify of the world's conquering King– Jesus. And being that prophecy is the illumination of the mysteries of heaven's infinite, eternal treasure, the words are alive and active. They do not pass away, reaching both behind and forward to Jesus himself who has, is, and will fulfill all prophecy. The moon did not foretell of the military victory in the lands of Persia that night; the God of Abraham, Isaac, and Jacob had done so through his chosen prophet many years prior. That prophet was a religious Hebrew

man, an astrologer and dreamer himself in a foreign nation–
Daniel.

Nearly 250 years before the rise and fall of Alexander III of
Macedon, a man by the name of Daniel (meaning "God is my
judge" in Hebrew) observed the moon which shone over the land
of Babylon. He likely did so from the royal house and did so on
many occasions considering that God had given him the gift of
wisdom and knowledge, keen perception and devout servanthood
(Dan. 1:4). The God of the Jews had granted Daniel favor with
Nebuchadnezzar, the cruel, earthly king who had destroyed
Jerusalem and enslaved the Jews. Daniel, a Babylonian Magi but
Hebrew at heart, was appointed to serve the pagan king as advisor,
government administrator, and prophet. It would be the latter role
that would have a long lasting impact on both the Babylonians, the
Jews, and the world.

God may have allowed the people of Judah to be taken into
foreign captivity, but he did not allow the familiar voice of the lion
of Judah to be taken out of them. The voice of God cannot be
silenced, even in the most chaotic and crushing of times. The
sheep know God's voice and in Daniel's day, the voice of God was
heard through dreams, oracles, miracles, and prophecies released
by his prophets. Even these ways in which God spoke to the Jews
and the pagans in the Old Testament are prophecies of the future.
The same God who never sleeps nor slumbers is *still* speaking.
Jesus, the Son of God, told his disciples, "Heaven and earth will
pass away, but my words will never pass away" (Matt. 24:35). The
word of God is a sound which cannot and will not be silenced and
it can still be heard today in the form of dreams, oracles, miracles,
and prophecy.

Even though Daniel's prediction of Alexander the Great's
rise and fall was fulfilled, could it be that this prophecy was a

prophecy of a coming prophecy? Or more broadly speaking, that the prophecies of ancient prophets like Daniel, Ezekiel, or Joel would speak to the New Testament prophecy found in the second chapter of The Book of Acts, which itself would foretell the future of the end times?

If so, the prophecy of Joel as partially fulfilled at Pentecost in Acts 2 connects the past, present, and future; a now and not yet prophecy that has yet to be wholly fulfilled and when it is, it will cease all prophecies once and for all. A prophecy of the soon-coming day when the sun will rise with healing in his wings and the night will be no more. When the moon will bleed out to its death and signal a sure victory for the waning morale of God's warriors.

Could it be that the Blood Moon Prophecy was foretold at the beginning of time…and for the conclusion of it?

PART I:
The Prophecy That Was

Chapter 1

The Birth of the Moon and War

Then God said, "Let there be lights in the expanse of the sky to separate the day from the night. They will serve as signs for seasons and for days and years. They will be lights in the expanse of the sky to provide light on the earth." And it was so. God made the two great lights–the greater light to rule over the day and the lesser light to rule over the night–as well as the stars. God placed them in the expanse of the sky to provide light to earth, to rule the day and the night, and to separate light from darkness. And God saw that it was good. Evening came and then morning: the fourth day.

Genesis 1:14-19, HCSB

In the afternoon of July 16th, 1969 there was a worldwide hush. It was as if Earth was holding her breath while eyes from all nations gazed into TV screens, peered into the sunny sky, or glued their ears to the radio. The reverberations from the Apollo 11 space mission had sparked loud and heated conversation among leaders of all nations while exciting the hearts of children and American families to a reality that always seemed like a dream. Could man *really* land on the moon? The crew's humbling silence as they boarded the Saturn V rocket at Kennedy Space Center in Florida on that muggy afternoon seemed to forecast the dense silence they would soon experience. But the silence of space would only be temporary, for in just four days post takeoff, the American space team's lunar landing would be accompanied by the ear splitting applause and triumphant cheers by onlookers hundreds of thousands of miles away.

After transferring to the lunar module *Eagle*, Astronauts Neil Armstrong, Buzz Aldrin, and Michael Collins landed in a mare they named "The Sea of Tranquility" before placing their fleshy feet on the rocky surface of the moon. Commander Armstrong ventured out of the spacecraft and into the unknown first, Aldrin and Collins following suit. Armstrong, the first human to step foot on the moon, broke the silence of space through his transponder to NASA in the famous statement, "One small step for man, one giant leap for mankind." Aldrin followed Armstrong in his poetic exclamation, *"Beautiful, beautiful. Magnificent desolation."* While the rugged peaks and pits around them told an ancient story of destruction, the lunar accomplishment of mankind told a story of hope and projected a forecast of tranquility.

The moon in all its magnificence has drawn intrigue since the beginning of mankind. The snow-colored luminary mass suspended among a mysterious, ebony expanse is both captivating and perplexing. How is such an object floating in what seems to be a watery sky, why does it "disappear" as the sun rises, why does it change shapes through the month, and does it have any other effect besides casting a silver glow across our planet? These questions have inspired men and women for ages, sparked imaginative tales and myths, created superstitions and even birthed explorative adventures such as Apollo 11.

While the sun burns furiously, forwarding life as we know it, the moon seems lifeless. Yet this could be far from the truth. The moon affects time, tides, and light. It affects all of creation in both negative and positive ways and it holds ancient secrets that are greater than any space mission from earth could reveal. Armstrong, Aldrin, and Collins were not the first humans to bring life to the lifeless moon. Ancient civilizations had been doing so for thousands of years, attaching stories of life and death, even their worship, to the luminary mass.

God's making the moon was riskier than any earthly space mission and bloodier than any earthly battle. There is much more to the moon than a quick midnight glance. And while a lifetime of observing and studying the moon would not reveal all the natural forces hidden behind it, I believe there is a hidden spring of spiritual mysteries that are available to anyone willing to venture outside of this world to find it. To begin our exploration of the moon and its impact on the natural and spiritual world, we must begin where all things naturally begin– birth.

One's birth is a shining moment, a spark of divine fusion between passion and zeal; a God-given time to live and breathe, to arise and dance, to lie down and rest. Birth begins in thought and imagination, in dream and vision. To birth something can have both literal and figurative meaning. By Oxford's definition, "birth is the emergence of a baby or other young from the body of its mother; the start of life as a physically separate being."[1] And since birth connects all life together, it is of no surprise then that writers, artists, and poets have personified the cosmos and our world with the image of human birth for millennia. Stars "are born" from the death of other stars. Ideologies and concepts are "birthed" into inventions, music, scientific advancements, literature, business platforms, etc. The picture of birth is one of old and young, blood and beauty, pain and joy. It captures creation and time.

Despite being inanimate objects, the sun, moon, and stars had a birthdate, too. They were created by God for the earth. They serve a purpose. They were ultimately created to point life form on the earth to its Creator. But as time would unfold, the moon in all of its phases would mirror and influence the fluctuating yet consistent waves of humankind. Before we dive into the moon's turbulent Sea of Tranquility, we must first dive into God's word. To fully understand the significance of the heavens and what occurs in them and how they affect earth, one must turn to the most vivid, reliable source known to mankind–the Bible. The very words in the Bible were produced out of The Holy Spirit's life-giving power and

[1] Oxford English Dictionary, "Birth," https://www.oed.com/dictionary/birth_n1?tab=factsheet#19947800

therefore serve to reveal the life-giver himself. Birth begins with Christ and from him were *all* things, including the moon.

Genesis to Revelation

The graphic imagery of birthing as applied to the cosmos is not as apparent in the book of Genesis as it is in, of all places, Revelation. God declares the end from the beginning (Isa. 46:10) and so to fully grasp the connection between cosmology and Christology is to read God's word in its entirety, from beginning to end, or I suppose, end from beginning.

In the twelfth chapter of the revelator John's account of the end of the world, an interesting event occurs, has occurred and will occur. Recall that prophecy is the testimony of Jesus (Rev. 19:10), who himself stretches across past, present, and future and knows no end. Therefore prophecy can span time and cross through dimensions. It was, is, and will be. The following passage demonstrates the "was, is, and will be" functionality of prophecy and it will be important for the beginning and ending of this book:

> "A great sign appeared in heaven: a woman clothed with the sun, with the moon under her feet, and a crown of twelve stars on her head. She was pregnant and cried out in labor and agony as she was about to give birth. Then another sign appeared in heaven: There was a great fiery red dragon having seven heads and ten horns, and on its heads were seven crowns. Its tail swept away a third of the stars in heaven and hurled them to earth. And the dragon stood in front of the woman who was about to give birth, so that when she did give birth it might devour her child. She gave birth to a Son, a male who is going to rule all nations with an iron rod. Her child was caught up to God and to his throne. The woman fled into the wilderness, where she had a place prepared by God, to be nourished there for 1,260 days" (Revelation 12:1-6, HCSB).

While in heaven, John sees a woman who is "pregnant and cried out in labor and agony as she was about to give birth" (v. 2). The woman was carrying something that had yet to be revealed and it had to be, per the passage, something incredible as a fiery red dragon waited to "devour her child" (v. 4). We are told that when the time had fully come, the woman *gives* birth to a Son who *is going* to rule nations "with an iron rod" (v. 5). She *was* pregnant, *gives* birth, and the son *is going* to rule. The past, present, and future parts of an ancient mystery unfolding is evident from the vision, but who exactly is the woman and what and/or who was she carrying?

The woman in this particular part of Revelation is the Virgin Mary. The fiery red dragon is Satan. The war between humanity and Satan is over a person, the son– *Jesus*. Mary, carrying the Son of God, is "clothed" in the sun revealing her own humanity, *not* her divinity. Interestingly, the vision begins with Mary's future where she will be in heaven with the moon under her feet. But before that can occur, she had to carry and deliver the divine Jesus who draws the fury of Satan. After the Son of Man is born, he is not devoured but rather prevails. He assumes his position in power as Son of God again in heaven, while Mary goes to a place prepared for her by him. Thus in this vision Jesus fills her, covers her, and redeems her. It's a beautiful victory. But there is more to this delivery. Mary also *births* a movement and not just any movement; she births a *war*.

The war was conceived in the cunning of the serpent at the fall of Adam and Eve in Genesis, the battle manifested at the Messiah's birth, and the battle for human souls continues to this day and will persist until the fulfillment of all prophecies. Following this miraculous birth is a great war between Michael and his angels and the dragon and his followers (Rev. 12:7-12). But this war's outcome was determined at its conception. The serpent is cast down by Jesus and defeated by Jesus, thus Jesus is at the beginning, center, and end of this spiritual war. I will discuss the significance of this vision in greater detail in Part III. In the first part of this book, I want to focus on the dragon and the woman but not the woman Mary, the other woman of Revelation and her connection to the moon. To start, a study of the physical moon and its beginning is important.

Genesis 1:1-5 informs us that on day one of earth's timeline, God said "Let there be light," and light was on the earth and that light was separate from darkness. It is on day one that "day" and "night" are established and earth's timeline begins. On day two God created the sky and on day three he created the dry land, seas, plants, and trees. It is on *day four* that God speaks the cosmos into existence. This strategic layout of creation was always to reveal Jesus. John's Gospel links this creation account to Jesus, opening his entire book with the famous words:

> "In the beginning was the Word, and the Word was with God, and the Word was God. He was with God in the beginning. All things were created through him, and apart from him not one thing was created that has been created. In him was life, and that life was the light of men. That light shines in the darkness, and yet the darkness did not overcome it" (John 1:1-5, HCSB).

John made the connection and he saw the distinction between day one and day four. His opening is a rebirthing of the original creation account where now Christ is not only revealed in Genesis but also connected to it. In fact, Christ *is* the source of all creation. He is the one who initiated time and he is the one who will terminate it. He created the heavens and the earth and he will be the one to recreate them (Rev. 21:1). He is the light source who lights up eternity and who lit time at its conception. The light of

Christ came *before* day four of his creation, *before* the day when the sun, moon, and stars were born.

Genesis 1:2 informs us that light was at the beginning of creation, but it isn't until verse fourteen that we are told about the lights of the sky. This perplexing repetition of light is not coincidental but concealing. Clearly there is a supernatural light that exists outside of natural light, a supernatural power that reigns supreme over even the brightest, hottest star. It is also worth noting that vegetation *preceded* the lights of the sky. There is a significance in the creation layout.

On day *four* God creates the lights in the sky to provide a natural light for the earth. It is in this light that a spectrum of color is given, plants are fed, and days and seasons are marked in a physical way. These natural lights are the sun, moon, and stars yet only the Hebrew word for stars, *kokab*, is explicitly used. Actually, the words "moon" and "sun" are not even mentioned in Genesis 1. And if we believe that every single word of the Bible is positioned by God, then perhaps there is a reason that these two words are not used in Genesis 1. Maybe God was concealing a mystery on day four.

The Law of First Mention

The law of first mention, or the first place in Scripture that a word or doctrine is revealed, is a guideline that some use for studying the scriptures. This type of study is to ease in a beginner to a more complex theological concept by building off the simplicity of a concept or word's first biblical mention. Many, myself included, would assume that the words "moon" and "sun" are in the first chapter of the Bible. That is the chapter where all things were created, is it not? But to my surprise, this was not the first place where the Hebrew word for moon, יָרֵחַ or *yareach*, was recorded. A word study will reveal that the first mention of *yareach* is actually in

Genesis 37. The luminescent light of the moon and its purpose is recorded in Genesis 1, but the actual moon itself is not revealed until Chapter 37 and it is actually revealed *in a dream*.

> "Then he [Joseph] had another dream and told it to his brothers. 'Look,' he said, 'I had another dream and this time the sun, moon, and eleven stars were bowing down to me.' He told his father and brothers and his father rebuked him. 'What kind of dream is this that you have had?' he said. 'Am I and your mother and your brothers really going to come and bow down to the ground before you?' His brothers were jealous of him, but his father kept the matter in his mind" (Gen. 37:9-11, HCSB).

The dream Joseph had was paramount to the prophecy that would come forth, the prophecy of *kingship*.

To summarize the story, Joseph, a favorite son of Jacob (later renamed Israel), was born to Jacob and Rachel in Jacob's old age in Padan-aram or "the highland."[2] At around seventeen years old, Joseph's family moved from the highlands of Padan-aram to Canaan. It is in this foreign land that Joseph has a peculiar, prophetic dream. One night as he sleeps under the stars, God gives him a dream of the sun, moon, and stars bowing down to him. The dream amplifies the jealousy of his brothers who then plot his removal, throw him into a pit, sell him into slavery to the Egyptians, and then falsify his absence through a fake murder coverup. After this sudden and heartbreaking betrayal, Joseph then spends around thirteen years in Egypt with a portion of that time spent in prison for a crime that he didn't commit! There is power in a dream!

But while a dream put him in prison, dreams also brought him out of prison. After correctly interpreting one of Pharaoh's dreams, he finds favor with Pharaoh who then promotes him to a

---

[2] The "Land of Aram" is described by Abraham in Genesis 24:4 as "my land." This land is in modern day Syria.

second-in-command position in the kingdom. Joseph was born in "the highland," put in a low pit, and then became a highly respected member of Egypt. And the redemption story doesn't stop with Joseph. Recall that in his initial dream the sun, the moon, and the stars bowed down to him. So after a revealing of his identity to his brothers in the midst of a severe famine, a reconciliation takes place between he and his family and he supports them in the midst of famine from the riches he received in his elevated, high status as second-in-command (Gen 37, 39-47). Joseph's descendants remain in Egypt for hundreds of years, eventually becoming slaves in the land, before Moses, "Israel's redeemer," shows up on the scene (Exodus 2).

The story of Joseph is rich with irony and deep with themes of justice and mercy and the events began with a dream containing the sun, the moon, and the stars. It is in Joseph's life-altering dream in the land of Canaan that the first mention of the word "moon" appears in the Bible.

The land where Joseph was born versus the land where he dies contains a mystery and his prophetic dream uncovers a portion of it. Canaan and Egypt were geographically neighboring countries thus creating a trade conduit for exchange between resources, slaves, and religious beliefs and practices. While Egypt was the larger, more advanced empire, the Canaanites brought their own dish to the table, particularly the dish of deities which the Egyptians, already a spiritual people, consumed. This area of religious influence was the greatest contribution Canaan gave to Egypt in which many Canaanite deities were "accepted into the Egyptian pantheon."[3] The intermingling of cultic worship practices in an area teeming with mythological and mystic beliefs would produce a perverse and idolatrous "spiritual" reality. The more the gods mingled, the more idolatrous the cult became.

---

[3] James Wiener, "Egyptian Relations with Canaan," 7 Jul. 2016, https://etc.worldhistory.org/interviews/egyptian-relations-canaan/

Of those gods was The Moon Goddess whose demanded worship brought with it extreme perversion and deceit. Thus Joseph, who belonged to a set apart monotheistic people who worshiped *one* God, received a peculiar dream from the creator God in the land replete with many gods. Additionally, he has a dream regarding the cosmos, especially the *moon*, bowing to him. Years after Joseph, Moses forbids the Israelites to worship the sun, moon, and stars (Deut. 4:19). Clearly, the Israelites were familiar with polytheistic foreign beliefs. So it is of no surprise then that Jacob rebukes Joseph when he tells him his dream. The idols of the pagans do not live nor do they worship mankind or vice versa. But even though Jacob rebukes Joseph, Jacob doesn't dismiss his son's dream. Perhaps Jacob, a dreamer himself (Gen. 28:10-17), sees the significance of such a dream in the land of Canaan, and maybe, even if to a limited extent, sees the impact this dream will have in future prophecies.

The first "appearance" of the moon in the Bible then is in this prolific dream. Its first mention is in Joseph's night vision concerning the Twelve Tribes of Israel and their preservation by their covenantal God. Its last mention is in a day vision by the exiled John on the isle of Patmos concerning the great end time battle between the dragon and God's children at the conclusion of time. As the moon illuminates the light of the sun in the natural, Joseph's dream illuminates the truth in the spiritual. Joseph's prophetic dream of kingship would be a foreshadowing of the ultimate kingship of Jesus, the world's Messiah, who overcame darkness once and for all, will keep his covenant, and will forever reign above the sun, moon, and stars.

But we cannot stop at the surface level. There are more messages to be uncovered in Joseph's dream. Where he received the night vision plays a vital part in discovering why the moon's first mention in the entire Bible is in Chapter 37, in the land of

Canaan, a dim land whose people were addicted to the moon and yet a land whose set apart people would bring a brighter ending.

Chapter 2

Called Out and Caught Up

*When you look to the heavens and see the sun, moon, and stars—all the stars in the sky—
do not be led astray to bow in worship to them and serve them. The Lord your God has
provided them for all people everywhere under heaven. But the Lord selected you and
brought you out of Egypt's iron furnace to be a people for his inheritance, as you are
today.*

Deuteronomy 4:19-20, HCSB

The Jewish Calendar

T he moon does not actually produce light of its own. It is
merely a large luminary mass that reflects the sun's light.
Unlike the moon, the sun does produce light and was set in
place perfectly by God to light the days on earth, give light source
to the vegetation, to give warmth to creation. And though science
over time has revealed more to us about the functions and abilities
of life and the universe, Genesis 1:14 attributes a distinct purpose
for the sun, moon, and stars—*time*. "They [the natural lights] will
serve as signs for seasons and for days, and years," thus human life
is meant to function within the parameters of time (Gen. 1:14).
Anything outside of this time would and could only be the source
of something supernatural. Spiritually speaking, those born again
into eternal life with Jesus Christ receive that supernatural light
upon conversion and then become luminaries that reflect, like the
moon, Christ's supernatural light in the darkness. So while there
are many moons in our solar system, it is the moon assigned to
earth that serves a specific purpose for time and light .

Further examining the natural purpose of the sun and
moon, one of the ways in which God brought order to chaos was
in the setting of the sun and the rising of the same (Ps. 113:3). The

sun and the moon were to mark the beginning and ending of a day, month, and year. Psalm 104:19 declares, "He made the moon to mark the seasons; the sun knows its time for setting." For the Jewish people, the calendar is different from that of the Romans and Greeks; the calendar is lunar based not solar based. This distinction for the Jewish people was to separate their timing from the timing of the pagan world, a world which followed other gods and even named their days after them. For example, "Sunday," or dies Solis, was named by the Romans after their sun god.

For the Israelites weekly timeline, the first day of the week was when the first light appeared (Gen 1:2-3). From that first day, six days followed. Like the Gregorian calendar, the Hebrew calendar has seven days in a week, but whereas the Gregorian day begins at midnight, Jewish days begin at *sundown*. As for months, the Jewish months begin at the appearance of a crescent moon. This new moon represented harvest and bounty, marked the beginning of a new month, and was celebrated with sacrifices and feasting. Each month contains 29 ½ days making Jewish years either 12 or 13 months long. A yearly lunar cycle–the moon rotating around the earth versus the earth rotating around the sun– produces 354.36 days in a year versus the 365.25 days in a solar cycle/Gregorian year. Therefore to correct the difference, the Jewish calendar has an additional year, or "pregnant" year, that is added to keep festival appointed times in order.[4] A shofar was and is still blown at Rosh Hashanah, the Jewish new year, and at the conclusion of Yom Kippur, The Day of Atonement (Psalm 81:3). The new moon was always accompanied with celebration, sound, and feasting.

The feasts which were held to celebrate the new bounty of each month were a set apart time when the people of God were to be grateful for his provision, remembering their deliverance and

---

[4] The addition of an Adar II occurs seven times every nineteen year cycle.

renewal, praising him for his creation and his covenant. The
luminary phases of the moon as it moved around the earth,
transitioning from darkness to full light back to darkness,
symbolically represented their falling away from God and being
restored to him.[5] And just as the moon was lesser to the great light,
the sun, Israel would be lesser among the nations but reflect God's
great light to the world. The moon was not to be worshiped but to
showcase God's supreme authority, power, and dominion.
Additionally, the sun and moon were to be used by his creation for
his purposes, more specifically, used by his set apart people for
appointed feasts and festivals as signs of the times.

A Set Apart People

All people, saved and not saved, are still within God's timing.
Whether one follows the Gregorian calendar, the Jewish calendar,
or no calendar, doesn't matter nearly as much as whether one pays
attention to the progression within time. To be truly set apart for
God has nothing to do with a calendar or waxing moon or a setting
sun but has everything to do with worship, and more critically, *who*
one worships.

As God's creation, every human being was born to worship
(Deut. 6:13). Even atheists and pantheists worship. Regardless if an
atheist acknowledges it, he or she expresses some sort of reverence
either toward earth, the universe, nature, the human body, etc. So
each day and each night, people either worship God or they don't.
They attach their faith to a divine being or they attach it to
themselves. For the Jews the feasts, festivals, the sacred assemblies
and holy convocations in the Old Testament were a time of set
apart worship by a set apart people to the one and only God–
Yahweh (YHWH). They were to attach their faith to a real God

---

[5] Bill Cloud, "The Feasts of Israel: The Mystery of the Seven Feasts of Israel,"
International School of the Word, https://isow.org/.

who loved them. These special activities marked them as unique and kept them hopeful.

Though the Old Testament patterns of worship were established thousands of years ago, the significance of them still persists. Some traditions were fulfilled when the law was fulfilled at Calvary, such as sacrificing a lamb to atone for sins during Passover, but some festivals have yet to be fulfilled, such as the Feast of Trumpets. Even in their establishment, the appointed feasts and festivals and the religious acts performed during them served as foreshadows and prophecies of Christ and of the end time events. Again, the end declared from the beginning. And yet, even in the passing of the law and the impending fulfillment of all prophecy and knowledge, there is present revelation to be excised from the feasts and festivals.[6]

The ancient feasts instituted by God linked the Israelites with their ancestral past, their present, and their future. Even if a person does not participate in the Jewish festivals today, they can still see the signs in them. This time link and the signs to follow were crucial for the Israelites. As authors Ann Spangler and Lois Tverberg state,

> "The purpose of the feasts was to give the Jewish people an opportunity to rejoice at the way God had provided and then to offer something back in return. The feasts were a tangible way for them to remember God's faithfulness and care."[7]

The lunar calendar did not set the people apart, it set their worship apart. For God's people, their worship was to be to him,

---

[6] "Love never ends. As for prophecies, they will pass away; as for tongues, they will cease; as for knowledge, it will pass away" (1 Cor. 13:8, ESV).

[7] Ann Spangler and Lois Tverberg, *Sitting at the Feet of Rabbi Jesus: How the Jewishness of Jesus Can Transform Your Faith* (Grand Rapids, MI: Zondervan Academic, 2009), 114.

for him, and all about him. When YHWH chose Abraham and made a covenant with him and his descendants, it established a chosen lineage that was to be called out among the world and to be caught up in God's presence forever.

To separate the Hebrews from the other pagan societies was to reiterate God as the one true God, a God who is faithful and *holy*. God's people were to reflect his holiness in their separation from polytheistic, idolatrous worship (Lev. 20:26). In God's marriage to a particular group of people—a people drawn out of darkness—was also, paradoxically, to divide. Jesus touched on such division in Luke 12:49-56:

> "I came to bring fire on the earth, and how I wish it were already set ablaze! But I have a baptism to undergo, and how it consumes me until it is finished! Do you think that I came here to bring peace on earth? No, I tell you, but rather division. From now on, five in one household will be divided: three against two, and two against three...He also said to the crowds, 'When you see the cloud rising in the west, right away you say, 'A storm is coming,' and so it does. And when the south wind is blowing, you say, 'It is going to be hot,' and it is. Hypocrites! You know how to interpret the appearance of the earth and sky, but why don't you know how to interpret this present time?'"

The division wasn't to outcast people or instill hatred toward a particular people group but to make a distinction between light and dark, between good and evil, between belief and unbelief, between legalism and love; to separate the gods of this world from the one true God. To be one in Christ is not to be divided with believing brothers and sisters, rather it is to be separated from the world. To be set apart for his purposes is to be a worshiper of YHWH alone, to seek the face of the God of Abraham, Isaac, and Jacob, and to give the triune Godhead (Father, Son, and Holy Spirit) all glory. Just as it was for the Israelites who were separated out from the polytheistic culture, this uncoupling with the world will inevitably bring division from the world.

The Israelites were set apart to follow YHWH and they were to worship him daily and gather at certain times of the year for communal worship. In fact some of the Jewish Pharisees, Sadducees and scribes would take this separation to a fundamentalist extreme, worshiping the signs and the sacred tradition rather than pursuing present love. They had been blinded by the natural light and in turn lost their supernatural light. Jesus asked them, "You know how to interpret the appearance of the earth and the sky, but why don't you know how to interpret this present time?" (Lk. 12:56). The God of Light stood in front of them, yet they did not see him. They were missing the ultimate sign, the one who put the sun and moon in its place!

While some missed Jesus' visitation, others did not. And so it is the same today. Some see the spiritual truth and others do not. Some hear his voice and some do not. For the ancient Israelites, the signs were bound to the natural elements of the world and in the sky, but for believers in the present time, the signs are bound in God's word which is alive and active (Heb. 4:12). And I believe as more Christians are set apart by God and more are baptized by The Holy Spirit's fire, as more spiritual eyes are opened, the more signs will begin to appear: natural and supernatural signs in dreams and visions, in miracles and wonders. And one of the signs revealed in God's word that will present itself as the time of the end draws near, the time when Jesus will return to finalize a separation of Satan from humanity, is *the blood moon*. All will see it in unity but interpret it in division.

Foreign lands and Foreign gods

The names of regions in the Bible should be noted as it was territory and the riches of the land that initiated pilgrimages and wars throughout history. Moreover, certain lands held certain cultures and belief systems, both good *and* bad. The names of landmasses, bodies of water, caves, etc. should all be taken into account when studying the Scriptures.

The territory in which events occurred in the Bible were important then and are important now. The complex nature of prophecy with its many parts and pieces makes even the seemingly minute detail major. Geographical locations not only play a part in the natural realm—such as agriculture, weather patterns, economic trade, and war— but they also play a part in the spiritual realm. The topography along with the names of regions, rivers, mountains, and cities contributed to the patterns of daily life as well as the plans and purposes of God in the earth and in the heavenlies.

From Jebus to Jerusalem

Take for example the most important city in the Bible and the world– Jerusalem. The name means "the city of peace" and is referred to at times in the scriptures as Zion, Mount Zion or the City of David. But to stop at the name is to miss the prophetic significance of it. The pre-Davidic land later known as Jerusalem was inhabited by the Jebusites, a Canaanite tribe descended from Ham, and was called Jebus.[8] But prior to becoming Jebus, it was known as Salem where King Melchizedek, the high priest and king, blessed Abram/Abraham (Gen. 14:19-20). At Canaan's root was an ancient blessing and mystery. As time went by, the city took on the Canaanite name Jebus, but its blessed destiny for the people of YHWH never changed. Perhaps it was this city's blessed destiny that attracted such stark division.

The Canaanites were a people group steeped in paganism. Their worship centered around many gods, especially El/Ba'al ("the father of the gods") and Asherah ("the mother of the gods")

---

[8] Gerald Flurry, "The Incredible Origins of Ancient Jerusalem," January-February 2023, *Let the Bones Speak*, https://armstronginstitute.org/843-the-incredible-origins-of-ancient-jerusalem.

and they were known to practice abhorrent religious acts such as temple prostitution and child sacrifice (Jer. 19:5, Deut. 23:17). The Jebusites of Canaan held a stronghold in the area until King David's foray. The Deuteronomic history of 2 Samuel explains the siege of Jebus as follows:

> "The king [David] and his men marched to Jerusalem against the Jebusites who inhabited the land. The Jebusites had said to David, 'You will never get in here. Even the blind and lame can repel you,' thinking, 'David can't get in here.'
>
> Yet David did capture the stronghold of Zion, that is, the City of David. He said that day, 'Whoever attacks the Jebusites must go through the water shaft to reach the lame and blind who are despised by David.' For this reason it is said, 'The blind and the lame will never enter the house.'
>
> David took up residence in the stronghold, which he named the City of David. He built it up all the way around from the supporting terraces inward. David became more and more powerful, and the Lord God of Armies was with him. King Hiram of Tyre sent envoys to David; he also sent cedar logs, carpenters, and stonemasons, and they built a palace for David. Then David knew that the Lord had established him as king over Israel and had exalted his kingdom for the sake of his people Israel" (2 Samuel 5:4-12, HCSB).

The land of Jebus was a well of water in the midst of a dry area as it contained a main water source from the Gihon spring. This resource made it a desirable and sought after land. For years the Canaanites controlled the region, building their strongest fortress in Jebus. And their personalities matched their fortress. They gloated that even the blind and the lame could not enter. Yet, as it would turn out, it was their venerated gods who had actually blinded them. Ba'al, the Canaanites "father of gods" who was also known as the "The Prince of the Earth," could not protect them against David. Additionally, the Canaanites marine goddess "mother of gods," also known as "She Who Walks on the Sea," could not protect her fortress of water.[9] The Canaanites' insults were only turned upon their own heads as David and his men used water shafts to blindside their foes and overtake the city. The story of David's capture of Jebus is a monumental moment in his kingship and the Israelites story. In the Old Testament, "The City of David" would become the foci of Old and New Testament prophecy.

Not only is paying attention to geographical locations important when studying scriptures, but names are also vitally important. An etymology of the name Jerusalem connects it to Genesis 14 and the high priest and King Melchizedek, king of Salem. Salem is translated as "peace" or "completeness" and deemed the birthplace of blessing.[10] Once King David acquired the land, he built an altar which would later become the site of Solomon's Temple, built by his son Solomon. The name Solomon comes from the Hebrew word *shalom* or "peace" and the words Salem and Solomon share the same root word– *peace*.[11] Jerusalem then becomes the "City of Peace," which was blessed by God for Abraham and his descendants, secured like the stars.

The influence of Melchizedek and his kingship of Salem is seen both in Old Testament and New Testament writings. Gerald Flurry states,

> "The Jewish Qumran community of the second and first centuries B.C. actually believed—as revealed by the text of the Dead Sea Scrolls—Melchizedek to be a *divine* being who would 'atone for' and 'forgive the

---

[9] Britannica, "Asherah," *Encyclopedia Britannica*, 22 May 2024, https://www.britannica.com/topic/Asherah-Semitic-goddess.
[10] Stephen J. Binz, *Jerusalem, the Holy City* (Waterford, Connecticut: Twenty-Third Publications, 2005), 2.
James Hastings, *A Dictionary of the Bible Volume II: (Part II:I-Kinsman), Volume 2* (Honolulu, Hawaii: University Press of the Pacific, 2004), 584.
[11] Flurry, "The Incredible Origins of Ancient Jerusalem," https://armstronginstitute.org/843-the-incredible-origins-of-ancient-jerusalem.

wrongdoings of all their iniquities,' a being who at the 'end of days' would usher in 'the day of salvation which God spoke through Isaiah the prophet' (11QMelch)."[12]

In the New Testament, the author of Hebrews, obviously a well-schooled Jew, devotes an entire passage to Melchizedek describing him as, "without father, without mother, without descent, having neither beginning of days, nor end of life…" (Heb. 7:1-3) and "resembling the Son of God" (Heb. 7:3). Jesus, revered as The Son of God with no beginning nor end as well as the Son of Man due to his Davidic lineage, is our high priest and conquering king who defeated the gods of the Canaanites and, most importantly, defeated the death, blindness, and lameness that the worship of such gods brought. And he continues to do so today.

Eschatologically, Jerusalem/The City of David/Mount Zion was not just an elevated city on earth but an eternal city in heaven, a sacred place where God dwells. The Jerusalem of this world will one day be renewed and glorified in the new heaven and new earth (Rev. 21, Isa. 52:1). It will become the city of *eternal* shalom peace, full of God's rich blessings, inhabited by his people who are *eternal* temples for his glory. Thus Jebus, a once paganistic land of the Canaanites, regained its rightful place as the blessed "City of Peace" under King David and it will happen again *permanently* under an everlasting peace in the eschaton upon the Root of David's return.

As deep and wide are the trees' roots and as long are the rivers in the land, so are the meanings of those lands. Land is apparently important to God. Specifically, Jerusalem is important to Jesus who promises to return to this sacred place from where he ascended, to The Mount of Olives located in Jerusalem (Zech. 14:4, Acts 1:1-10). With the chosen priesthood (believers in Christ)

---

[12] Flurry, "The Incredible Origins of Ancient Jerusalem," https://armstronginstitute.org/843-the-incredible-origins-of-ancient-jerusalem.

comes the chosen land (The New Heaven and New Earth), a status reserved only for Jesus' worshipers and a territory reserved only for his believers.

To be set apart for God at times required the removal of the people out of a territory while at other times it required the removal of the adopted territorial religious practices and beliefs out of the people. To remove the practices of the Canaanites out of the Israelites was just as tough as removing the Egyptians practices out of the Israelites. The stubborn, persistent worship of idols became the main stronghold for the Israelites in the Old Testament and even continues among believers worldwide today. But just as King David recaptured the city that had originally been blessed by Melchizedek, so too will Jesus redeem his people out of the strongholds of this world, bringing them into his eternal blessing and peace.

Set Among The Reeds

Another example of God's perfect redemption for his chosen people is in the Exodus story. It testifies of the love of a God who orchestrated the deliverance of his people out of darkness and sustained them after their salvation, even when they forgot him. The story also shows God's heart is for *all* people to be set free, even the pagans. I have briefly discussed Mary, the mother of Jesus but there is another mother who is noteworthy in the beginning of the Hebrew story. And she, like Mary, will reveal clues to The Blood Moon Prophecy as well as contrast the *"other"* wicked woman of Revelation.

Moses, the man chosen to be Israel's redeemer, was bravely and sacrificially placed by his biological mother, Jochebed, into a basket in an attempt to save him from the infanticide of the Hebrew baby boys under Egyptian Pharaoh Ramses II. This basket, unlike Hollywood depictions, did not float down a river but was rather strategically placed by Jochebed "among the reeds" by the bank of the Nile (Exodus 2:4, HCSB). This particular riverbank was, as the story tells us, used by the Pharaoh's daughter to wash herself. It is on the riverbank where the princess saw the surviving Hebrew boy and desired to keep him. Moses' sister, Miriam, witnessed her baby brother's rescue by the Egyptian princess and suggested to her that he be nursed by his mother. The princess agreed and allowed Jochebed to nurse him. In this tender and limited time with his biological mother, he received the foundation for his future–the rocking and nourishment of his Hebraic heritage, lullabies written on his heart. But Moses was destined to grow up in the Egyptian royal house and for a reason.

After weaning him, Moses was brought back to the princess who became his adoptive mother. This woman was bat-Pharaoh ("daughter of Pharaoh), or as the Torah portion of the Shemat calls her, Bithiah.[13] It is Bithiah, the pagan princess of Egypt, who named the boy Moses, meaning, "I drew him out of the water" (Exod. 2:10). Thus in a sense Moses had two beginnings, a Hebraic one and a paganistic one, but he had only *one* ending–*mercy*. Moses grew up by the mercy of God under Bithiah's stewardship in the Egyptian royal palace until he eventually ran from Egypt's evil and found his father, the god of mercy, on Mount Horeb. Moses was "drawn out" of a paganistic land where he was set apart by God to return to Egypt and deliver the enslaved Israelites. But some Jewish legends hold that it wasn't just the Israelites who found deliverance when he returned.

As stated before Moses was strategically placed among the reeds, foreshadowing his future set apart status as a Hebrew among the Egyptians. His position in power stemmed from his position in

[13] The Shemot is the second of The Five Books of Moses and includes the Israelites slavery in Egypt, their Exodus, the giving of the Torah, the sin of the golden calf, and the construction of the Tabernacle.
The Torah is Hebrew for "teaching" or "instruction" and refers to the first five books of the Bible, also called the Pentateuch.

God's plan, not the princess' power. Yet even the pagan princess, Bithiah, who worshiped Isis and Osiris, the gods of Egypt, was positioned in God's redemptive plan. As she washed in the Nile, she saw the boy and chose to save him. It is this choice clothed in compassion that will actually clothe her in mercy. Bithiah, according to some rabbinical teachings and interpretations of Caleb's genealogy in 1 Chronicles, was saved with the Israelites during the Passover because she chose to save Moses.[14] It was the God of Israel, not the Egyptian false gods, that would actually wash *her* with the lamb's blood, *drawing her* out of the grip of the Nile, and making a way for her to spend an eternity with the God of mercy as a *true* princess.

The Egyptian princess was rewarded with both life and a new name per some rabbinic writings. *Leviticus Rabbah*, a mid-first millennium A.D. midrashic collection, explains this unusual name for an Egyptian princess by identifying her as the woman who saved Moses's life (1:3).[15] The Talmud understands this scripture to connect her with the Judahites (*yehudiah* or "Jewess") and the *Megillah* 13a. explains her new name of Bithiah was given ultimately because she repudiated idol worship.[16] The fascinating story of Bithiah's redemption, while not technically proven, is interesting.

Another name was reported for bat-Pharaoh by 1st century Roman-Jewish historian Flavius Josephus in his *Antiquities of the Jews* and by the author of The Book of Jubilees (Jubilees 47:5). Both

---

[14] "Ezrah's sons: Jether, Mered, Epher, and Jalon. Mered's wife *Bithiah* gave birth to Miriam, Shammai, and Ishbah the father of Estemoa. These were the sons of Pharaoh's daughter Bithiah; Mered had married her..." (1 Chronicles 4:17-18, HCSB, emphasis added)

[15] Malka Z. Simkovich, "Pharaoh's Daughter: A Woman Worthy of Raising Moses," TheTorah.Com, 2002, https://thetorah.com/article/pharaohs-daughter-a-woman-worthy-of-raising-moses

[16] Simkovich, "Pharaoh's Daughter," https://thetorah.com/article/pharaohs-daughter-a-woman-worthy-of-raising-moses

authors claim that the princesses' name was actually Thermutis (Θερμουθις), the Greek name of Renenutet, the Egyptian snake deity.[17] While there are different beliefs about bat-Pharaoh, there is one undeniable truth: the princess of Pharaoh came from a serpent worshiping line and was chosen out from among them to help save Moses. Both avenues of belief prove that her name was important and so was the choice she made.

The classic Shakespearean question, "What's in a name?" describes this undeniable depth and connection between one's name and one's soul well. Identity is the basis of every life decision. Bithiah's love for Moses and her action connected to his name would reflect the way Moses would live his life; a life of mercy, love, and daring rescue for the Jewish people. As deep as the seas was the depth of Moses' name.

The life of Moses and the lives of the women who helped him would serve as a prototype for the ministry and life of Messiah Jesus who delivered God's people once and for all, fulfilling everything Moses began. Even the events surrounding the birth of Moses would serve as a prophetic picture of the demonic infanticide that would also be at work during Jesus' birth. Moses' biological mother, Jochebed, was a Hebrew who followed YHWH. Jesus' biological mother was also a woman whose covenantal identity was in YHWH. The two women (Jochebed and Mary) mirrored one another in their purpose in God's sovereign

---

[17] David Flusser and Shua Amorai-Stark, "The Goddess Thermuthis, Moses, and Artapanus," *Jewish Studies Quarterly* 1 (3): 217–33, JSTOR 40753100.; Flavius Josephus, *Antiquities of the Jews Books 1-19*, trans. William Whiston (Cambridge, 1737).
The Talmud is a large volume of compiled ancient teachings and commentaries on the Mishnah or Oral Torah. There are two Talmuds: the *Jerusalem Talmud* (A.D. 400) and the *Babylonian Talmud* (A.D. 500). The *Babylonian Talmud* is considered authoritative by Jews today. See also Spangler and Tverberg, *Sitting at the Feet of Rabbi Jesus*, 25 and 29.
Megillah is any of the five sacred books of the Ketuvim (the third division of the Old Testament) in scroll form that are read in the synagogue in the course of certain festivals.

covenant. Both women delivered children under tyrannical rule and both women played an essential role in God's redemptive story. But what about Bithiah, Moses' adoptive mother? Did she also serve as a prototype? And if so, how does she fit into The Blood Moon Prophecy?

If we view her story through Josephus' lens, then we see her as a light who exposed the gods and goddesses at work behind the assassination attempt of Moses; a snake spirit that sought to kill Israel's redeemer. On the other hand, if we examine her through the Jewish tradition which taught that she was saved with the Israelites, Bithiah would serve as a prototype for the Gentile, who in surrender to YHWH could find a new identity and purpose in the God of Israel. Paul later wrote of such mercy in his words to the Romans, "For there is no difference between Jew and Gentile– the same Lord is Lord of all and richly blesses all who call on him, for 'Everyone who calls on the name of the Lord will be saved'" (Romans 10:12-13, c.f. Acts 2:21, NIV). Using the birthing imagery and building upon the Jewess theory, Bithiah herself was delivered out of the hands of a deadly snake spirit and into the hands of a perfectly positioned life-giving redeemer.

While Bithiah gripped Moses' small fingers that day on the river Nile, the grasp of the evil spirit who had been spiritually holding Bithiah's hands began to loosen its snaky grip. When the Nile was turned to blood by Moses, who himself was a prototype of Jesus Christ, it prophetically signified the impending bloody death of another woman of the Nile, the same woman John the revelator sees while caught up into heaven; the dark, wicked woman of Revelation, a drinker of blood who conceals herself behind *the moon*.

Chapter 3

The Wine of Babylon

Then the Lord said to Moses, "Pharaoh's heart is hard: He refuses to let the people go. Go to Pharaoh in the morning. When you see him walking out to the water, stand ready to meet him by the bank of the Nile. Take in your hand the staff that turned into a snake. Tell him: The Lord, the God of the Hebrews, has sent me to tell you: Let my people go, so that they may worship me in the wilderness. But so far you have not listened. This is what the Lord says: Here is how you will know that I am the Lord. Watch. I am about to strike the Nile with the staff in my hand, and it will turn to blood. The fish in the Nile will die, the river will stink, and the Egyptians will be unable to drink water from it."

Exodus 7:14-18, HCSB

Life is in the blood but in the case of the first plague in Egypt, death was in the blood. The river where the blood runs means everything. As Aaron, Moses' biological brother, stretched out his staff over the Nile river, an eerie event occurred that would rattle the bones of the living and the dead. The first plague when the river turned to blood would symbolically represent *many* parts of Scripture but it would also foretell of a present prophecy and a prophecy still to come which I call *The Blood Moon Prophecy*.

The moon has always played an important part in religions. Though secondary to the sun, the moon was and still is acknowledged in religion, and in pagan cultures it was and still is worshiped. But the moon was originally created to showcase God's majesty, his creativity, and his supreme power. King David wrote of God's creative magnificence in this way:

"When I observe your heavens, the work of your fingers, the moon and the stars, which you set in place, what is a human being that you remember him, a son of man that you look after him. You made him a little less than God, and crowned him with glory and honor. You made him ruler over the works of your hands; you put everything under his feet…" (Psalm 8:3-6, HCSB)

The sun, moon, and stars were never created to be worshiped. The God who made them was to be worshiped.

In the following chapters, I will be speaking in both natural and spiritual terms. When I speak of The Moon Goddess, please understand that I am referring to the spirit at work behind the worship of the moon not the physical moon itself. The symbolism used in the scriptures, and even in this book, are to conceal mysteries for the sake of preserving the prophecy and the prophet. Many of God's prophets spoke in cryptic and symbolic terms so that they would not be killed by national leaders who disagreed with their words and so that their writings would not be destroyed. Viewing symbols and metaphors with a spiritual lens will help you work through apocalyptic writings such as Ezekiel, Daniel, Zechariah, and Revelation as well as understand The Blood Moon Prophecy as it relates to end time events.

The Blood of the Nile

Recall the name that Josephus and *The Book of Jubilees* used for the daughter of Pharaoh was *Thermutis*, the Greek name of *Renenutet*, the Egyptian snake deity. As I stated before, the name of Moses' adoptive mother differs between rabbinical teachings, but one thing is for sure: that the pagan woman was from a polytheistic religion is undebatable. Josephus' naming informs us of a few pieces of information that will be helpful with The Blood Moon Prophecy: (1) The religion of the Egyptians and their myriad mythology had a massive impact on other polytheistic religions, including the Greeks; (2) There is a connection between the snake goddess, the river Nile and the moon; (3) Names of ancient deities can be interchangeable with other deities across cultures and time.

Moon worship goes back millennia to the fertile crescent region of Mesopotamia and has persisted into modern times. Like the actual moon which reappears day after day, so do the ugly gods attached to its worship appear day after day. But as we will come to find out throughout the remainder of the book, their end was foretold at their beginning.

Wine and Blood

Blood in the Bible, particularly in prophetic and apocalyptic writings, is often symbolized by wine outside of its literal, life-giving meaning (Lev. 17:11). The wine as a trope represents two contrasting expressions. On the one hand, wine can represent blessing in the form of life, abundance, prosperity, reward, and joy.[18] On the other hand, wine can symbolize God's wrath and judgment in the form of plague, destruction, and eternal torment.[19] The latter is the one depicted in the scene in Exodus and, as always with God, for a reason.

The snake's attachment to Renenutet of the Nile in the Exodus story is ironic. Prior to the Nile turning to blood in Exodus 7, a showdown took place between the magicians of Pharaoh and Moses and Aaron. In this dramatic scene, the sorcerers of Egypt attempt to compete with Moses and Aaron. Aaron throws down his staff which turns into a snake and the occultists do the same. Aaron's staff consumes the sorcerers' staffs, signifying that YHWH is the all-powerful, undefeated God. Exodus 7:11 informs us that

---

[18] Judges 9:13; Isaiah 24:11; Zechariah 10:7; Psalm 104:15; Ecclesiastes 9:7; 10:19, Luke 22:20

[19] Obadiah 16, Jeremiah 25:15, Isaiah 51:17, Revelation 14:10

Aaron's snake actually *devoured* the other snakes. Thus it is extremely ironic that Aaron extends the same staff over the river Nile, connected to the snake deity, to perform another miracle. The death of the river and the victory of God's people was foretold in the prophetic act the day before!

But there is more to Renenutet than the cobra. Ancient Egyptians associated this goddess with grain, harvest, and grapes.[20] She was called the "mistress of provisions," the"mistress of food," and the goddess who "maintains everyone."[21] She was also strongly associated with breastfeeding and milk, being that she provided nourishment. Of the food, or drink thereof, she was venerated for grapes in the form of wine. She was often depicted in wine making scenes in tombs and her shrines could be found in Egyptian vineyards. Additionally, her image was found on stamps and stoppers for wine.[22] This goddess was *filled* with wine and even nourished the young and old of the land with it. Her husband in Egyptian mythology was Sobek, represented by the Nile. The two produced a son, Nehebkau, who is represented as a primordial snake and connected with the afterlife. The vine of this goddess had various offshoots all of which led to the afterlife of death.

As Aaron stretched his victorious staff over the river Nile, he and Moses did so to prove a point to Pharaoh, to the sorcerers and priests of the Egyptian gods, and to the "gods" themselves. While Pharaoh, who believed himself to be a god, may not have fully understood the significance of the plagues, the priests and

---

[20] Paolo, Marini, "Renenutet: worship and popular piety at Thebes in the New Kingdom," *Journal of Intercultural and Interdisciplinary Archaeology* (2) 2015, 73-84; Geraldine Pinch, *Egyptian mythology: a guide to the gods, goddesses, and traditions of ancient Egypt* (New York: Oxford University Press, 2003).

[21] Massimiliano Franci, "Isis-Thermouthis and the anguiform deities in Egypt: a cultural and semantic evolution," *A Journal of Intercultural and Archeology* (2) 2016: 35-40.

[22] Evelien Denecker and Katelijn Vandorpe, "Sealed Amphora Stoppers and Tradesmen in Greco-Roman Egypt" in *BABESCH*, 82(1): 115-128, DOI:10.2143/BAB.82.1.2020764

priestesses of the gods in the land certainly made the connection. Each plague was an insult to their god. The plague of the bloody Nile was an insult to Hapi, Isis, and Renenutet. The plague of frogs was an insult to their god Heqet, the plague of the gnats was an insult to the god Set, the plague of hail was an insult to Nut, Osiris, and Set.[23] And so the punches to the gods continued for ten plagues. Each one served a purpose and the first plague of the Nile turning to blood was a hard hit to Isis and a firm warning to her followers.

The most important river to the people of that time, the Nile produced the reeds and papyrus used for writing, it provided fish which fed the river's ecosystem and the people, it helped transport goods and was used as a bathhouse. As it turned to blood, the Nile as the Egyptians knew it vanished. The first plague had devastating effects. When Bithiah and her maidens found Moses among the reeds, they could not have imagined that years later he would stand at the riverbank again among the reeds and perform a sign of death. The final plague would be the judgment and vindication for the onslaught of all the Hebrew babies–the death of the firstborn.

The first miracle was serious and it foreshadowed the Egyptians' end. The river turning to blood wasn't contained to just the Nile, Exodus 7:19 tells us that *all* the water sources turned to blood, even water in wooden and stone containers! The water in these containers would be bitter, like a bitter wine, and give no reward for the labor that went into filling them.

Even more astounding is that the Hebrew words used for "wooden" and "stone" in this verse are עֵץ, or *ets* and אֶבֶן, or *eben*, respectively. The word *ets* is used over 74 times for "tree" in the Bible and the word *eben* is used for "stone rocks," "weights,"

---

[23] ZA Blog, "What the Bible Tells Us about the 10 Plagues of Egypt," Zondervan Academic (2018), https://zondervanacademic.com/blog/what-the-bible-tells-us-about-the-10-plagues-of-egypt

"hailstones," and even "charm."[24] The word *ets* is particularly used in Genesis for the Tree of Life and the Tree of Knowledge of Good and Evil (Gen 1-3). These wood containers and stony vessels throughout Egypt were used to store water and were often used in temple worship and likely even used to wash literal blood from the hands of those sacrificing in the temples. These vessels that were heavy with sin bore a great weight of judgment.

As Jesus, the mediator of the New Covenant, performed *his* first miracle, it had great implications and prophesied to a serious ending, too. In the second chapter of Saint John's Gospel, Jesus turns water in stony vessels into fresh wine at a wedding. This astounding miracle is indicative of the miraculous power of God, his power to give life and the power to take it away. And as Jesus would hang on a tree, water and blood pouring from his side, he exhibited this power: that anyone who worshiped him as Lord would dwell with him beside still waters forever and they would be filled with The River of *Living* Water (Psalm 23, John 7:38). Jesus became the vessel for us so that we might not taste the blood of death.

But for those who do not choose Jesus, the water represented in the form of blood does not foretell of an eternal life in paradise but rather the eternal wrath of God. Those who worship the evil spirits behind idols will drink from a different cup, the cup of judgment. For the Egyptians, this cup of wrath came in the form of a bloodied, deadly river. The fish, which were the Egyptians main protein source, all died (Exod. 7:21). God was making a statement to the Egyptians and their gods: it is YHWH who provides the fish. Except for possibly Bithiah, the bloody miracle would not be enough to convince them that YHWH was God. One would think that such a supernatural phenomena would

---

[24] James Strong, *Strong's Exhaustive Concordance of the Bible* (Peabody, MA: Hendrickson Publishing Marketing, LLC, 2007), H68 and H6086.

certainly bring a man or woman to their knees in humility, but that wasn't the case. So what possessed the stony hearts of the people?

The worship of The Moon Goddess.

Her wine had blinded the Egyptians just as it had blinded the Canaanites at Jebus. The goddess had gripped minds for thousands of years. Her deceptive spell went all the way back to her commander, Satan, the serpent in the Garden of Eden who made Adam and Eve question their identity in God and tempted them to eat of The Tree of Knowledge of Good and Evil. And as the human population grew and spread throughout the earth, the remembrance of the garden and its rivers of life waned like a waxing moon and the search for another manmade god created in a manmade garden began. In time the worship of foreign gods became not so foreign as The Moon Goddess walked through the open door and onto the stage of the world. But the door of access for her was not found in Eden like it was for Satan, her master. No. Her entrance came through a manmade door located in *Babylon*.

The Tower in Shinar

The lust for power and receiving that power from a higher being rose to its short lived peak at The Tower of Babel or The Tower of Babylon mentioned in Genesis 11:1-9. In this story we are told by the author of Genesis (Jewish and Christian tradition teaches the author to be Moses) that the offspring of Adam and Eve eventually spread across the earth and originally spoke the same language. At one point in early history, the people gathered in the land of Shinar on the Euphrates river (modern day Iraq) and settled there.

Outside of the garden and in the new land, the people began to make bricks of stone and asphalt and then used these bricks to build a tower in the city that would reach into the heavens.

"And they said, 'Come, let's make oven-fired bricks...
And they said, 'Come, let's build ourselves a city and a
tower with its top in the sky. Let's make a name for
ourselves; otherwise, we will be scattered throughout the
earth'" (Gen. 11:3-4).

The people longed for a higher view and a higher reach and they
craved an increase in power and knowledge. Omniscient God saw
the tower and, knowing their motives, went "down" to the people
(obviously God was above all thought to be gods) and "confuses"
their language, scattering them throughout the earth (Gen. 11:7).
The city is then renamed Babylon. Its tower's name, Babel, is
derived from the root word *balal* or "confuse." The city would
become an epicenter for confusion in Mesopotamia. The confusion
would lead to many deities, many forms of worship, and many
paths of religious thought. But all of those paths, all of the evil
spirits behind the deities worshiped, originate with one evil being
known as Satan, or *the accuser* (Job 1:7-9), the serpent from Eden.

Underneath the rule of Satan, come the fallen angels, the
principalities, powers, rulers of the darkness of this age, and
spiritual hosts of wickedness in high places who he uses to steal, kill
and destroy (Eph. 6:12, John 10:10). The high ranking
principalities of darkness operate behind three major deities of the
ancient world. The three false gods mentioned frequently in the
Bible are Ba'al, Asherah, and Moloch. Their names would change
from culture to culture. Each of these gods and the demonic
powers operating underneath them are from the same origin–the
fall of Satan–and they all have the same ending–the fall to eternal
torment.[25] Even though they are represented by different names
and images across time and cultures, these powers of darkness all

---

[25] "And the devil, who deceived them, was thrown into the lake of burning
sulfur, where the beast and the false prophet had been thrown. They will be
tormented day and night for ever and ever" (Revelation 20:10, NIV).

have the same fate. Their purpose from the garden until the end of the world is to do the work of Satan, whose ultimate goal is to bring as many souls to Hades with him as he can before Jesus returns.

The unclean spirits saw doubtful, prideful, identity-confused people and took advantage of the situation, using man to build a spiritual tower that would only bring about mankind's separation from each other and widen mankind's separation from God. The minions of Satan's malicious intent were exposed in Genesis in the lands of Shinar but throughout history, they would take on different forms and identities to conceal their demonic agendas. The Mesopotamian gods of Babylon influenced the Egyptians, the Canaanites, and other pagan civilizations in both the Old and New Testament. The land of Shinar, known as the birthplace of Babylon, played an important role in the scattering of the people and spreading the gods they worshiped across the world.

A Twisted Marriage and The Birth of Babylon

The name *Shinar* is actually derived from the worship of The Moon Goddess. In Genesis 10:8-12, Nimrod, a son of Cush who was son of Ham (one of Noah's three sons), was a "powerful hunter in the sight of the Lord" and his kingdom started with what would become Babylon (Gen 10:9). The English translation of the Hebrew almost makes it sound as if Nimrod was a mighty man, but the literal translation of the Hebrew is just that he was a physically strong man who excelled in hunting. In actuality Nimrod was not a spiritually "strong" man in the sense of morality. His name in Hebrew means "to rebel."

According to some legends, Nimrod was married to or at least had sexual relations with with a woman named Semiramis, a brothel owner from Uruk and queen of Assyria from 811-806

B.C.[26] This historical queen was well known in the ancient world for her grand building projects. She is credited with founding the ancient Armenian city Shamiramagerd, meaning "City of Semiramis."[27] Greek historians Herodotus and Strabo claim she built many earthworks around the Euphrates river and her name was applied to many monuments throughout the Ancient Near East. Roman historian Ammianus Marcellinus (330-400 B.C) credits her as the first person to castrate a young man into eunuch-hood.[28] If Marcellinus' statement is true, then it strongly suggests she was also a temple priestess. Per some legends, Nimrod would sleep with her upon his return from battle.

Ancient stories also describe her as secretive, dominating, and hypersexual. She was known to command total authority and indoctrinated many into her worship. Sumerian mythological renderings show her ascending to heaven as a dove where she became a fertility and queen goddess over all of the heavens. Semiramis, the queen of Uruk, was deified in the sight of the peoples and became the goddess she was said to have worshiped, *The Moon Goddess*.

The Moon Goddess was known as *Inanna* by the Sumerians, *Ishtar* by the Babylonians, *Isis* by the Egyptians, *Asherah/Ashteroth* by the Canaanites, *Venus* by the Romans, *Aphrodite/Selene/Luna* by the Greeks, *Diana/Artemis* by the Ephesians, *Rhiannon* by the Celts, *Sina*

---

[26] Dr. Nathan Merrell, "Nimrod, Semiramus, and the Mystery Religion of Babylon," https://findinghopeministries.org/nimrod-the-mystery-religion-of-babylon/; c.f.
Steven Merrill, *Nimrod: Darkness in the Cradle of Civilization* (Maitland, FL: Xulon Press, 2004); Annette Griffin, "What Do We Know About Semiramis, Nimrod's Wife?" 22 Jan. 2024, BibleStudyTools.com, https://www.biblestudytools.com/bible-study/topical-studies/who-was-semiramis-the-wife-of-nimrod.html

[27] Louis A. Boettiger, "Studies in the social Sciences: Armenian Legends and Festivals," *Studies in the Social Sciences: Armenian Legends and Festivals* 14 (1918): 10-11.

[28] Ammianus Marcellinus, *History, Volume I: Books 14-19.* Translated by J. C. Rolfe. Loeb Classical Library 300 (Cambridge, MA: Harvard University Press, 1950); Herodotus 1: 184. 1 (Rawlinson, LCL).

by the polynesians, *Coyolxauhqui* by the Aztecs, *Cybele* by the Phrygians. The prophet Jeremiah addressed her as *"Queen of Heaven"* (Jer. 44:19-23). Her aliases are lengthy but they are all the same spirit hiding in different craters of names and mythologies. So as it turns out, Renenutet, the Egyptian snake deity of the Nile who is syncretized with Isis, is just another form of The Moon Goddess, Inanna, or the deified version of Semiramis of Shinar.

Concerning Semiramis mythology, per the Greek historian Diodorus, Semiramis was the daughter of a noble fish goddess of Ascalon named Atargatis. The legend of Atargatis holds that she drowned herself in the sea leaving Semiramis, her daughter, an orphan. Semiramis was then fed by doves until Simmas, the royal shepherd, found her.[29] Notice the similar imagery of fish, her divine conception, and her assumption into the aristocracy of Syria to the images in the New Testament of Jesus, the saving shepherd who gives people access to the royal throne of heaven and makes fishers out of men.[30] The blatant mimicry is astounding. Eusebius, an ancient biblical scholar and historian, identified Semiramis as the wife of Nimrod. His writings inspired Alexander Hislop, a Scottish minister of the 1800's. In *The Two Babylons*, Hislop supported and used Eusebius' claim to defend his argument that the spirit of Babylon is the same spirit across polytheistic religions and is the same spirit behind papal worship.[31]

While the Bible only mentions Nimrod three times, his influence would be long lasting and affect world history. Nimrod, who had likely acquired respect from those around him because of

---

[29] Joshua J. Mark, "Sammu-Ramat and Semiramis: The Inspiration and the Myth," *World History Encyclopedia*, https://www.worldhistory.org/article/743/sammu-ramat-and-semiramis-the-inspiration-and-the/.

[30] Hebrews 13:20, Matthew 4:19, Ephesians 2:18

[31] Griffin, "Who was Semiramis" https://www.biblestudytools.com/bible-study/topical-studies/who-was-semiramis-the-wife-of-nimrod.html; c.f. Alexander Hislop, *The Two Babylons* or *The Papal Worship Proved to be the Worship of Nimrod and His Wife* (1858), Archive.org, https://archive.org/details/theTwoBabylons.

his hunting ability, was not a man of benevolence. Remember, Nimrod was a Cushite, a spiritual son of Ham, the cursed son of Noah (Gen. 9:18-27) whose name meant "rebel." He occupied and managed the lands that would become the center of harlotry, idolatry, and detestable practices.

While some historians deny this tale of Semiramis and Nimrod, there are interesting parallels between ancient gods and goddesses among these early civilizations. Some scholars and theorists suggest that Nimrod was Gilgamesh in the *Epic of Gilgamesh*, a demigod and possibly even a Nephilim.[32] The Assyrian and Babylonian cuneiform writings in the epic of Gilgamesh speak of Uruk where Semiramis was said to live.[33] Ishtar, the moon goddess spirit who Semiramis worshiped, is even a character in the epic.

Even more fascinating are the carved images of the ancient gods and goddesses. Specific features can be noted between Inaana/Semiramis/Ishtar and other gods and goddesses found in other cultures outside of ancient Babylon. Carvings depicting the goddess as wearing a crescent moon headdress with a backdrop of the sun and stars were not scant in Sumerian iconography. Inaana was also often depicted riding a lion, having large or many breasts, and possessing wings like an eagle. An examination of all the ancient polytheistic religions reveals eerie and uncanny similarities between their deities, their worship practices, their art, and their mythologies.

---

[32] "Now it came to pass, when men began to multiply on the face of the earth, and daughters were born to them, that the sons of God saw the daughters of men, that they were beautiful; and they took wives for themselves of all whom they chose. And the LORD said, 'My Spirit shall not strive with man forever, for he is indeed flesh; yet his days shall be one hundred and twenty years.' There were giants on the earth in those days, and also afterward, when the sons of God came into the daughters of men and they bore children to them. Those were the mighty men who were of old, men of renown" (Genesis 6:1-4, NKJV).

[33] Utah State University, *The Epic of Gilgamesh*, https://www.usu.edu/markdamen/ane/slides/m102_ot2.pdf

Inaana plaque courtesy of the British Museum, 2003; "Burney relief", "Queen of the Night"

A further study of Semiramis reveals that her name is actually the Hellenized form of the Sumerian word, *"Samar Amat,"* or *"Sammur-amat"* meaning "gift of the sea." The Hebrew word for Samar Amat is *Shinar*. The Tower of Babel was constructed in the lands of Shinar or one could say, the lands under the influence of a marine-born Semiramis, the worshiper of Ishtar who was, per mythology, the priestess of the moon god, Sin.[34]

The darkness behind this "moon" goddess deity was and still is the same across the world. She was connected with fertility, drunkenness, water, the sea, the moon, war and promiscuity. It was this spirit which influenced men to construct The Tower of Babel. This structure would function as the Queen of Heaven or The Moon Goddess' center of worship and provide a spiritual access point for Satan and the Babylonian goddess to come and go on the earth.

Unlike the pyramids of Egypt, many assume the Tower of Babel was a ziggurat which lacked indoor chambers. The structure was specifically designed for ascension and the main ziggurat of

---

[34]Louise Pryke, "Ishtar," World History Encyclopedia, 10 May 2019, https://www.worldhistory.org/ishtar/#google_vignette

ancient lands was where the patron deity was said to reign. The ziggurat of Shinar was one of complexity and much effort, cost, and time. Essentially, the ziggurat functioned as "the gate of the gods."[35] While there is not enough evidence to support the notion that this tower was built by Nimrod and Semiramis, priestess of The Moon Goddess, it was, according to the text of Genesis, a tower built by prideful people to exalt themselves into a realm God *did not* want them to occupy.

Despite the missing pieces in the story, there is too much evidence as it pertains to ancient worship of Ishtar, a manifestation of The Moon Goddess, to deny that Babylon is connected to the perverse practices of this spirit. The origin of moon goddess worship was in Babylon. And it is my belief that the Tower in Shinar was built to make way for her to descend into earth through the ascension of her priestess into the second heaven. In contrast to scholar John H. Walton who does not believe that people ascended ziggurats but that they were built for gods and goddesses to ascend and descend, others argue that a person *did* ascend, and that person was the high priestess to that deity.[36] As the priest or priestess would sit at the top making blood sacrifices, she would receive revelation from the deity. I tend to believe both sides arguing that the Babylonian spirit is the Queen of Heaven who entered through a man made gate via blood sacrifices and continues to come and go in the earth where she has access.[37]

---

[35] Walton, *Ancient Near Eastern*, 79-83.

[36] John H. Walton, *Ancient Near Eastern Thought and the Old Testament Second Edition* (Grand Rapids, MI: Baker Academic, 2018), 16. Harriet Crawford notes that historian Herodotus claimed there was a shrine at the top of the ziggurat but erosion has prevented archeological evidence from being found; Harriet Crawford, *Sumer and the Sumerians Second Edition* (New York: Cambridge University Press, 2004).

[37] An actual Ishtar Gate would be constructed under King Nebuchadnezzar II functioning as the main entry into Babylon around 604-562 B.C.

From Babylon The Moon Goddess worked her way into the nearby clans and lands. To assume that Queen of Heaven worship occurred only in Babylon and died with ancient Babylonians is to be deceived. In all of the descendants of Shem, Ham, and Japheth, the worship of Semiramis can be found. From Japheth would come the Dodanites/Rhodanites who would eventually inhabit much of Greece and the islands of the Agean and promote Ba'al and Ishtar worship through Zeus and Aphrodite. Even Shem whose descendants would include the patriarch Abraham, was influenced at some point by her worship, but it was the cursed root of Ham that really propagated paganism.[38] It was Nimrod who started Babylon (Gen. 1:10) and it would be from these lands that Ishtar worship would pulse through the veins of men and women who were spellbound by her.

The blood of her worship dripped down the generational lines. Mesopotamia, considered the "Cradle of Civilization," bore more than just human expansion; it birthed the expansion of paganism and polytheism. The language of the land where the Queen of Heaven had gained a foothold to confuse the people was broken up and scattered, but her shapeshifting and chameleonic disguise only intensified. The domino mask she wore concealed her through the ages as she took on different embellishments and colors, but the wickedness behind the mask remained the same.

Mimicry and Mockery

The mask of The Moon Goddess is mimicry and mockery. Satan, her master, can only attempt a copy of God's work. In Satan's limited power, he cannot create anything himself. His tactic is a wily takeover through cunning deceit. Like a serpent, he twists the

---

[38] Terah is mentioned in Genesis 11:26–32 as a son of Nahor, the son of Serug, descendants of Shem and, per Joshua 24:2, lived beyond the Euphrates and worshiped other gods.

truth and causes confusion. Then his most destructive maneuver is to pit man against man. Satan loves a bloody war. One of the ways he inspired wars was through mythological tales. The legends of ferocious and mighty deities and demigods were woven into mens' mindsets, some even believing they were descendants of such gods. Satan dangled shiny, delectable baits that lustered with lies in front of these stories. Additionally, he drew on the biological and innate nature in man and woman for childbearing, worship, and connection with a creator.

He drew upon the foundational biology of mankind to mimic the work of God by influencing demonic-inspired mythologies centered around false gods who had emotions and biological similarities with men and women. Creating a fantasy world clouded in mysticism, he also pulled on the innate desire for humans to tell stories and be a part of a story. And to complicate and confuse matters even more, Satan tangled truth and a lie so as to blur the lines between mythology and reality. The mythologies men and women began to tell, first orally and then through written form, of their surrounding world would actually, to a large degree, incorporate a spiritual world around them whether they knew it or not. The counterfeit to their reality was propagated through mimicry. Of significance is his mimicry and underpinning attempt to mock the virgin birth, and since I have been expounding upon the birth imagery it is only fitting to discuss it as it pertains to The Queen of Heaven or The Moon Goddess.

The virgin birth of Jesus was and will be the only virgin birth of all time and the birth was purposed and willed by God at the very foundation of the world. The incredible miracle could only come from the miraculous God who spoke time into existence. Predating Mary's yieldedness to the Father, before her profound assignment to carry the Messiah, and prior to her labor and delivery of the Son of Man, the earth was already trembling with labor pains for him. The Jew and Gentile, whether knowingly or unknowingly, were in labor pains prior to Mary's. What were the people of the earth laboring for exactly? They were laboring for a savior who would deliver them from the curse of separation from God.

The separation, the pain, and the turmoil came at the fall. And as men and women turned away from God to idols, either in the form of oneself, the Queen of Heaven, Ba'al, Moloch, the Nile, the moon, a pinecone, a dog, the list goes on, the pain intensified. And from the conception of Babylon came the false narrative of a virgin birth. Per Hislop's findings, Semiramis supposedly gave birth to Tammuz through supernatural sun rays of her deceased husband, Nimrod. She then incestuously marries her son Tammuz (also known as Dumuzid), believing he is Nimrod reincarnated.[39] While there are many skeptics who argue that Semiramis' power died with her and while many deny that Nimrod married her or deny that the two ever produced the child Tammuz, one cannot deny the fact that such deification was prominent, powerful, and persistent then and now. These figures certainly influenced belief systems, ceremonies, art, and worship.

Many other polytheistic cultures would repeat this false virgin birth story. But in each rendition, the spiritual child The Moon Goddess produced was a stillborn; it was always *death*. Operating as a mediatrix for mankind to reach their "god," she lured men and women deeper into her womb and as they went deeper, the demented concept of the ultimate abomination would take root in man's mind–child sacrifice.

The Moon Goddess was not the typical mother. Despite her being associated with fertility, childbearing, and sexuality, she was usually believed to be a "virgin" goddess who controlled fertility but also could murder anyone who stood in her way at any time, even her own children. Examples include Cōātlīcue, the "snake"

---

[39] Alexander Hislop, *The Two Babylons*, https://archive.org/details/theTwoBabylons.

goddess among the Aztecs, who they believed gave birth to the moon and stars, and Artemis, the virgin goddess of the moon among the Greeks who placed Orion and Scorpius constellations in the sky.[40] Despite these goddesses being virgins who represented childbearing and in some myths had miraculous virgin births of many children (like the one of Cōātlīcue), they would *require* blood, particularly children's blood, to appease them.

From the lands of Shinar would follow the influx of pagan worship of false religions that would secretly lure men and women in through the lust of the eyes, lust of the flesh, and pride of life. The concept of man ascending to the highest heaven on his own to appease the gods via the works of his hands would permeate the nations. The image of The Queen of Heaven "ascending as a dove" from the ziggurat in Shinar would attempt to mock the one true God who did not require man to ascend through good works, but himself descended as a dove upon the earth to bring mankind up with him through faith. But God cannot be mocked (Gal. 6:7-8) nor can he be confused. The contradictory expressions between personalities and the natures of these gods continue to manifest themselves through the confusion and chaos, lawlessness, schism and division present in our world today, but as knowledge and truth are revealed by the Holy Spirit, their strongholds and their dominions will begin to break. Babylon and the spirits under her will soon be no more.

---

[40] Mark Cartwright, "Coatlicue," 28 Nov. 2013, WorldHistoryEncyclopedia.org, https://www.worldhistory.org/Coatlicue/; Britannica, "Coatlicue," *Encyclopedia Britannica*, 17 Oct. 2021, https://www.britannica.com/topic/Coatlicue; Mike Lynch, "Sky Watch: Orion and Artemis and forbidden love," 14 Feb. 2016, Twin Cities Pioneer Press, https://www.twincities.com/2016/02/14/sky-watch-mike-lynch-orion/

Chapter 4

The Many Faces of the Moon

Then one of the seven angels who had the seven bowls came and spoke with me:
"Come, I will show you the judgment of the notorious prostitute who is seated on many
waters. The kings of the earth committed sexual immorality with her, and those who
live on the earth became drunk on the wine of her sexual immorality." Then he carried
me away in the Spirit to a wilderness.
I saw a woman sitting on a scarlet beast that was covered with the blasphemous names
and had seven heads and ten horns. The woman was dressed in purple and scarlet,
adorned with gold, jewels, and pearls. She had a golden cup in her hand filled with
everything detestable and with the impurities of her prostitution. On her forehead was
written a name, a mystery: BABYLON THE GREAT, THE MOTHER OF
PROSTITUTES AND THE DETESTABLE THINGS OF THE EARTH.
Then I saw that the woman was drunk with the blood of the saints and with the blood
of the witnesses to Jesus. When I saw her, I was greatly astonished.

Revelation 17:1-6, HCSB

For the sake of consistency, I will refer to The Queen of Heaven as The Moon Goddess moving forward. Remember that this goddess is a high-ranking principality under Satan's rule and bids his doing to twist, pervert, kill and destroy humanity. She and the demons she manages in the earth are spirits of lust, perversion, rage, gender confusion, idolatry, war, jealousy, promiscuity, witchcraft, and death. This is not an exhaustive list. She is the Babylonian Queen and the Babylonian Mother of Prostitutes mentioned in Revelation. And her main goal is to seduce souls into her hell in an attempt to launch an attack against YHWH who created those souls. She feasts on power and washes it down with blood. It is no wonder then that every time the Israelites bowed down to her or incorporated her worship practices into theirs it led to severe consequences. When a man or woman chooses to serve this god, or any others aside from Christ, they are assuming there is "another way" to achieve some higher knowledge, enter into an eternal paradise, or reincarnate into a better afterlife. But Jesus is the only way. To fall for her nymph melody is to fall prey to the very mythological outcomes of the doomed, blinded, spellbound sailors of folklore.

Before we begin our journey through ancient history to unmask this spirit and to effectively build upon the impact Egypt and other civilizations' moon goddess worship have had in the world, a basic understanding of cosmic geography should be laid.

Cosmic Geography

Most Christians, Jews, and Muslims today will claim that they believe in a heaven and a hell. Heaven is said to be "above" and hell "below" and the earth rests somewhere in the middle. The Lord and his angels inhabit a paradise, known as heaven, a spiritual realm of perfect peace. After dying, a believer (or children before the age of moral awareness) enters that heaven for eternity. Unbelievers go to a designated place called "hell" by their own choice. Originally reserved for Satan, the fallen angels, and all unclean spirits, hell is an eternal place of torment and darkness where the worm dieth not, the fire never goes out, men grind their teeth in agony, and hope is not found (Isa. 66:24, Mk 9:48, Rev. 20:14-15). For the Christian who acknowledges spiritual warfare, there is more to the picture than this simple, three-tiered construct. There is the highest heaven where God the Father and God the Son dwell and reign. There is also a second heaven where spiritual hosts of wickedness and territorial principalities dwell. And there is hell which is either in the center of the earth (believed by some) or in an outer darkness (believed by others). Even in polytheistic religions, similar hierarchies have been assumed. This tiered construct in the mind is an ancient one.

Understanding our placement in the cosmic geography is important. For the Egyptians and other ancient civilizations, "the sun moved through the sky during the day and then moved during the night into the underworld, where it traversed under the earth to its place for rising for the next day. Neither the sun nor the moon was recognized as a physical object; they were gods and lights."[41] Their cosmic geography was metaphysical, Ra (the sun god) sailing in the cosmic waters of heaven during the day and the cosmic waters of the netherworld at night. The Moon Goddess arched above the sky bearing the stars on her chest.[42] In ancient thought the gods and goddesses were confined to and administered their powers from a place outside earth.

For the Mesopotamians, Egyptians, and Canaanites, the sun set in the west and entered the netherworld each day, the moon controlled the monthly and yearly calendar, and the stars and planets were used in omens, astrology, and storytelling. The belief of what happened in the sun's journey and the moon's phases played a significant role in the religious practices.

With an ancient cosmology understanding, I would now like to break down The Moon Goddess' worship throughout the ancient world, beginning with the Sumerians. My goal is to show how this spirit, though different in mythology and names in different regions, is actually the same spirit across time and cultures.

Mesopotamia and the Sumerians

Adding to what I have already discussed concerning Semiramis and Ishtar, the Sumerian moon goddess was known as *Inanna*.

---

[41] Walton, *Ancient Near Eastern Thought*, 133.

[42] Walton, *Ancient Near Eastern Thought*, 133; c.f. Horowitz, *Mesopotamian Cosmic Geography*, 120,265; W.G. Lambert, "The Cosmology of Sumer and Babylon" in *Ancient Cosmologies*, ed. Blacker and Loewe, 62.

Inanna was also the goddess of sex, fertility, war, love, sensuality, and power who became *Ishtar* to the Babylonians, Akkadians, and Assyrians. She was the most worshiped deity in the Sumerian pantheon and her temples could be found across Mesopotamia. Her symbols included the lion, eagle wings, and an eight-pointed star and she was associated with the planet Venus in astrology. Her cult practices were sex-focused with many temple prostitutes performing sexual duties on behalf of the deity.

This spirit was double sided, too. She could be a woman or a man, her emotions were bipolar, and she could live or die. Her festivals and cultic rites demonstrated the perverted and confusing parts of her mythology. *Gala*, a set of male priests in the temples of Inanna, were required to take on female names, sing in female voices, have homosexual intercourse, cross dress, and even castrate themselves through erratic self-mutilation.[43] In the Akkadian worship of Ishtar, similar practices were done by priests called the *kurgarrū* and *assinnu*.[44]

Though the goddess was associated with sex, war, fertility, and love, she was not the goddess of marriage.[45] In fact, this spirit hates marriage and thrives in strife. She was also known to be invoked by incantations and chants, erotic dances, and prostitution and if she was displeased with any act, she was said to seek revenge in wrath and terrify and confuse those who disappointed her. One of the hymns dedicated to her declares, "She stirs confusion and chaos against those who are disobedient to her, speeding carnage

---

[43] Gwendolyn Leick, *Sex and Eroticism in Mesopotamian Literature* (New York, NY: Routledge, 2013), 285.

[44] Will Roscoe and Stephen Murray, *Islamic Homosexualities: Culture, History, and Literature* (New York, NY: New York University Press, 1997), 65-66.

[45] Jeremy Black and Anthony Green, *Gods, Demons, and Symbols of Ancient Mesopotamia: An illustrated dictionary* (The British Museum Press, 1992), 108-109, 182.

and inciting the devastating flood, clothed in terrifying radiance."[46] Her "family" in the Sumerian pantheon was even incestruous with many texts hinting at a sexual relationship between the sun god and her brother, Utu.[47] Despite her not being associated with marriage, some myths claim she was married to Dumuzid, later known as Tammuz, who is her proposed son in her other form of Semiramis.[48]

"Substitute king ritual" was also prevalent in ancient Mesopotamia. The sacrifice of humans was an identifying marker of The Moon Goddess.

> "In this case, omens, usually an eclipse, would indicate that the deity was displeased with the king. If the divination priests concluded through their arts that the omens suggested that the king's life was in jeopardy, he would step down from his throne and a substitute would be enthroned for a period of time to be determined, usually a maximum of one hundred days. Chosen by the diviners, he was enthroned, dressed like the king, and given the royal insignias (crown, mantle, weapon, scepter). He was given a queen, who eventually shared his fate. He played the role of the king by presenting offerings before the altar and burning incense. At the same time, he was made to recite omen litanies and thereby take the evil omens on himself. The final act by which the transference of the evil omens was accomplished came at the end of the period when the substitute was put to death. Thus the omens were canceled and the king and his prince were redeemed. The substitution was seen as a way of allowing the gods to do what they wanted to do. The omens had indicated that the gods desired to act against someone. The ritual was not intended to fool the gods but to give them a ready victim on whom to carry out their intentions. It would never be known in this case what the gods

[46] Enheduanna pre 2250 BCE, "A hymn to Inanna (Inana C)," *The Electronic Text Corpus of Sumerian Literature*. 2003, lines 18–28. 4.07.3.

[47] Louise M. Pryke, *Ishtar* (New York and London: Routledge, 2017), 36-37.

[48] Diane Wolkstein and Samuel Noah Kramer, *Inanna, Queen of Heaven and Earth: Her stories and hymns from Sumer* (New York City, New York: Harper & Row Publishers, 1983), x-xi.

had been angry about. It only gave them a target to inflict their anger on, which would result in their appeasement."[49]

It is of no surprise that The Moon Goddess, Ba'al, and Moloch required human life to satisfy their appetite being that their entire goal is to destroy mankind. The detestable practices of this goddess, especially human sacrifice, traveled out of Mesopotamia and into the world, including Egypt, a land whose king would perform the largest massacre of Hebrew boys in the Old Testament. Egypt with its long and winding Nile would, in fact, play a large role in the travel of The Moon Goddess.

Egypt's Isis, Osiris, and Horus

Being that Egypt was greatly influenced by Mesopotamia, it is a great starting place for understanding the beliefs and practices of polytheistic worship, particularly the worship of The Moon Goddess. The Egyptians were master recorders, mathematicians, artists, and sculptists. They were also extremely spiritual. One need not look further than the three pyramids of Giza to know the Egyptians were skilled and intelligent for their time. And despite conspiracy theorists, the template of those pyramids did not come from aliens (except if a person claims fallen angels as aliens). No. Their mythologies and sculptural inspirations came from the principalities under Satan's rule–Ba'al (Ra), The Moon Goddess (Isis), Tammuz (Horus), along with many more. The ancient Egyptians were a smart people and the spirits knew it.

In ancient Egyptian mythology, Ra the sun god had four children: Osiris (son), Isis (daughter), Nephthys (daughter), and Set (son). The tale goes as follows: Osiris married Isis and Nephthys

---

[49] Walton, *Ancient Near Eastern*, 101; c.f. S. Parpola, *Letters from Assyrian and Babylonian Scholars*, SAA 10 (Helsinki: University of Helsinki Press, 1993); c.f. Discussion in J. Bottero, "The Substitute King and His Fate," *Akkadica* 9 (1978): 2-24.

married Set. Osiris, the firstborn, was to inherit Ra's kingdom. Set becomes envious and plots to usurp the throne by killing his brother. He builds a sarcophagus to Osiris' measurements and when Osiris returns from his journey, Set has him play a game of who can fit in the sarcophagus. When Osiris is in the sarcophagus, Set slams the lid and buries his brother alive in the Nile River. This coffin then floats into Byblos (modern day Syria and Lebanon).

The king of Byblos finds the sarcophagus, which had a beautiful acacia tree growing out of it, and puts it into the temple to be worshiped. Meanwhile, Isis is distraught at her husband's absence and sets out with Nephthys to find him. Using magic, Isis finds the sarcophagus and retrieves it, then using her ankh, she breathes life into Osiris' dead body and he is resurrected. She sleeps with Osiris and posthumously produces Horus, "the all-seeing eye," who becomes the savior child of Egypt. But the story doesn't end there.

Set, infuriated by his dead brother's abduction, sets out across the land to try and stop Isis and Nephthys. He stumbles across a cave and finds his brother alive and well. Angry, Set murders Osiris again, scattering his body parts throughout Egypt. He specifically takes the "golden manhood" of Osiris and throws it into the Nile river where it is eaten by a crocodile. Isis and Nephthys return and, to their dismay, find Osiris missing. Knowing what Set did, they then set out to gather all of Osiris' body parts. They find thirteen but cannot find the missing manhood, so they attempt to make him one out of wood and dirt, but this attempt is a lousy one. Isis then uses her magic again through a fanning of her wings to resurrect him a second time.[50]

---

[50] Jan Assmann, *The Search for God in Ancient Egypt*, Translated by David Lorton (Ithaca, NY: Cornell University Press, 2001); Geraldine Pinch, *Egyptian Mythology: A Guide to the Gods, Goddesses, and Traditions of Ancient Egypt* (Oxford University Press, 2004).

Osiris then becomes the Judge and God of the Underworld. Horus becomes associated with the pharaoh who was considered to be a reincarnation of the deity. In other renderings, Horus takes on the officiating priest in rituals. Isis becomes The Moon Goddess who is connected to fertility, motherhood, and the Nile.[51] Pharaohs were believed to have nursed from her breasts and the people were won to her allegiance through her healing spells. The Moon Goddess concealed her deathly motive behind a masquerade of "miracles," healings and prophecy. She filled her followers with a deceptive wine and numbed their conscience to a state of marble until their hearts mirrored the massive monuments they built in her honor.

These monuments consisted of obelisks, pyramids, the Sphinx, and temples. The obelisks were Ba'al and The Moon Goddess' greatest display of hubris. The phallic symbols were called *tekhenu*, meaning "to pierce," by the Egyptians. They were constructed with a gold cap and represented Osiris' manhood. Per legend, each day when the sun would rise over the top of the obelisk, it would reflect off the gold and "shower" the land. When this occurred, it was believed that the sun god was procreating with The Moon Goddess (Isis) and regenerating the earth. At night as the moon would rise over the obelisk, it again cast a light across the land to remind the people that The Moon Goddess was procreating at that moment and giving the earth power. While some would say these are nothing but dead ancient myths, the phallic objects were not limited to Egypt and there are modern day obelisks found and worshiped in the world today including the Washington Monument, Cleopatra's Needle in Central Park NYC, Place de la Concorde in Paris, and the Column of the Immaculate Conception in front of the Vatican.

---

[51] Walton, *Near Eastern Ancient Thought*, 323.

Vatican Obelisk in St. Peter's Square in Vatican City.

The ritualistic practices surrounding Egypt's moon goddess Isis were perverted, horrific, abhorrent, and bloody. One historical document revealing pieces of her practice is found in *The Golden Ass* also called *Metamorphoses* written by the late second century Roman author Apuleius. In his novel the protagonist, Lucius, was transformed into a donkey, fell asleep in Greece and awoke to a full moon. He then prayed to the moon, calling upon the goddess, and Isis appeared. She declared herself the greatest of all goddesses and told him to attend the Navigium Isidis, a feast in her honor occurring nearby. There he was instructed to eat roses to restore him to a human form. After this transformation he decides to join the local Isis temple and undergo initiation.

Scholars are divided on whether Apuleius' book was a satire or an actual account of his devotion to the goddess, but most agree that the novel reveals to a moderate degree the temple cult practices. Initiation involved paying money to the temple, fasting and repenting, and being brought to near death.[52] What happened in the most inner part of the sanctuary was kept a secret. The rites mentioned in the novel are intentionally cryptic, but historical findings of Egyptian (and later Greek) initiation rites and temple practices reveal the details of the rites. See this example from Britannica Encyclopedia:

> "The initiation ceremonies usually mimed death and resurrection. This was done in the most extravagant manner. In some ceremonies, candidates were buried or shut up in a sarcophagus; they were even symbolically deprived of their entrails and mummified (an animal's belly with entrails was prepared for the ceremony). Alternatively, the candidates were symbolically drowned or decapitated. In imitation of the Orphic myth of Dionysus Zagreus, a rite was held in which the heart of a victim, supposedly a human child, was roasted and distributed among the participants to be eaten.
>
> The baptism could be either by water or by fire, and the rites often included actions that had an exotic flavor. Sulfur torches were used during the baptism ceremony; they were dipped into water and then—contrary to the expectations of the observers —burned when drawn out of the water. In a dark room a script would suddenly become visible on a wall that had been prepared accordingly. Instructions still exist for producing a nimbus effect—the appearance of light around the head of a priest. The priest's head was shaved and prepared with a protective ointment; then a circular metal receptacle for alcohol was fixed on his head; it was set aflame in a dark room and would shine for some seconds. In the Dionysus and Isis mysteries, the initiation was sometimes accomplished by a 'sacred marriage,' a sacral copulation. Two cases are known in which a priest speaking from the statue of the god ordered a

---

[52] Jaime Alvar translated by Richard Gordan, *Romanising Oriental Gods: Myth, Salvation, and Ethics in the Cults of Cybele, Isis, and Mithras, Spanish Edition* (Leiden: Brill Academic Publishing, 2008), 336-337;
Hugh Bowden, *Mystery Cults of the Ancient World* (Princeton, NJ: Princeton University Press, 2010), 166-167;
Jan N. Bremmer, *Initiation into the Mysteries of the Ancient World* (Berlin: Walter de Gruyter, 2014), 114.
Arthur J. Hanson, *Metamorphoses (The Golden Ass), Volume II: Books 7-11* (Harvard University Press, 1989); see also Walter Burkert, *Ancient Mystery Cults* (Harvard University Press: 1987).

credulous woman to come to the temple and be the god's concubine, the part of the god being enacted by the priest."[53]

Isis with Horus, bronze figurine of the Late Period; in the Egyptian Museum, Berlin.

The bait the goddess used was shrouded in "mysteries" where men and women who knew the secrets and participated in unique initiation rites felt a sense of belonging and control. Her practices took on other forms and names throughout the ages. Some were more modest, appealing to a more sophisticated crowd, while other temples and rites were licentious and excessive, like the temple worship of Cybele and Lilluth which required men to bring themselves to the point of orgasm before self-mutilating their genitalia. Blood sacrifice, which was prominent throughout all Ancient Near Eastern religions, was the ultimate open door to curses and greater darkness.

The Sumerians had opened a door to Satan's dark realm. The Egyptians opened more, including Pandora's Box.

The Greeks and Romans

In one of the most famous Greek mythologies, Pandora, the first woman on earth, received a box from the gods which contained all of the evil in the world. Upon her opening the box, all the miseries

---

[53] Reinhold Merkelbach, "Mystery Religion," *Encyclopedia Britannica*, https://www.britannica.com/topic/mystery-religion

of life were released into the world.[54] The metaphor "Pandora's Box" is now used as a proverbial phrase to mean a source of vast complications and troubles. The story might not be far off when one considers what spilled out of the vestibule of The Moon Goddess' temples. Her corrupt practices spread from the lands of Egypt, Canaan, and Babylon to Greece and Rome, to Asia and Indonesia, and ancient Europe. Meanwhile, similar practices were occurring in the future "new world" of the ancient Americas.

The offshoots of all of Noah's sons were at some point in time participating in sun and moon goddess worship. While it is hard to pinpoint one people group who began pagan worship in the lands that once encompassed the Roman empire and ancient Greece, we do know that all originated with the sons of Noah. We are told in Genesis 10:1-5 and 1 Chronicles 1:1-7 that Japheth's descendant, Dodanim (or Rhodanim in some translations) settled in what is now modern Greece and the coastal islands of Greece including The Island of Rhodes. His other descendants would spread from the Caucasus eastward into Central Asia and westward through Asia Minor to the coastlands of Europe and possibly even China. The Roman and Greek world powers would come from Japheth's line, leaving a lasting imprint on the world.

Dodanim/Rhodanim

Both Rhodes and Dodona, though separate land regions, were under the influence of pagan worship. Dodona was a historical sanctuary site in Epirus (a historical land region shared between modern Greece and Albania) and its earliest mention is by Homer in *The Iliad* who associates it with the Greek god Zeus. According to historian Plutarch, a temple was erected for the worship of Jupiter/Zeus at Dodona and it quickly became the hub of oracles. Though it did not surpass the ancient grandeur of the Oracles at Delphi in Ephesus, it did pre-date Delphi, functioning as a hotspot for

---

[54] Britannica, The Editors of Encyclopaedia. "Pandora". *Encyclopedia Britannica*, 28 May. 2024, https://www.britannica.com/topic/Pandora-Greek-mythology.

prophecies and pagan temple worship. The religious practices of The Moon Goddess were seen early on in Greece.

Historian Herodotus claims he was told by priests at Egyptian Thebes in the 5th century B.C., "that two priestesses had been carried away from Thebes by the Phoenicians." These Thebes priestesses were "the first founders of places of divination in the aforesaid countries" who called themselves the *pleiades* or "doves" at Dodona because of their "strange sounding language."[55] Later in this chapter, we will see that the infamous Jezebel in the Book of Kings was a Phoenician woman who hosted The Moon Goddess. But here again we see the mimicry of the dove being used in a strange way. Recall that the dove in the Sumerian tale of Inanna (also Semiramis) is that she was fed by doves at her birth following her fish mother's abandonment and then upon her death ascended like a dove. The Thebes priestesses were simply operating under the same spirit.

The largest outward sign to the world that the sun god (Ba'al) and The Moon Goddess were operating in the inward parts of men throughout Greece could be seen in massive monuments such as the Temple of Artemis and Diana, annual festivals such as the Athenian Pandia, and statues such as the Colossus at Rhodes. The Colossus at Rhodes was a colossal statue of the sun god, Helios, that was said to be located on the Island of Rhodes. A monument around the size of the Statue of Liberty, its legs bridged the entry way for incoming mariners. After twelve years of construction, the statue stood as a large graven image for 54 years before it toppled over by an earthquake in 226 B.C.[56] The temple of Artemis was also considered a wonder of the world and was the largest marble Greek temple ever built. The grandiosity of these statues and monuments was short lived though as all were

---

[55] Herodotus, *The History of Herodotus*, 4 vols. trans. George Rawlinson (New York: Tandy-Thomas Co., 1909). Vol. 2. 2:54–57.

[56] Adda Bruemmer Bozeman, *Politics and Culture in International History: From the Ancient Near East to the Opening of the Modern Age* (Piscataway, NJ: Transaction Publishers: 1994), 108.

destroyed either by earthquakes or war. It is ironic that The Moon Goddess and Ba'al who hide themselves behind fixed objects in the sky not made by human hands cannot hide for long in man made structures on earth.

Cybele, Demeter, Rhea

In ancient Greece, Demeter was the goddess of harvest and fertility, the daughter of Rhea who was the mother of Zeus. Cybele, the Anatolian and Phrygian moon goddess, made her way into Greece and was widely accepted. As a hermaphrodite, Cybele, or Mater Deum Magna Idaea (Great Idaean Mother of the Gods) was both male and female and the goddess of all life in Greece around the 5th century B.C.[57] She eventually assimilated to Demeter and Rhea, her cultic practices mingling with those of Demeter and Rhea. Along with a eunuch priesthood, Cybele's ecstatic dancing and orgiastic celebrations of Inanna of Mesopotamia were common in Dionysus/Bacchus (god of fertility, wine, and pleasure) and Pan (god of shepherds and hunters) worship as was bloodletting, a practice seen in the Bible among the prophets of Ba'al (1 Kings 18:28).[58]

Aphrodite/Venus

Cybele also took on the name of Aphrodite in Cyprus, Cythera, and Corinth. As men and women pilgrimaged, so did the spirits behind their polytheistic beliefs. Moon goddess worship traveled through mountains, vineyards, and valleys, and, for Greece

---

[57] Britannica, "Great Mother of the Gods'," *Encyclopedia Britannica*, 6 Jun. 2024, https://www.britannica.com/topic/Great-Mother-of-the-Gods.

[58] Jenny Wade, "The Castrated Gods and their Castration Cults: Revenge, Punishment, and Spiritual Supremacy," *International Journal of Transpersonal Studies* 38(1), https://doi.org/10.24972/ijts.2019.38.1.31.
Lynn Emrich Roller, *In Search of God the Mother: The Cult of Anatolian Cybele* (Berkeley and Los Angeles, California: University of California Press, 1999), 228-232.

especially, across the ocean. The marine goddess, her statues, and her cult greeted and entertained visitors in the ports. She didn't even have to look for the people to worship her, as she had used her dark magic to brainwash the majority. Her fantasies and mysticism had lured them in. Kings and warriors would travel from distant lands to hear her prophecies and sleep with her concubines.

Though The Moon Goddess had disguised herself yet again with another name and through a different people group, her associations and practices were the same. She was known to the Greeks as Aphrodite and to the Romans as Venus. She was the goddess of sexual love and beauty, fertility, seafaring, and war. Hesiod, an early Greek poet, claimed in his *Theogony* that she was "born from the white foam produced by severed genitals of Uranus (Heaven)."[59] In Greek mythology she was promiscuous, adulterous, and murderous. She served as the prostitute's patron deity and the philosopher's idol. She bathed in perversion, idolatry, and lust and pushed her followers to do the same. Homer called her the daughter of Zeus and Dione. She was a cognate of Astarte, Ishtar, and Inanna. The Moon Goddess of the Babylonians had merely been Hellenized, and the people had fallen yet again into her trap. Homer wrote of her this way,

> "What life is there, what delight, without golden Aphrodite? She spoke and loosened from her bosom the embroidered girdle of many colors into which all her allurements were fashioned. In it was love and in its desire and in its blandishing persuasion which steals the mind even of the wise."[60]

Her main centers of worship were Paphos, Amathus, the island of Cythera, and Corinth. Today she is worshiped in Neopagan religions including the Church of Aphrodite, Wicca, and Hellenismos but is also hidden behind secret societies such as Freemasonry and Knights of Pythia, The Illuminati, and other worldwide religions such as Shintoism, Islam, and Hinduism.

---

[59] Britannica, "Amathus," *Encyclopedia Britannica*, 17 Oct. 2023, https://www.britannica.com/place/Amathus.
[60] Homer, *Iliad*, Translated by Samuel Butler, 14.193 (Barnes and Noble Publishing, 1995).

The goddess, like nearby Cybele, did not limit herself to a gender. She was considered both male and female which fuzzed the lines between reality and biology and further opened Pandora's Box to the myriad of sexual confusion and perversion that permeated her cult. Truth then became obsolete and with it morale. If she could be both genders or genderless, then her devotees could be as well. She was considered the inspiration of male homosexual relations, pederasty (men attracted to boys), and eroticism. Her esteemed "beauty" was symbolized with swans, sparrows, doves, and pomegranates but the stench of her foul worship could not be beautified nor deodorized.

From the Classical period to the Hellenistic and Roman periods, her worship included festivals and processions, feasts, sacrifice, and sex. The main festival, the Aphrodisia, was celebrated on the fourth day of the month of Hekatombaion (3rd week of July to 3rd week of August). The festivities included temple purification with the blood of sacrificed doves, bathing of her statues, and worship in her shrines. Notice again the mockery of the sacrifice. Her desired sacrifice was that of a dove– which is associated with The Holy Spirit in Matthew 3:16– and her *forbidden* sacrifice was that of a polluted goat. The sacrifice of a goat to atone for sin was associated with the Passover for the Jews.

Behind her mimicry was malicious intent. She was determined to break men and women. Her status as mother of prostitutes was well known in the ancient world. She "mothered" the *pornai* or "cheap street prostitutes" used by pimps and the *hetairai*, the more "expensive, well-educated" prostitutes.[61] Corinth was said to have housed the "most skilled" of the *hetairai*. Even more sickening was her condoning of minor sexual relations. But the most wicked act of all was the sacrifice of children. According to an archeological find in 2014, there were many child sacrifices in ancient Carthage, a major Phoenician port city located on the northern coast of Africa that was repackaged in the Roman empire

---

[61] Monica S. Cyrino, *Aphrodite (Gods and Heroes of the Ancient World)*, (New York and London: Routledge, 2010), 41-42.

under Julius Caesar.[62] Not to mention the children conceived by temple prostitutes who oftentimes were aborted, killed, or groomed for her cult.

The Moon Goddess, just as she had done in ancient Mesopotamia, had taken on new forms and, now through the proliferation of manmade mythological deities, masked herself and her abhorrent practices behind many different gods and goddesses. For the Greeks she was Aphrodite as well as Selene (the actual deified new and full moon goddess) and Artemis and Hecate (the goddess of witchcraft). For the Romans, she was Venus and Luna. She may have manifested differently in different cultures but her vile acts were consistent in the cities where she was venerated. And one of her most coveted powers was that of fortune telling.

The Oracles at Dodona and Delphi

Witchcraft and sorcery were the nucleus of moon goddess worship. Remember that Nimrod's name means "to rebel" and recall the prophet Samuel telling King Saul in 1 Samuel 15:23, "For rebellion is as the sin of witchcraft, and stubbornness is an iniquity and idolatry." The core of her worship is rebellion.

In Leviticus 19:31, God instructed his people, "Do not turn to mediums or seek out spiritists, for you will be defiled by them. I am the LORD your God." Her worship was and is witchcraft and idolatry. The dark magic of her spells, incantations, hexes, and hypnotism were her way to manipulate and control, to mind-bind and captivate. One of the most practiced forms of her magic was fortune telling or the ability of her priests and priestesses to foretell the future. Unlike the true prophets of YHWH, her prophets and prophetesses gained their knowledge and information illegally. So while some of her prophecies could turn out to be "true," she and her consort Ba'al were actually false prophets, having given the people elicited information to lead them into a trap.

---

[62] "Ancient Carthaginians really did sacrifice their children," 23 Jan. 2014, University of Oxford, https://www.ox.ac.uk/news/2014-01-23-ancient-carthaginians-really-did-sacrifice-their-children

Stories of her prophecies and oracles are prevalent throughout the ancient world. The two hotspots where her magic was practiced were The Oracles at Dodona and The Oracles at Delphi. In Dodona, the oracle shrine was the seat of Gaia/Dione (mother earth) and Zeus and, per Herodotus, a gray-headed priestess remained there who spoke with black doves from Egypt and interpreted sounds of leaves, doves, water, and tree branches.[63] In these peculiar acts, she (or another priestess of Zeus and Dione) would then release a mystic prophecy of what was to come. This oracle, per Herodotus, produced a "strange" sound. These caws of her rebellion wouldn't stand, however. The Moon Goddess prophecies had a foothold in Dodona for a time but her sounds were eventually muted by Emperor Theodosius in 393 B.C. who uprooted the sacred oaks and banned pagan sites and festivals.

The second and most famous oracle shrine was the one at Delphi in Ephesus. It was here that priestesses called Pythia (named after the Python snake) were said to have spoken directly with the Greek god Apollo (sun god). The Pythia and her officiants before and after her gained much influence in the ancient world as farmers and businessmen would seek the goddesses' prophecies about harvest seasons while kings and warriors would seek out the women for oracles concerning future battles. Of these kings would be the famous Spartan king Leonidas who would die in battle against Xerxes the king of Persia, the same Xerxes in the Book of Esther. Roughly 200 years later, Alexander the Great would seek out the famous Delphic priestess. It is said that some 500 oracular statements were given at Delphi. Acts 16 informs us that the Delphic oracles were still present and operating in the infancy of Christianity.

But The Moon Goddesses' services were not free. The temple overseers demanded fees and exchange of goods for her services. Additionally, on the days when she would give her oracle, provisional cakes were required as well as the slaughter of a beast. These "cakes" were not new to the true prophets of God.

---

[63] "The Oracle Shrine at Dodona," VisitGreece.gr, https://www.visitgreece.gr/experiences/culture/archaeological-sites-and-monuments/the-oracle-shrine-at-dodona/

"'The sons gather wood, the fathers light the fire, and the women knead dough to make cakes for the queen of heaven, and they pour out drink offerings to other gods so that they provoke me to anger. But are they really provoking me?' This is the Lord's declaration. 'Isn't it they themselves being provoked to disgrace?'" (Jer. 7:18, HCSB).

"Then the Lord said to me, 'Go again; show love to a woman who is loved by another man and is an adulteress, just as the Lord loves the Israelites though they turn to other gods and love raisin cakes'" (Hos. 3:1, HCSB).

Priestess of Delphi (1891) by John Collier

The concept that food would be spiritually consumed by the gods to appease them was not uncommon. The gods of Ephesus, just as with the gods of Babylon and Egypt, were unstable, unreliable and unpredictable. Bad omens and natural disasters were signs of the gods wrath and displeasure. For their devotees, if food wouldn't appease their outrage, people certainly would.

The practice of human sacrifice to please and pacify the gods permeated Greek and Roman religions. Even gladiators were given over in sacrifice to gods along with many of the prophetesses and prostitutes themselves who worked the temples. To appease the gods with natural food and drink, human sacrifice, incense and sex, was erroneous to God. The "sweet" cakes and what they represented were detestable. Ezekiel, a prophet of YHWH, summed up the rancid raisin cakes in his prophetic act in Ezekiel 4 in which he kneaded bread and cooked it over human dung as a picture of the peoples' rebellious acts and marriage with foreign gods.

The food The Moon Goddess required could not go without a drink. Her meals were washed down with blood, either in the form of sacrificial animals, battles of men, or even, as stated above, her priestesses themselves. Plutarch describes how the priestesses' trances for revelation were often physically exhausting and could lead to death just a few days after the event.[64] I will discuss the Pythia priestesses and their poisonous platter of prophecy in greater depth in Part II. But for now, I want to turn to the Canaanites, the archaic ancestors of the Greeks and Romans; the ones who were just as blood thirsty, if not more than their Greeks and Roman successors.

In fact, on the Canaanite menu was a special cocktail–the blood of God's prophets.

The Canaanites

To holistically appreciate the impact the Canaanites had on the world, one must go back to the beginning of the world. The Canaanites progenitor really begins with Noah's son, Ham, who I have mentioned was a cursed son of Noah. But why was he cursed? And what did the curse of Canaan have to do with The Moon Goddess? To answer these questions, I will begin with a peculiar scene which takes place in Genesis 9; a scene that is, to say the least, intoxicating.

While much could be deciphered from Genesis 9:1-28, I am going to stick to the parts that I believe pertain to the theme of this book. In the story Noah and his three sons came out of the ark following the destructive flood. After many days in a confined boat

---

[64] Plutarch, "De Defectu Oraculorum (Περὶ τῶν Ἐκλελοιπότων Χρηστηρίων)," Translated by F.C. Babbitt, Vol. V Loeb Classical Library Edition, 1936.

surrounded by only water, Noah, likely ecstatic to be on land once again, begins a garden, a vineyard in fact. This vineyard took time to grow. Vineyards are typically well established at or around three years time. The author of Genesis doesn't tell us what occurred during this length of time, but we can assume that excavation work, planting, tending to, harvesting, and fermentation had to all take place. We can also assume that Noah had the seeds to begin the vineyard. So, after much time and work, Noah, "a man of the soil," drinks the wine of his vineyard, becomes drunk, and uncovers himself inside *his* tent. His youngest son, Ham, sees his father naked and tells his brothers outside. Shem and Japheth take a cloak and place it upon their shoulders, forming a privacy screen. They then walk backwards, covering Noah's nakedness while their faces were turned away from their father. In honor of Noah, they took the responsibility and cloaked him while keeping their faces from looking, a look that could kill. By seeing their father in his drunken state, they might have seen the outside–a battered ark per se–but neglected the heart of the man– the survivor on the inside.

Ham's actions brought the consequence of a curse. In an attempt to ridicule his father in his numbed state of mind would bring about Ham's own ridicule in his father's sober state. Though Noah's actions may seem absurd, Ham had no right to judge his father's choice. The vineyard was *Noah's*, the tent was *Noah's*, and the covenant was with *Noah*. If Ham was close enough to see even his father's nakedness, possibly even spying, then his proximity should have revealed the promise. Ham should have known the covenant God made with Noah just before he began his vineyard, a covenant of redemption and justice, of mercy and love. In the time since he stepped foot off the ark, Ham had forgotten about the God he served, a God of mercy and justice. Tarry had stripped his faith and his pride had taken his honor. It harkens Hebrews 4:13, "No creature is hidden from him but all are naked and exposed before him to whom we must give an account." In judging his father's exposure, Ham's heart would be exposed. The flood had not washed away his critical and condemning heart. It would be from Ham's cursed bloodline that the Canaanites would emerge.

The Curse of the Canaanites

After learning of Ham's actions, Noah—now sober—sees with X-ray vision his children. The prophet Noah cursed Ham's son Canaan and declared him to be "the lowest of slaves to his brothers" and two more times declared Canaan to be Shem's slave (Gen. 9:24-28). Recall that Shem was the forefather of Abraham, the man who God would expound upon his covenant and later fulfill his covenant through Jesus. Canaan, though still under the covenant of God promised to his grandfather Noah, would not be the one chosen for the future lineage of Jesus. A look really can kill. This curse would not be broken until Jesus, God's one and only son, hung naked and exposed on the cross for mankind's sins; a nakedness that showcased not a drunken, numbed God but a sober, alert God whose heart has always been for redeeming his people.

But while curses can be broken, the covenant cannot. And in God's covenant with Noah, He makes clear the requirement: to be fruitful and multiply the earth with new life and any life taken away through bloodshed will be punishable by death.

> "However, you must not eat meat with its lifeblood in it. And I will require a penalty for your lifeblood; I will require it from any human; if someone murders a fellow human, I will require that persons life. Whoever sheds human blood, by humans his blood will be shed, for God made humans in his image" (Genesis 9:5-6, HCSB).

The shedding of human blood was, is, and still is a violation against God's commandments and the eternal punishment, if not saved and forgiven under the renewed covenantal blood of Jesus, is death.

The curse of Canaan was copied from generation to generation, passing through Nimrod the builder of Babylon and Nineveh, Mizraim who would be the progenitor for the Philistines, and Sidon and Heth who would father the Amorites, Girgashites, Hivites, Arkites, Sinites, Arvadites, Zemarites, and Hamathites. From these "ite" clans, the sons of Canaan would spread out, the curse going with them. In time the Canaanites would occupy land from the eastern Mediterranean Sea to the Brook of Egypt and the Jordan River Valley, modern day Lebanon, Israel, and parts of

Jordan and Syria. The land was vast and its men became mighty, their "strong" hearts beating with jealousy and pride for their kinfolk.

Occupying the Promised Land, they stood as enemies against the Israelites for centuries. The Canaanites, while a seemingly narrow people group, was actually composed of various ethnic and cultural groups as it spread across the lands. Of these Canaanites would come the Phoenicians who had not only carried the curse but had accepted paganistic religions. Eventually, Sodom and Gomorrah and Tyre and Sidon, biblically sin ridden cities, would emerge bringing the judgment of God through hellfire and brimstone.[65] Through the intermingling via trade and pilgrimage, The Moon Goddess would work her way into the minds and hearts of the offspring of Noah. And through the marriage of Semiramis and Nimrod, she would create her own type of crooked covenant, a covenant of death.

The Canaanites, or the group of people who inhabited the land of Canaan, would take on the worst of her ways. It was in the Canaanite lands that temple prostitution was common practice and child sacrifice was exercised.[66] In mind warping her cultists through drunkenness and love for money, her followers entered into the covenant of death, marrying themselves with the abhorrent prostitute herself, the one mentioned in Revelation 17. The shedding of innocent blood to appease her appetite would inevitably bring God's judgment. God forewarned even those under the Abrahamic covenant *and* those reborn in Christ, that if they accepted or supported her practices they would receive a similar judgment (Jer. 10:1-5, 1 Cor. 5:11).

The Moon Goddess marked herself as Asherah among the Canaanites and as Astarte or Tanit among the Phoenicians. Her

---

[65] Two beautiful stories of God's grand love and his faithfulness with Noah's sons and their offspring are seen in the book of Jonah and the Book of Genesis. In Jonah's story, God commands the prophet to go to the Ninevites (a wicked and idolatrous nation) and preach repentance. The Ninevites repent and are saved by God (Jonah 3:10). In Genesis 19, God spares Lot, Abraham's son, out of the wicked city of Sodom and Gomorrah.

[66] S.G.F Brandon, *Dictionary of Comparative Religion* (New York City, NY: Charles Scribner's Son, 1970), 448.

counterpart, Ba'al, the storm god, was just as present. Together these spirits would produce an idolatrous following. Possessing open human vessels, they would work their magic to brainwash victims and produce more unrighteousness. Through the use of willing humans, they would hide themselves behind fortified walls and pretty, painted faces but were always, through YHWH's agents, *exposed*.

Jericho

The Canaanites and their gods held a foothold in the land that was promised to Abraham until Joshua, a man chosen by God, arose to possess it. Joshua or *Yeshua* in Hebrew meaning "God is our salvation," was sent by Moses to spy out the land of Canaan, particularly Jericho, which had been building fortresses and walls for years. After forty days of spying, Joshua and the other selected men return to give a report. The men describe a large city that is possessed by many, including the Nephilim (Josh. 13:33). From the report, we know that the land was possessed by giants, or Nephilim, the offspring of "sons of man" with the fallen angels (Genesis 6:1-4). Though much could be interpreted from their report, one thing is for certain: the city of Jericho was a massive-walled city guarded by massive men.

For Joshua and Caleb, the size of the enemy paled in comparison to the size of YHWH, who had delivered the Israelites out of the hands of the Egyptians by miraculous wonders and sustained them by his righteous right hand in the wilderness. Joshua was not intimated and was thus chosen by Moses to lead the Israelites into the Promised Land. Under Joshua's hand, "God is our salvation," the Battle of Jericho was fought and won. But under the surface of this battle lies an important connection with The Blood Moon Prophecy in Acts 2 and a foreshadowing of the end time battle in Revelation.

Remember that there is always more in a name. The name Jericho in Hebrew is *Yeriḥo* named after the moon god of early Canaanite religion, Yerach. Later, these names would be changed to Ba'al and Asherah/Ashteroth. But Jericho was itself the "moon city" and its chief deity, the chief of the pantheon, was the moon god. The fact that Nephilim were present is of no surprise when one considers the spiritual darkness that filled the city. What took place behind those walls would have included moon worship practices: sacrificing to idols, eroticism, temple prostitution, gender alteration, and child sacrifice. These practices were masked behind charm and beauty, stealth and grandeur but underneath the charm of the goddess was a rageful, mercurial, tyrannical spirit that would slaughter the masses. See this description of the spirit based off the Keret Epic, an ancient Ugaritic poem:

> "At its best there can be little doubt that there was a certain amount of aesthetic charm about Canaanite literary and artistic portrayal of these goddesses; in the Keret Epic, for instance, the hero's betrothed is poetically described as having 'the charm of Anath' and 'the beauty of Astarte.' At its worst however, the erotic aspect of their cult must have sunk to extremely sordid depths of social degradation. Besides being patronesses of sexual life these interesting ladies were also goddesses of war. Anath or Astarte is depicted in Egyptian representations of the New Empire as a naked woman astride a galloping horse, brandishing shield and lance in her outflung hands. In the Baal Epic there is a harrowing description of Anath's thirst for blood. For a reason which still escapes us she decided to carry out a general massacre: 'With might she hewed down the people of the cities, she smote the folk of the seacoast, she slew the men of the sunrise (east).' After filling her temple (it seems) with men, she barred the gates so that none might escape, after which 'she hurled chairs at the youths, tables at the warriors, footstools at the men of might.' The blood was so deep that she waded in it up to her knees - nay, up to her neck. Under her feet were human heads, above her human hands flew like locusts. In her sensuous delight she decorated herself with suspended heads, while she attached hands to her girdle. Her joy at the butchery is described in even more sadistic language: 'Her liver swelled with laughter, her heart was full of joy, the liver of Anath (was full of) exultation (?).' Afterwards

69

Anath 'was satisfied' and washed her hands in human gore before proceeding to other occupations."[67]

Recall that Satan is a copier and can only produce counterfeit. The mythological stories of the moon goddess and her cohort Ba'al (or El in early Canaan) were filled with subtle mockeries of YHWH. The Legend of Keret, also known as the Epic of Kirta, is an ancient Ugaritic poem (c. 1500-1200 B.C.) paralleling the events that occurred at Jericho under Joshua's siege. A brief summary of the epic tells of Keret, a king in need of an heir to the throne, who is instructed by El in a dream to sacrifice and then wage war against another kingdom, taking the princess as his wife in order to make a son. Keret does as told but hosts a feast first before setting out in the following order: men of war first, the people following, the trumpeters last. On the way, he stops at a shrine to Atharit "the sea goddess" and makes a promise to her that he will give her gold and silver if the mission succeeds. He instructs all who follow him to be quiet until the last day. At the end of two six-day intervals, a loud sound is made by the trumpeters on the seventh day before arriving at Udum where he finds his future queen. Though the mission succeeds, Keret fails to repay the goddess her dues and is struck by her with a terminal illness.[68]

Looking at the Bible's historical account of the Battle of Jericho, there are undercut insults to the epic. Joshua is given the city to possess and take over (Josh. 6:2). To begin his battle, the Lord instructs Joshua to have men march around the city for six days, while seven priests carry seven rams-horn trumpets in front of the ark. On the seventh day, they are to march seven times while the priests blow the ram horns. On the seventh and final march, the trumpeters were to sound the trumpet with a long blast and have the men make a war cry. Joshua obeys the Lord and, after completing the assignment, the walls of Jericho collapse at the sound and Joshua's men ransack the city, saving Rahab (a prostitute

---

[67] William Foxwell Albright, *Archaeology and the Religion of Israel* (Louisville, KY: Westminster John Knox Press, 2006), 68-94; c.f. Dr. Dave Livingston, "The Fall of the Moon City," 2003, http://davelivingston.com/mooncity.htm
[68] S. H. Hooke, *Middle Eastern Mythology* (North Chelmsford, MA: Courier Corporation, 2004), 87-89.

who protected spies sent by Joshua) and her family and the gold and silver in offering to the Lord.

The parallels reveal more to the story of the battle. There was again, like the plagues which mocked each god of Egypt, a pointed message to Ba'al and The Moon Goddess. God cannot be mocked and so while the cultists of the moon deity were performing their mythologically inspired barbaric rituals, God was raising up an army on the outside who would tear down her stronghold through the power of their God. And it would be God's son, Jesus or *Yeshua Hamashiach*, who would possess divine kingship through *his own* sacrifice.

It is not by coincidence that the leader of the Israelites in the Old Testament, the *Tanakh*, mirrors the divine savior in the New Testament, the *B'rit Hadasha*. Like the princess who was taken by force in the moon god's counterfeit story, the savior of the world, Jesus, would sacrifice himself so that all could come to him by freedom of choice, not by force. His extension of salvation would bridge the *Tanakh* and the *B'rit Hadasha*, saving both Jew and Gentile. Rahab, a prostitute (and possibly a moon goddess prostitute), would be a foreshadowing of the Messiah's worldwide sacrifice as she and her household were saved by her faith in the saving God. And not only would God save her out of the darkness, he would also bring down the walls that kept her from the Promised Land and save her from the sword of death. In fact, it would actually be from Rahab's bloodline that the Messiah would come, as she would be the ancestor of King David (Matt. 1:5)!

And like the days of Joshua, The Moon Goddess, the prostitute of prostitutes, will be exposed and destroyed once and for all. And because we serve a God who keeps his covenant, before her final destruction, God will extend his salvation and deliverance to the ends of the earth, to all of those who might be in the pit of her craters, if they accept his saving hand through faith.

Jezebel

Another significant appearance of The Moon Goddess in Scripture is in the infamous story of Jezebel and it is her story that plays a large part in unmasking The Moon Goddess' ultimate agenda. The prophets Jeremiah and Ezekiel write about her vile practices of her sordid worship like child sacrifice and false prophecy. She craved blood and power. The author of 1 Kings (likely Jeremiah) reveals her ultimate vendetta–to silence the prophets of God.

In the first book of Kings, we are introduced to a mighty prophet of God named Elijah. It is through God's chosen and *true* prophet Elijah and his selected warrior Jehu that the false prophets, including Jezebel herself, and the god and goddess these servants worshiped would be exposed and destroyed. But Elijah was not the only prophet who had stood against the wicked woman Jezebel, as we will see.

Jezebel, a human woman possessed by the spirit of The Moon Goddess, was married to King Ahab, a king of Judah in the time of Israel's division. 1 Kings 16:30-34 informs us that Jezebel was the daughter of Ethbaal king of the Sidonians who served Ba'al and Asherah. Like her father, she too worshiped the deities and in such great measure that she sought to control the kingdom by eradicating all YHWH worship by any means necessary. She used sex and money to cunningly charm her way into greater power, stepping on her weak husband Ahab to do so. She was dominating and vocal but also sly and secretive. It was under Jezebel's hand that God's prophets were to be exterminated, leaving many surviving prophets to hide in caves (1 Kings 18:1-15). It was also under her craftiness that she manipulated the unjust death of Naboth (1 Kings 21:1-16). She also employed seduction to try and escape her death, "painting her eyes" and "fixing her hair" (2 Kings 9:30). But her seductive tactics failed and she was eventually plunged to her death by Jehu before being consumed by wild dogs.

Before her death though, Jezebel's ultimate goal was to establish national Ba'al and moon goddess worship and one of the ways in which she tried to accomplish this was through the silencing of God's prophets by means of murder. The prophet Obadiah's conversation with Elijah in 1 Kings 18 informs us that many prophets had been killed by Jezebel, up to 100. But why the prophets specifically?

It was through God's prophets, those chosen before birth to be his mouthpiece to the people, that God would warn, encourage, and direct his people. So to silence the prophet was, per Jezebel, to silence YHWH. If she shut the mouth of the prophet then she could open the mouth of The Moon Goddess and Ba'al to lie and devour. As Jesus told The Church of Thyatira in Revelation 2, to tolerate her is to fall into her idolatrous practices and her sexual immorality and God is against such tolerance.[69] Jezebel may have died at Jehu's hand but the spirit which possessed her persists.

The cup at Jezebel's table was and is filled with fermented, filthy wine. It was a mixture of sexual perversion, lies, murder, and greed. Recall that The Moon Goddess was another representation of the Egyptian snake deity Renenutet, the goddess of wine. The wine in her cup was the blood of the innocent, the blood of the children, and the blood of God's prophets. To drink of her cup meant dire consequences, to entertain her practices was to look into the painted eyes of death. Her manipulative maneuver to acquire Naboth's vineyard for herself and Ahab so that they could drink fermented grape juice was really not to drink Naboth's wine but *his blood*. The spirit which possessed Jezebel was none other than The Moon Goddess who intoxicated her members with a counterfeit cup filled with bitter wine.

> "On her forehead was written a name, a mystery:
> BABYLON THE GREAT, THE MOTHER OF
> PROSTITUTES AND THE DETESTABLE THINGS
> OF THE EARTH. Then I saw that the woman was
> drunk with the blood of the saints and with the blood of
> the witnesses to Jesus" (Revelation 17:5-6, HCSB).

The "other" woman of Revelation is the Babylonian spirit, The Moon Goddess who murdered the potential prophets of the Hebrew babies in Moses' day, the outspoken prophets in Elijah's

---

[69]At times I capitalize "The" in The Church to make clear that I am referring to The Bride of Christ, or the churches together under the headship of Christ. Additionally, I will at times capitalize the "H" when referring to God as "Him" to differentiate between man and God.

73

day, murdered John the Baptist, murdered the saints of the early church, and who today murders through abortion, beheadings, sexual diseases, murder, overdoses, genocide and suicide.

Revelation informs us that this evil spirit will be the driving force behind many deaths prior to Jesus' return. But even though her ceremonial wedding banquet celebrating her drunken marriage with corrupt men may run over with the blood of God's people, the blood of Jesus in the cup of his fury and wrath will soon be poured out eternally over her. The Bride of Christ will drink from the cup of joy; The Moon Goddess, the cup of torment.

And not only her, but her twisted groom, Ba'al, will drink it, too.

Ancient Europe, Asia, and Americas

The Moon Goddess was not limited to the Ancient Near East. Her impact was worldwide and her practices have been discovered in all continents. Remember that a spirit is a spirit and the spirit of The Moon Goddess manifests in different forms, taking on different names throughout all cultures. This is one way in which Satan deceives the whole world (Isa. 14:16). Realizing this, it is no surprise then that her practices are seen in all landmasses of the ancient world, from the lands of Shinar to the advanced Roman empire to the mountainous tribes in the Swiss Alps. While many are familiar with the Sumerian, Egyptian, Greek, and Roman forms of this spirit, there are many other ancient civilizations which performed her ritualistic practices.

As the sons of Noah and their descendants multiplied and spread out through the world, they took with them the practices of the lands of Shinar. Eventually these ancient ancestors made their way through the lands of Europe, Asia, India, and through the Bering Strait to the Americas. Animalistic polytheism was popular as was demigod worship. Other identifying signs of The Moon Goddess worship were found in human sacrifice, sexual orgies and temple prostitution which has been found in nearly all fertility goddess worship throughout the ancient world.

Later Roman sources would give more information as to the secretive practices of the pagan world in ancient Europe. The Slavs worshiped Devana, the Celts worshiped Rhiannon, the Scandinavians (Norsemen) worshiped a masculine form of the spirit named Máni, ancient Germanic tribes worshiped Ēostre which may be where our modern day term "Easter" is derived.[70] In fact our modern Easter egg tradition in the Western world has a not so colorful past, a practice that did not originate with Christianity. Being that Ēostre was a Spring fertility goddess, her practices were centered around sex in which prostitutes would be given over to men in orgies, similar to that of Ishtar festivities. Per folklore, following these spring equinox festivals, pregnant women would offer their infants as a sacrifice to the goddess of fertility the following spring. Legend has long attributed the eggs connected to Ēostre with the eggs of Ishtar which were eggs dipped in the blood of slaughtered infants conceived during those orgies. While there are few resources about the subject, evidence does show a connection between eggs, hares, and paganism and since the practice of dying easter eggs came out of ancient polytheistic tribes of Europe, it may be safe to assume that Ishtar and Ēostre are one in the same. Isis, another presentation of The Moon Goddess, was also called "the egg of the Goose."[71] Again, the fact checkers may not agree, but the perverse and hypersexual customs of The Moon Goddess do not aid the doubter's case.

In Asia similar practices were being performed but under the guise of a different set of deities. Emphasis was placed upon nature and ancestral worship. Mysticism, necromancy, shamanism, and sorcery were common among ancient Asian religious practices and still are today. Buddhism, Taoism, and Confucianist teachings and doctrines arose bringing an emphasis on the self, meditation, astrology, transcendentalism, and feng shui. The human body, animals, dead relatives, land masses, and natural events could be a god and could be worshiped. In ancient China The Moon Goddess

---

[70] Etymology research cannot confirm this but the similarities are striking.

[71] "Pompeii Excavation Indicates Birds Were Important in Isis Cults," 21 May 2023, Science Forbes.com, https://www.forbes.com/sites/grrlscientist/2023/05/21/pompeii-excavation-indicates-birds-were-important-in-isis-cult/

took the form of Chang'e and was believed to be the most beautiful goddess among all of the gods. Interestingly, this goddess was depicted with a white hare, a common association with Easter as mentioned above.

The rabbit symbolism with The Moon Goddess doesn't stop in Asia or Europe. A body of water could not limit the marine spirit's influence. The full moon's shadowing created an image of a "Rabbit in the Moon" to the ancient Aztecs and Mayans and was thus associated with the goddess of the moon, who was known as Metztli (one of Coatlicue's children) to the Aztecs and IxChel for the Mayans.[72] These goddesses also represented water, fertility, sexuality, and midwifery to both civilizations. For the Mayans, IxChel was The Moon Goddess who represented water, weaving, fertility, and midwifery. In the Incan culture, Mama Quilla was The Moon Goddess who was also in charge of women's menstrual cycles.

Of the most brutal manifestations of The Moon Goddess outside of Babylon was in the ancient Mesoamerican Aztec civilization which occupied central and southern Mexico in the 15th and 16th centuries. The moon was central to this vibrant and violent people group. The Aztecs were also known as Tenocha from an eponymous ancestor Tencoh and Metzliapán, meaning "Moon Lake."[73] Their venerated "Mother of the gods," Coatlicue, gave birth to the sun, moon, and stars and her rituals were darker than space, they were *wicked*. Depictions of her feature a face with two fanged snakes, a skirt of snakes topped with saggy breasts, and her hand holding a necklace made of human hearts and a skull.[74] This virgin goddess conceived many children who, per complex mythology, murdered each other, even brutally butchering siblings and casting their body parts off mountains.[75] It is even possible that

---

[72] Scholar J. Eric S. Thompson does not believe IxChel and the Maya Moon Goddess are the same deity. See his book *Maya History & Religion* for more information on this counter argument.

[73] Britannica, "Aztec," *Encyclopedia Britannica*, 22 Jul. 2024, https://www.britannica.com/topic/Aztec.

[74] Britannica, "Aztec" https://www.britannica.com/topic/Aztec.

[75] Cartwright, "Coatlicue," https://www.worldhistory.org/Coatlicue/.

women sacrificed themselves to this goddess to put the sun into motion.[76]

Statue of Coatlicue displayed in the National Museum of Anthropology in Mexico City.
Statue of Coatlicue displayed in the National Museum of Anthropology in Mexico City.

The list of The Moon Goddess' forms through history is lengthy, but the protocols of her worship and her venerated qualities are similar: animal and human sacrifices, temple worship and offerings, temple prostitution, nature worship, and magic were performed to the goddess of sexuality and fertility. Her representation of fertility was perfidious considering much of her sacrifices involved death and disease and male mutilation to *prevent* offspring. The twisted marriage between The Moon Goddess and Ba'al did not produce fruit but instead produced rotten, vulgar eggs dipped in blood.

---

[76] Dr. Lauren Kilroy-Ewbank, "Coatlicue," Khan Academy, https://www.khanacademy.org/humanities/art-americas/early-cultures/aztec-mexica/a/coatlicue#:~:text=The%20myth%20notes%20that%20several,by%20offering%20their%20own%20lives.

Chapter 5

A Wedding to Remember

After this I heard something like the loud voice of a vast multitude in heaven, saying, "Hallelujah! Salvation, glory, and power belong to our God because his judgments are true and righteous, because he has judged the notorious prostitute who corrupted the earth with her sexual immorality; and he has avenged the blood of his servants that was on her hands." A second time they said, "Hallelujah! Her smoke ascends forever and ever!" Then the twenty-four elders and the four living creatures fell down and worshiped God, who is seated on the throne, saying, "Amen! Hallelujah!" A voice came from the throne, saying, "Praise our God, all his servants and the ones who fear him, both small and great!" Then I heard something like the voice of a vast multitude, like the sound of cascading waters, and like the rumbling of loud thunder, saying, "Hallelujah, because our Lord God, the Almighty, reigns! Let us be glad, rejoice, and give him glory, because the marriage of the Lamb has come and his bride has prepared herself."

Revelation 19:1-7, HCSB

Prior to the sound of a new baby's cry as it emerges from the womb of its mother is the laughter from the womb of a wedding. Then, following the mother's labor cries of her birth comes her own laughter. Ceremonial rejoicing caps both ends of the creation of new life. Before the work and labor that goes into making new life is the enjoyment of the husband and wife together. And this design was established intentionally by God. The beginning of mankind's story is a wedding in the Garden of Eden, the first marriage in the world between Adam and Eve (Gen. 2), and the end of mankind's story on earth is an eternal wedding, the marriage between the bride of Christ with her bridegroom, Jesus himself (Rev. 19:6-9). The laborious life that happens in between our beginning and end *is* capped by joy. God rejoiced at our physical conception just as he celebrated at our spiritual rebirth. Again, the same is for his church which will be "reborn" in the eschaton and celebrated with the greatest wedding of all time.

The birthing motif is a constant throughout the Scriptures, but we mustn't forget that before the birth and after the birth is a wedding. The celebratory matrimony marks the beginning of a lifelong union between the bride and the groom. It is an anticipatory celebration as well, prophesying to the future hope that will be found in their intimacy. The wedding between Christ and his bride (The Church) is one of deep love, steadfast faith, and enduring patience and God celebrates this wedding with song, dance, and *feasting*.

As already mentioned, the table prepared for God's victorious bride features a glorious meal. We know that this meal is the bread of God's word broken for us and the everlasting wine of God's love poured out for us. But as with any feast, the food and the drink is only as enjoyable as the company it is shared with. So who is the company? All the saints in Christ will feast together with Jesus! And though he won't be sitting at the table, the enemy and his hosts of wickedness will be watching, too. As God's saints feast in joy with Jesus, Satan and all of those who worshiped him will be eating and drinking from the table of torment. We won't see them nor will we care about them, but we will taste the sweet lack of their presence as we sit in the fullness of Christ's presence and his joy.

The Miracle at Cana

The tastiest wine is the aged one. The one that has been stored for time, patiently tended to, and crafted in perfection, aged in barrels of fragrant wood that themselves came from trees which took years of aging, processing, and tending to; trees grown in the best soil, vines fertilized with the best nutrients. Thus the wine served at the wedding feast for Jesus and his bride will be unlike any wine ever served. The body of our Lord, the Ancient of Days, our vinedresser who patiently tends to his bride, preparing her for his return will provide *himself* as the wine. Likewise, he is saving his finest wine of wrath for the enemy. In the same measure he was crushed for the sins of man, so will the same measure be poured out. God is perfectly, harmoniously homeostatic.

Considering that the story of man and woman with God began in a garden with a wedding, it is of no surprise then that the first miracle Jesus performed during his earthly ministry involved a wedding and the fruit of the vine–wine. Recapping the story found in John 2, Jesus and his disciples attend a wedding in Cana of Galilee. During the ceremony, Jesus' mother goes to her son in need of a solution to a problem: the guests have no wine. Jesus obliges in order to reveal his glory to his disciples (v. 12). He tells the servants of the wedding to fill the jars with water to the brim (v. 7). He then instructs them to draw out some of the water and take it to the headwaiter. The servants obey, and while they and Jesus' disciples know about the miracle, the headwaiter does not. He tastes the wine and is astounded at its taste. He responds, "Everyone sets out the fine wine first, then, after people are drunk, the inferior. But you have kept the fine wine until now" (v. 10).

The first miracle of Jesus' earthly ministry involves a wedding and wine. There is much to be drawn out of this text, but what is of importance in regard to this book is that Jesus' disciples and his servants *knew* the water had turned to wine. Additionally, they fill the jars with water *to the brim*. Jesus' followers hear his word and obey. They fill the jars with water to the point of near overflow and this new wine is, per the headwaiter, the best wine. Thus as the world nears its end, Jesus is saving the best for last. When he adds his weight of glory to vessels, that is humans who follow him, the water of life will inevitably spill over, creating an outpouring of God's miracles, signs, and wonders. As Joel's prophecy notes, this incredible weight of glory is the Ancient of Days himself, The Holy Spirit, filling people. Those who have been filled with The Holy Spirit's wine will *know* the signs, the miracles, and the wonders; but most importantly, *who* is behind them.

This knowledge will be critical in the last days, for many people, including the Antichrist and false prophet, will rise up falsely prophesying, adding to or taking away from scripture, twisting doctrines to tickle ears, and per 2 Thessalonians 2:9 and Revelation 13:13, perform wonders even calling down fire from heaven (Matt. 24:11, Deut. 4:2, Rev. 22:18-19). Therefore, knowing the Shepherd's voice, recognizing the signs, and discerning the spirits will all be needed for those who are living in the last days.

Following this miracle in Cana is the story of Jesus cleaning out the temple, so I do not believe this orientation is coincidental, rather it is the outpouring of the Holy Spirit upon his people that will precede the cleansing of the earth, especially the churches as described in Revelation.

The second set of servants who harken the instructions of Jesus will be his angels who will administer justice on the earth. This is when the stone vessels, like those in the land of Egypt, those belonging to false gods–The Moon Goddess, Ba'al, Moloch–will be filled, not with water, but with *blood*.

The Twisted Groom

In Joseph's dream the sun and the moon represented the marriage between his father, Jacob (the sun) and his mother, Rachel (the moon). The stars represented his eleven brothers. Recall that the enemy is a copycat who mimics whatever he sees God doing, adding his demented twist so as to deceive and destroy men. Thus in Satan's story, the sun god Ba'al marries The Moon Goddess. This twisted marriage produces demonic lies of lust which form a web to entice and then entrap the sons and daughters of men. These lies have persisted through the ages, but as the revealing of God's bride begins–that is, as the time of the end draws near for the bride to meet the bridegroom–the light of The Church will expose the darkness of this world, and even more importantly, purge out the dark blemishes *within* The Church. In fact as the days on earth darken, the enemy will attempt his most powerful tools of mimicry to lead many astray and, if it were possible, even the elect astray (Matt. 24:24). But it *will not* be possible for them who believe God's word and who know of the enemy's devices. Satan's tools and schemes have been and will continue to be his distorted images of the birth, life, death, and resurrection of Jesus; the eradication of marriage between man and woman; and the corrupted voice of false prophets.

Ba'al and Tammuz

The twisted groom of Satan's story is Ba'al, the storm god of the Canaanites. Joel informs us that the sun will be darkened and the moon will be turned to blood before the great and terrible day of the Lord (Joel 2:31). Per Joel, the dark groom will be darkened, and so if we look at his prophecy through an acrostic, multi-dimensional and apocalyptic lens, then we must examine this part of the prophecy in conjunction with The Moon Goddess who is herself a luminere of the sun deity's evil. To disregard one is to miss the entire blood moon prophecy.

Ba'al, though subordinate to El in the Syro-Palestinian pantheon, is the most mentioned and active pagan deity in the Old Testament scriptures. Remember that the god and goddesses of antiquity were different across tribes and tongues but were similar in nature. Their structure was and is satanic, their influence going back to Semiramis. They are spirits without gender. The sun and moon were not always male and female and some cultures even reversed the anthropomorphic nature (i.e. Japanese Shintoism or Mesopotamian Sin/Suen moon god). But again these are spirits, so they essentially do not have a female or male body. This explains the typical "de-gendering" of men and women priests and priestesses in sun and moon god cultic rituals. The cultists mimicked the genderless gods they served. By adding feminine pronouns to the moon deity, I am simply pulling from the Scriptures description of its promiscuous nature. Being that we are biologically wired to be male or female, these types of attributions are helpful in our processing of a spiritual world.

Bearing this in mind, Ba'al was a spirit that manifested like the moon goddess in various ways throughout the ancient world. While different facets of the principality's character or powers were divided to different deities, the head of the mythology was the sun god. For the Canaanites, Ba'al was in charge of the rain cycles and was therefore connected to fertility. His symbol was the bull. For the Mesopotamians, the symbol for the moon god, Sin, was a bull. For the Egyptians, the sun god was Amun-Re, who was "a syncretistic formulation between the primeval creator god and wind god Amun and the sun god Re."[77] Yet the image of the sun

---

[77] Walton, *Ancient Near Eastern*, 332.

was associated with the Aten. Thus behind all the different names, depictions, and associated mythologies were the spirits connected to sun and moon worship. The idiom "the devil is in the details" can be applied here; behind every detail of these false deities is the devil. It is that simple.

In Canaanite mythology, El was married to Ashteroth, "the queen of the mother gods."[78] Excavations of the ancient city of Ugarit (modern day Ras Shamra, Syria) reveal Ba'al eventually replacing El as the king of the gods.[79] Ba'al, along with his consort Ashteroth who was represented by a sacred fertility pole/tree, became the primary deity in Canaanite and Phoenician worship and his worship practices were similar to that of The Moon Goddess. Sexual acts with temple prostitutes were performed to mimic his marriage with The Moon Goddess (Deut. 23:17-19), child sacrifices were performed (Jer. 19:5), incense were offered to him (Jer. 11:3), even erratic dancing and self mutilation by his prophets were done to persuade him (1 Kings 18:28). Walton writes, "The shape of one's belief was less significant in the ancient world. It was not belief that counted, but performance of the cult."[80] The ritualistic acts of child sacrifice, murder, burning incense, and sex (homosexual and heterosexual) to appease or entice the gods to perform a duty (such as send rain for harvest) was the identifying stained garment of the religion. The performance of Ba'al or The Moon Goddess was in effect controlled by the performance (or lack thereof) of their worshipers. As evidenced by the false prophets of Ba'al in 1 Kings 18 who really weren't sure if their god would perform a miracle or not, their insane performance of cutting themselves to provoke him was to make up for their god's inability to perform. Satan, while hiding behind false gods and goddesses, used these abhorrent practices to make self-image and human ability the focus, making man believe his works could win salvation, in turn pitting man against himself and against other men. The wedding to Ba'al or the Moon

[78] Walton, *Ancient Near Eastern*, 322.

[79] Joshua J. Mark, "Ba'al," WorldHistory.org, 5 Nov. 2021, https://www.worldhistory.org/baal/#google_vignette

[80] Walton, *Ancient Near Eastern*, 93.

Goddess was one of weariness, worry, and waste. Needless to say, their wedding doesn't lead to happy ever after.

Interestingly, the "sun god" was a goddess in Canaanite mythology. Known as Shapshu, meaning "lamp of the gods," this goddess appears in tales of Ba'al in Ugaritic texts. While a "separate" deity in the pantheon of gods, the goddess still reveals the work of the spirits behind the sun and moon worship in paganistic religion and the connection between the two in the prophecy of Joel. The prophecy of Joel and its repetition in Acts 2 by Apostle Peter at the outpouring of The Holy Spirit are to be read together. The sun will be darkened and the moon will be turned to blood as a sign that the evil principalities at work behind sun and moon worship will be exposed. The perverse and sacrilegious practices that occurred within the inner, hidden parts of the temples did not escape the eye of YHWH. The consummation of the marriage with Ba'al by his priests and priestesses was not hidden from God. Ezekiel 8, which will be discussed in greater detail in Chapter 6, reveals that God was very aware of what was happening as were his prophets.

The True Groom and His Moonlit Bride

While the world grows darker with sin, the sanctified bride awaiting Christ's return grows brighter. The aurora of God's faithful one is likened to the moon, the sun, and the stars by the author of Song of Songs, Solomon– the king of great wisdom.

> "Who is this that appears like the dawn, fair as the moon, bright as the sun, majestic as the stars in procession?" (Song. 6:10)

The man of the song describes her–his longed for bride–poetically in song; a melody of miraculous wonder and captivating light. In the chorus to the song, the man introduces the woman with a fresh perspective. His question "Who is this?" highlights the beautified and transformed woman who is now even more of a sight to behold than previously in the song. Solomon describes the character of the bride as "fair as the moon" and "bright as the sun," painting a picture of the one day perfected and purified bride of Christ. Like Esther who was beautified for the king for months by soaking in oil, so too will the bride of Christ be prepared and purified for his return by soaking in his presence. The bridegroom is preparing his bride for a glorious reveal, an introduction to the chorus of the final song of Christ's cry for his beloved. Just as Jesus prayed under the moonlight in the garden before his crucifixion, so he continues to intercede for his bride day and night, that she might be ready for his soon-coming return (Rom. 8:34).

As Christ's beloved, each believer radiates the sun of righteousness (Mal. 4:2) who lights the fire in our spiritual lamps upon conversion. And, like the moon, each believer projects this light into a fallen world, expelling darkness and revealing Jesus. The jaw-dropping reveal of The Church will only intensify as the days draw closer to the groom's arrival. The world will not perceive the transformation; they will hear and see and not understand it (Mark 4:12). But like the virgins of wisdom in Jesus' parable in Matthew 25, those that tend to the light, who add the oil of God's presence to their fire daily, they will not be taken by surprise by his return. His bride *will* go out singing and rejoicing. Only the fools will mourn that which they did not know.

Chapter 6

The Prophets

Surely the Sovereign LORD does nothing without revealing his plan to his servants the prophets.

Amos 3:7, NIV

B efore we move to the second part of this book which deals with The Blood Moon Prophecy as it relates to our world today, the prophets of the Old Testament need to be discussed. Just as the Apostle Peter used the prophecy of Joel in his speech to forecast a future latter rain of revival, I will also use the prophets of old to point to the end time significance of The Blood Moon Prophecy. God always has a remnant in reserve who will, at his divine timing, rise up to be used for the purpose of pointing people back to him. And that is the point of this book and the ultimate goal as a prophetess of God–to expose darkness and point people back to the light of Christ. The Old Testament prophecies were pointing to the Messiah then, now, and to come and, with their words, I am going to do the same.

The Major Prophets

The four major prophets of the Bible include the writings of Isaiah, Jeremiah, Ezekiel, and Daniel. The twelve minor prophets include: Hosea, Joel, Amos, Obadiah, Jonah, Micah, Nahum, Habakkuk, Zephaniah, Haggai, Zechariah, and Malachi. "Major" and "minor" does not denote a ranking but refers to the amount of material found within these books. In this section I will pull parts from the four major prophets that I believe relate to The Blood Moon Prophecy.

Jeremiah

The Moon Goddess worship was nothing new to Jeremiah the prophet. It is actually Jeremiah who explicitly names The Moon

Goddess as the Queen of Heaven (Jer 7:18) and many times condemns her worship practices throughout his writings. And yet it is Jeremiah who captures the ultimate truth of God's original intent in creating the sun, moon, and stars when he wrote:

> "This is what the LORD says, he who appoints the sun to shine by day, who decrees the moon and stars to shine by night, who stirs up the sea so that its waves roar— the LORD Almighty is his name. If this order departs before me—this is the Lord's declaration—only then will Israel's descendants cease to be a nation before me" (Jer. 31:35-36, HCSB).

The celestial bodies were created and fixed to reveal God. That the sun, moon, and stars were created by God for His purposes is evident in the prophet's heavy and hopeful books, Jeremiah and Lamentations. The same God who named and appointed the stars their place has also set them in order and it is the same God who can make them cease their shining and rearrange their order.

Jeremiah spoke to and advised the people of God during their Babylonian exile. Recall that the Israelites had turned from YHWH repeatedly since their days of Egyptian deliverance and due to this had brought punishment upon their own heads (Jer. 6:19). Along with not adhering to the Sabbath day command, one of their major sins was worshiping false gods. In Jeremiah 44 the prophet addresses moon goddess worship. The people complained to the prophet, stating "...but from the time we ceased to burn incense to the queen of heaven and to offer her drink offerings, we have lacked everything, and through sword and famine have met our end." Because they associated the goddess with fertility and life, they vowed to Jeremiah that they would not stop sacrificing to her or worshiping her because when they did, the land became desolate. But God responds to the defiant and doubtful people through Jeremiah:

> "As for the incense you burned in Judah's cities and in Jerusalem's streets— you, your ancestors, your kings, your officials, and the people of the land—did the Lord not remember them? He brought this to mind. The Lord

can no longer bear your evil deeds and the detestable
acts you have committed, so your land has become a
waste, a desolation, and an example for cursing, without
inhabitant, as you see today" (Jer. 44:20-23, HCSB).

God explains to them why their land is desolate and why they die
by sword and famine. It is because *they chose* to worship the gods
and goddess. They brought disaster upon themselves. Because of
their rebellion and their insistence on following other gods, death
consumed their land. As a result of sacrificing children in fire to
Ba'al and even resorting to cannibalism in the midst of a famine,
the people were judged and punished (Jeremiah 19). Yet despite
their frayed faith, God's covenant of redemption remained intact.
He would not forsake them. And so throughout Jeremiah's writings
we see the heart of Jesus, a just God who is also merciful and
patient.

The same is true today. God is still merciful and he
administers his justice in righteousness. He continues to speak
through his people today, to the sheep who know his voice, and
will, like Jeremiah, warn those who are bound to the ways of the
world so that all might come to repentance before his return.[81]
While there will be miracles, signs, and wonders in the heavenlies
on the earth before Christ's return, the greatest sign will be the love
of Jesus' followers and their trust in him. Jeremiah frequently
reminded the backslidden and fearful Israelites to trust in YHWH.
In Jeremiah 10:2 he specifically tells them to not be moved in fear
by the movement of the heavenlies.

"Do not learn the way of the nations or be terrified by
signs in the heavens, although nations are terrified by
them, for the customs of the peoples are worthless" (Jer.
10:2-3, HCSB).

Jesus also told his disciples to be careful not to idolize the signs.

---

[81] "The Lord is not slow to fulfill his promise as some count slowness, but is
patient toward you, not wishing that any should perish, but that all should reach
repentance" (2 Peter 3:9, ESV).

"The Pharisees and Sadducees approached, and tested him [Jesus], asking him to show them a sign from heaven. Jesus replied, 'When evening comes you say, 'It will be good weather because the sky is red.' And in the morning, 'Today will be stormy because the sky is red and threatening.' You know how to read the appearance of the sky, but you can't read the signs of the times. An evil and adulterous generation demands a sign, but no sign will be given to it except the sign of Jonah.' Then Jesus left them and went away" (Matt. 16:1-4, HCSB).

From this passage in Matthew, we see the significance of the signs. The unbelieving nations will be terrified by them, but to those that believe, the signs will be a testament to God's justice and his mercy, to his power and his control. We are to be aware of the signs but not to worship them. We are to know what the blood moon means but we are not to forsake the advancement of the Gospel out of fear or complacency. We are to understand the significance of such prophecies but not miss the testimony of Jesus within those prophecies. Nor are we to be looking at the sky and not looking for God's lost sheep.

In the heart of Jeremiah and as God's church we are to deliver messages of hope to the lost, encouraging them to seek the Lord while he may be found while also exposing false gods. New age and occultists today attempt to read their horoscopes to predict the future, but God's people are not to participate in those practices. Instead, we are to trust God's word because it is *he* who holds the stars and our destiny. We are to promote justice and righteousness, love and mercy, humility and grace while we await his return.

Ezekiel

Ezekiel, a contemporary of Jeremiah and Daniel, was also privy to the knowledge of God's justice and mercy, especially as it pertained to the end times and like Jeremiah, he reminded the people that in the end they will *know* that God is the Lord. One of the ways in which the nations will know him will be through his signs, his wonders, and his awe-inspiring acts. The nations will also know him by his zeal, his passion, and his fury. I would humbly add to this that the nations will also know him by his prophecies being fulfilled.

Along with Jeremiah, Ezekiel was concerned with the nation's idolatry and prophesied of God's punishment when a person or nation disobeys His ordinances and statutes. Though Ezekiel prophesied to a different group of people than Jeremiah, both men wrote of impending judgment and eventual restoration of Israel. Following the second siege under the rule of King Jehoiachin in 597 B.C., Nebuchadnezzar (the king of Babylon) appointed Zedekiah as king. Zedekiah deported the royal family, the upper class, and priests one of whom was Ezekiel. Five years after Ezekiel's deportation, Zedekiah plans a revolt. Prior to the revolt and the last and final siege of Jerusalem by Nebuchadnezzar, Ezekiel is commissioned to be a prophet outside of Judah (Chapters 1-3). It is from these first three chapters in Ezekiel that we see a nation in turmoil, inwardly and outwardly; a nation which has forsaken YHWH to follow other gods. Ezekiel addresses the peoples' rebellion and informs them that it is this rebellion which will lead to the destruction of Jerusalem and The Temple.

Through symbolic acts and lengthy oracles, Ezekiel repeatedly attempts to point God's people back to YHWH by exposing their hardened hearts. For those whose hearts were not mortared with magic or malice, the promise of redemption would be their portion (Chapters 36-37, 40-48). But leading up to the destruction of Jerusalem, Ezekiel continually spoke the word of the Lord. He prophesied of a coming destruction but he is also foretold of a day when Israel would be reunited as one kingdom, ruled by an eternal king of peace in a renewed temple (Chapter 37). Undergirding all of Ezekiel's words of warning and his prophecies of a new Jerusalem is *God's sovereignty*. It is through his acts of justice and his unrelenting love that God will make his name known, and he will do so according to his own standards and in his own timing.

Ezekiel not only foretold of Israel's destruction in 587 B.C., but his writings are also apocalyptic. His vision of the glory leaving the temple (Chapter 10) followed by judgment and punishment yet ending with a renewed Jerusalem and God's glory returning once again to the temple are eschatological glimpses into the end of the age when God will again judge the nations, extending mercy to those who have not bowed a knee to an idol. The hope of glory–Christ in us–is a testament to the mystery of God's mercy and righteousness in the past, present, and future. Ezekiel's vision of a New Jerusalem reveals the ultimate heavenly end for Gentile and Jew. In the ashes there is beauty and a glorious hope. Such visions of a renewed Jerusalem were not limited to Ezekiel or Daniel. The New Testament writer John wrote of a similar spiritual encounter during his exile:

> "Then I saw a new heaven and a new earth; for the first heaven and the first earth had passed away, and the sea was no more. I also saw the holy city, the new Jerusalem, coming down out of heaven from God, prepared like a bride for her adorned husband" (Rev. 21:1-2, NIV).

Ezekiel's writings dealt with the present reality in Israel's day, when the people's hopes were dashed by their deportation and their city's destruction, but Ezekiel also forewarns and encourages a future judgment and restoration. Of the most inspiring of his prophecies is the day when the filthy practices of the pagans which had influenced the Israelites and angered God will be wiped completely from their guilty hands and hearts. Specifically, Ezekiel (like Isaiah and Jeremiah) addresses the abhorrent practice of child sacrifice.

In Elijah's day Jezebel slew God's prophets (1 Kings 18:13), in Moses' day Pharaoh brutally enslaved thousands of Israelites to build his temples and idols (Exod. 1:12), and in Jeremiah's day the followers of Ba'al burned children in the Valley of Ben Hinnom (Jer. 19:4). Ezekiel's day was no different. The same practices were happening and the same spirits of The Moon Goddess and Ba'al were behind the horrendous practices. Ezekiel 20:26 and 20:31 reveals that the Israelites had turned to treacherous acts, prostituting themselves with The Moon Goddess and Ba'al and had conceived evil plots, burning even their firstborn children in fire as an offering to the gods. These same practices continued through the New Testament era and they persist today. Modern day child sacrifice is evident in the millions of aborted babies in the womb, global child sex trafficking, gender mutilation, and child torture for Luciferian ritual practices (yes, this actually happens!). The death of the innocent is the blood of future prophets, priests, and kings being poured out to The Moon Goddess. But unlike the false gods, the giver of Life–YHWH–hears the cries of the innocent. Genesis 4:10 informs us that the blood itself cries out from the ground. All of the cries of the innocent will, as in Ezekiel and Jeremiah's days, be avenged.

Remembering that many of the human sacrifice, witchcraft, occultic and demonic practices had Egyptian origins, one can read Ezekiel 32-33 and 37 with a spiritually refined lens. In chapter 32, about 1 and 2/3 years after the fall of Jerusalem, Ezekiel released a prophecy of Egypt's destruction. As Israel's historic foe, Egypt will one day be condemned to an eternal fate of doom. The modern day country of Egypt is not what Ezekiel was alluding to, rather he was prophetically referencing the power structure and the cults tied to ancient Egypt: the worship of Isis, Horus, Ra and even Pharaoh himself who claimed to be divine. I propose that it is the worship of false gods that Ezekiel is ultimately addressing in Chapter 32 when he prophesied the fall of Egypt. The Moon Goddess and Ba'al who hid themselves behind the Egyptian pantheon will be eradicated .

Ezekiel describes the woe that awaits those who bow to the Egyptian idols and the ultimate fate of them that lower themselves to those gods; those that bow low to the false gods will eventually be cast to the lowest depths of the earth, Sheol. Ezekiel likens the Egyptian Pharaoh to the dragon who will be entrapped by a net and thrown into a field of torture (Ezk. 32:2-6). This interesting picture may perhaps be Ezekiel's way of connecting the Egyptian foreign practices to those practiced in Babylon during his time.

Not long after Moses delivered the Israelites out of Egypt's iron furnace, the Israelites acculturated again, assuming the practices of Babylonian pagan worship. In the Babylonian creation myth, Marduk, the god of Babylon, uses a net to capture Tiamat, the goddess of chaos (ANET:67). Ezekiel 32:3-4 may be a mockery of such a myth when Ezekiel prophesies,

> "This is what the Lord God says: I will spread my net over you with an assembly of many peoples, and they

will haul you up in my net. I will abandon you on the
land and throw you onto the open field…"

Egypt and Babylon were nearly one in the same when it came to
their idolatry and so would be their sentences upon judgment.

The dragons' power structure that oozed out of the sores of
the Egyptians and infected the Israelites would, per Ezekiel, be
judged. Egypt's demolition would have resounding painful effects
on the earth *and* in the cosmos. Ezekiel prophesies of God's
judgment against Pharaoh in this way:

> "When I snuff you out,
> I will cover the heavens
> and darken their stars.
> I will cover the sun
>   with a cloud,
> and the moon will not give its light.
> I will darken all
>   the shining lights
> in the heavens over you,
> and I will bring darkness
>   on your land.
>   This is the declaration
>   of the Lord God" (Ezekiel 32:7-8, HCSB).

While it is obvious that Ezekiel was addressing the Pharaoh in his
day, the apocalyptic nature of his prophecy foreshadows events of
the end times when the earth and the cosmos will be shaken. When
the time comes to deal with the dragon (who is Satan in
Revelation), The Moon Goddess (who is the Babylon Prostitute in
Revelation), the Antichrist and his false prophet, then cosmic
phenomena *will* occur. God will cover the sun with a cloud,
dimming its light which will cause the moon not to shine. These
signs will be indicative of the impending return of Jesus.

The symbolism which the prophet uses to address the
Pharaoh of that day can be applied symbolically to represent the
end time judgments. The repetitive judgment imagery of the sun
being obscured, all the stars being darkened, and the moon not
shedding its light as a sign to the earth that the end is coming is

characteristic of prophetic, apocalyptic forecasts in both Old and New Testament writings. And to this date, no such cosmic event has occurred. Knowing this then, it is relatively hard to confine the prophecies to an antiquated mold. Additionally, note that God says he will darken the sun with a "cloud." Being that clouds in biblical imagery often represented God's glory, the "cloud" which darkens the sun in the last days could foreshadow the impending return of God's glory in the final restoration of all things. Just as Ezekiel prophesied a time when the glory will depart from Jerusalem and then return, so too does the judgment pronouncement on Pharaoh reveal a time when the return of God's glory in the form of a cloud will point to the final judgments of God upon the earth.

The Israelites followed the pillar of cloud by day and the pillar of fire by night as they made their way to the Promised Land (Ex.13:20-22). The sign guiding them through the wilderness was the glory of God, not the sun or moon. His manifest glory was seen and followed. In the last days, God will cover the sun with his cloud, that is, with his glory. This covering will produce a darkness which will confuse those who have followed the sun god's ways. Their daily directives will be demolished. In turn the stars they used to cast horoscopes and predict the future will not be found nor will the moon have any sunlight to radiate, meaning the end cannot be marked from the beginning. The judgment will be round the clock. If we look at Ezekiel 32:7-8 apocalyptically, then it shares many aspects with the end time prophecy of Joel 2:28-32. Thus only those, like Ezekiel declared, who have not turned to the confusing, wicked ways of idol worship will be able to stand in the days of universal disassembling.

Ezekiel connects the Egyptian worship and its influence in his day to The Moon Goddess worship that began in Babylon centuries prior. The Holy Spirit reveals this connection to his prophet. Prior to the prophecy of Egypt's downfall, God carries the prophet Ezekiel into a visionary state showing him the inner workings of the Israelites' temple.

> "Then he [YHWH] brought me [Ezekiel] to the
> entrance of the north gate of the Lord's house, and I saw
> women sitting there weeping for Tammuz. And he said

to me, 'Do you see this, son of man? You will see even more detestable acts than these.'

So he brought me to the inner court of the Lord's house, and there were about twenty-five men at the entrance of the Lord's temple, between the portico and the altar, with their backs to the Lord's temple and their faces turned to the east. They were bowing to the east in worship of the sun. And he said to me, 'Do you see this, son of man? Is it not enough for the house of Judah to commit the detestable acts they are doing here, that they must also fill the land with violence and repeatedly anger me, even putting the branch to their nose? Therefore I will respond with wrath. I will not show pity or spare them. Though they will call loudly in my hearing, I will not listen to them'" (Ezekiel 8:14-18, HCSB).

In this vision Ezekiel observes women "weeping for Tammuz" before he is shown "even more detestable acts"– twenty-five men with their backs to the Lord's temple and their faces turned toward the sun. Tammuz, the sun-god of the Babylonians was, per the mythology, married to Ishtar. The mythology is complicated but the underlying theme of Tammuz' history is that he was "like a shepherd, beautiful in appearance and giver of life" who was resurrected from death to life. Again, another Satanic attempt at mimicking the story of the life, death, burial, and resurrection of Jesus Christ. Remember that one legend purports that Tammuz was the son of Semiramis, the queen of Babylon, who conceived him after Nimrod's death via supernatural sun-rays. Though the Bible is relatively silent on Nimrod and Tammuz, the effect Tammuz and the sun-god's false worship had on the Israelites was enough to bring about God's wrath. Ezekiel is shown women sowing tears for their false god in the month that Tammuz was claimed to have been banished to the underworld, the month which marked the dry season, and he is also shown twenty-five men who have turned away from YHWH to worship Tammuz. The women were weeping for the god of vegetation to send forth rain. The men were bowing down to the east in an attempt to bring forth the sun. Both of these symbolic acts of worship were not only useless but detestable. The women weeping at the gate was bad, the men in the temple were worse, but it was the violence that ensued from turning to such violent gods that was the ultimate sin against God (i.e. child sacrifice).

The women were weeping for a god they did not know. The blinded men were facing the wrong direction. Had they remembered Elohim, God the Creator, and how he had created the vegetation *before* the sun (Gen. 9:11-13), then perhaps they would have forfeited their foreign sun god who could not deliver. But while the people of God forgot their origins, God did not forget them. Hundreds of years later, God would send forth the true Shepherd, His beautiful Son, who would come not to be served but to serve, giving his own life as a ransom for many (Matt. 20:28). Jesus would be resurrected from death to life so that all who believe in his name would never die but live in the garden again with him forever. The resurrection power of Jesus is not reliant upon the weeping of women or the worship of men. The forecasted resurrection of Christ, his return to redeem his people, and his recreation of heaven and earth was the nucleus of God's redemptive plan all along.

The sovereign, omnipotent, redemptive nature of YHWH is displayed beautifully in John 20 when Mary sees the resurrected Jesus.

> "But Mary stood outside the tomb, crying. As she was crying, she stooped to look into the tomb. She saw two angels in white sitting where Jesus' body had been lying, one at the head and the other at the feet. They said to her, 'Woman, why are you crying?'
>
> 'Because they've taken away my Lord,' she told them, 'and I don't know where they've put him.'
>
> Having said this, she turned around and saw Jesus standing there, but she did not know it was Jesus. 'Woman,' Jesus said to her, 'why are you crying? Who is it that you're seeking?'
>
> Supposing he was the gardener, she replied, 'Sir, if you've carried him away, tell me where you've put him, and I will take him away.'
>
> Jesus said to her, 'Mary.'

Turning around, she said to him in Aramaic, *'Rabboni!'* – which means 'Teacher'" (John 20:11-16, HCSB).

Mary's tears of sorrow were turned to joy in the moment she realized that the tomb was truly empty. Jesus is *alive*. Jesus' tears of blood in the garden before his crucifixion were the shower of rain needed for eternal life. His broken body on the cross was the reverse of the curse that separated mankind from the light of life. His resurrection was the Way that when men turned back to it, to *His* direction, they would receive life and life more abundantly; their blind eyes would be opened. There was no need to weep for Jesus as the women wept for Tammuz nor was there need for men to bow down to the sun, for the God of the Jew and Gentile is *alive* and day and night the twenty-four elders of Revelation bow down to him!

Many years before Mary, Jesus had taken Ezekiel to the secret place, showing him the detestable acts of the Israelites. In showing Ezekiel the inner workings of the temple, God not only exposed the secrets of the enemy but also revealed his redemptive plan for the Jewish people. All of the parts and pieces of the visions and prophecies would come together post resurrection. In intimacy with the one true God, Ezekiel was shown the workings of the false gods and their followers. The dark practices of sun god worship were happening *inside* the people and *inside* the temples of God, and the prophet saw it before the exposure. In the New Testament, Mary, a woman who walked closely with the Lord, was shown the fulfillment of the Law and the Prophets. She witnessed the hope of glory. In the same way, similar occurrences will happen as the world grows closer to the return of Christ. The remnant who walks with the Lord and spends time with him in the secret place will arise and declare the word of the Lord. They *will* prophesy. The sun and its false worship *will* be darkened. The moon and its false worship *will* cease.

And like the remnant who will shout from the mountain tops of the things they've heard in the secret place, the occurrence of such cosmic acts will and must occur *publicly* per the prophecy. It will be a sign "in the sky" where every eye will be able to see it.

Some will believe what they see while others will not. Just as the erroneous acts committed against YHWH in the inner places of the temples during the Israelites days were revealed to his prophets, the inner sins committed inside The Church and the "temples" of men in the future will be exposed by God's prophets before "the great and terrible day of the Lord" (Mal. 4:5).

Daniel

Daniel, a man of unshakable faith and incredible spiritual giftedness, was a contemporary of Ezekiel who also prophesied to the Judaic diaspora as well as the Babylonians. Particularly, Daniel was a voice of council for King Nebuchadnezzar, the king of Babylon. Having been taken with some of the early deportees following the first siege of Jerusalem, Daniel, a Hebrew by birth, found himself in a foreign nation under the rule of a pagan king at around the age of twenty. He served in Babylon around 70 years, the prophesied length of captivity as foretold by Jeremiah in 25:11. He had a colorful ministry. He advised the king, endured hardship and persecution for his faith, interpreted dreams and visions, and prophesied God's judgment on the nation of Israel and his future judgment at the end of the age.

Even Daniel's name was prophetic, meaning "God *has* judged." Presuming this was his name at birth, the focal point of his ministry and his life's purpose would be pointing to the future judgment that Israel, the treasured nation among the nations (Deut. 7:6), would face. Additionally, Daniel was accompanied by three other Judahite boys: Hananiah, Mishael, and Azariah (Ezk. 1:6). While in Babylon, the four men had their names changed to fit the Babylonian beliefs: Daniel was called Belteshazzar, Hananiah was called Shadrach, Mishael was called Meshach, and Azariah was called Abednego. Each Babylonian name reflected a spiritual deity worshiped in the land and interestingly, the name Shadrach means "command of Aku," Aku being the moon god. Belteshazzar given to Daniel means, "Bel protects." Ironically, it is YHWH who protects Daniel in the lion's den and his friends in the furnace, causing Nebuchadnezzar to eventually exclaim the God of the Jews is the only God (Ezk. 4:34-37). Under the saving hand of

God, Daniel lived through the judgment and eventually saw the fall of Babylon to the Persian empire as well as the return of his people to their homeland (Ezra 1), thus Daniel's name spoke then, now, and to come; his earthly ministry functioning as an appetizer to a greater supper that has yet to begin.

His ministry on earth was powerful. The miraculous stories of surviving lions in a den (Dan. 6) and his friends survival in the blazing furnace (Dan. 3) speak to the supernatural protection that comes to those who serve YHWH with great faith; his visions and prophetic oracles speak to the intimacy of YHWH; his premonitions and his discernment speak to the spiritual battle taking place over regions and souls; and his prophecies speak of impending judgment and restoration of the nations and of Israel. In Chapter 12, the final chapter of the Book of Daniel, the prophet is given a word by the archangel Michael. It is this word that reveals the "not yet" aspect of Daniel's prophetic insight:

> "But you, Daniel, keep these words secret and seal the
> book until the time of the end. Many will roam about
> and knowledge will increase…Go on your way, Daniel,
> for the words are secret and sealed until the time of the
> end" Daniel 12:4, 9 (HCSB).

For Daniel, his end would be in Babylon as he would die there in his late 90's, but the visions and the future predictions would not die with him. In fact many would say that his predictions were fulfilled hundreds of years later, but I (along with many others) believe there are still parts of Daniel hidden that have yet to be revealed. I will explain what I mean using specific passages from Daniel that I believe pertain to The Blood Moon Prophecy including but not limited to Chapters 2, 8, 11 and 12.

In the second chapter of the Book of Daniel, the young seer is given an opportunity to exercise his spiritual gift of dream interpretation to the king. Recall that King Nebuchaddnezar II (also known as "Nebuchadnezzar the Great" to the Babylonians or "The Destroyer of the Nations" to the Jews) was the second king of the Neo-Babylonian Empire. He ruled from 605 B.C. until his death in 562 B.C. He was known for his military campaigns in the Levant, his extravagant building projects which included the famous Hanging Gardens of Babylon, his defeat of the Egyptian Pharaoh Necho II, and his destruction of Jerusalem in 587 B.C. Though Nebuchadnezzar is depicted as a military powerhouse, his infrastructure was still woven with wicked witchcraft (Ezk 21:21, Daniel 4:6-7) and his kingdom with idolatry. Jeremiah describes him as evil yet used by God to bring about judgment to the Jews (Jer. 27-29). He was ruthless, even gouging out the eyes of fathers just before he killed their sons. But as sons of the Father of all power and under His divine grace, Daniel and his friends found favor in the earthly king's sight and for a reason. It was this favor for Daniel that would make way for the prophet to speak to both Jew and Gentile and to release prophetic words of end times events which would persist past the king's death.

God used Nebuchadnezzar to bring about judgment and inadvertent restoration to the Jewish people. In the beginning of The Book of Daniel, God gave the king of Babylon a dream but God left the interpretation of it up to his prophet, Daniel. Summarizing the story in Chapter 2, after informing his magicians and sorcerers who offer no interpretation, the king issues a decree that the wise men of the nation be executed (2:12). Daniel hears of the king's plan and asks his friends to help him pray for God's mercy and wisdom concerning the king's dream. God answers Daniel in a night vision, explaining the mystery to him. Daniel is then brought to the king where he is commanded to tell not only the dream itself but also the interpretation. Fascinatingly, it is not until the prophet speaks that the dream Nebuchadnezzar had is revealed to the readers.

In the first dream, the reader is allowed into the room of revelation. Daniel tells the dream that Nebuchadnezzar was given: a colossal statue made up of various metals suddenly appeared before the king. The statue had a gold head, silver chest and arms, bronze belly and thighs, iron legs, and feet of iron mixed with clay. Each of these metals is progressively less valuable while also progressively stronger. In his dream, the statue was broken apart by a stone from the head down until all that remained was chaff. However, the stone that struck the statue becomes a large mountain, filling the earth (Dan. 2:31-34). Daniel interprets the dream, letting the king know that after his death, other kingdoms will arise and fall until an eternal kingship is established that cannot be destroyed (Dan. 2:36-45). The history to follow King Nebuchadnezzar's rule shows that the four kingdoms of this vision were the Babylonian, Medo-Persian, Greek and Roman empires. It was this first successful assignment with the king that sealed Daniel's favor and his ministry. Despite persecution that would follow, Daniel and his friends were preserved and given more opportunities to exercise their faith, wisdom, and knowledge.

In Daniel 8 the prophet is given a vision that expounds upon the future Medo-Persian and Greek empires. 250 years before Alexander of Macedon, God revealed to Daniel events that would occur among the nations. In the vision Daniel sees the demise of the Medo-Persian Empire which had conquered the Babylonian empire in 539 B.C. (the year Daniel died). In the first half of Chapter 8, God speaks symbolically to Daniel about the end of the Persian Empire using a ram and a goat. The ram had two horns, one longer than the other (Persians and Medes respectively), and was violent and relentless (8:20), but an unforeseen "goat from the west" appears who bears a horn between its eyes (8:5). This goat defeats the ram, rises to power, but loses the power in an untimely death. Though the Bible doesn't explicitly name the goat as Alexander of Macedon, most biblical scholars claim that it was indeed Alexander. The details are so amazingly accurate that critics of the Bible have a hard time defending their stance against it. Alexander did emerge from the west, defeat the Persian emperor Darius III, rise to great power, and die prematurely on June 11, 323 B.C. in, of all places, Nebuchadnezzar's palace at the age of 32.

The vision continued with the four kingdoms that would emerge from the goat's horn. These kingdoms would come out of Alexander's empire, "parceled to the four winds," but would not go to Alexander's descendants nor have the power he had (Dan. 11:4). These events did occur nearly two centuries after Daniel's prophecy. And we know that what these images represented because of the interpretation given to Daniel by the angel Gabriel:

> "The two-horned ram that you saw represents the kings of Media and Persia. The shaggy goat represents the

king of Greece, and the large horn between his eyes represents the first king. The four horns that took the place of the broken horn represent four kingdoms. They will rise from that nation, but without its power.

Near the end of their kingdoms, when the rebels have reached the full measure of their sin, a ruthless king, skilled in intrigue, will come to the throne. His power will be great, but it will not be his own. He will cause outrageous destruction and succeed in whatever he does. He will destroy the powerful along with the holy people. He will cause deceit to prosper through his cunning and by his influence, and in his own mind he will exalt himself. He will destroy many in a time of peace; he will even stand against the Prince of princes. Yet he will be broken–not by human hands. The vision of the evenings and the mornings that has been told is true. Now you are to seal up the vision because it refers to many days in the future" (Dan. 8:80-26).

The angel's information revealed the future of the nations not just in Daniel's day but many days after Daniel. But were they fulfilled at Alexander's untimely death? And if not, what does it have to do with The Blood Moon Prophecy? To answer these questions, we must look more extensively at the Greek "goat from the west" and the final chapter of Daniel.

Preceding the Persian emperor Darius III's defeat, there was–if you'll recall from the Introduction–a peculiar event. From both the Greek army and the Persian army, a blood moon was observed in the night sky before the critical Battle at Gaugamela. For the Greeks this blood moon represented a sure victory, while for the Persians it foretold their doom. Despite the negative omen, Darius went into battle anyway where he would die by his own people. Alexander won the Battle of Gaugamela and the prophecy given to Daniel was fulfilled. The young, shaggy King of Macedon surprisingly took the Persian empire and continued his conquests until his death at 32. The blood moon stood for more than a silly omen, it represented something more powerful. It was a sign in the sky for all to see that, whether interpreted correctly or incorrectly, would fulfill prophecy. More importantly, it pointed to the prophecy giver– YHWH. Though Daniel had been dead for more than two centuries, could the magicians of Alexander's day have known about the YHWH prophets' predictions, or could Alexander himself have known? Did they know about the ram and the goat? Perhaps they did.

Flavius Josephus, a Roman-Jewish historian, wrote in his *Antiquities of the Jews* of a compelling event that he claimed occurred in 332 B.C., years *after* Daniel:

> "...he [Alexander the Great] gave his hand to the high priest and, with the Jews running beside him, entered the city. Then he went up to the temple, where he sacrificed to God under the direction of the high priest, and showed due honor to the priests and to the high priest himself. And, when the book of Daniel was shown to him, in which he had declared that one of the Greeks would destroy the empire of the Persians, he believed himself to be the one indicated; and in his joy he dismissed the multitude for the time being, but on the following day he summoned them again and told them to ask for any gifts which they might desire. . ."[82]

Using Josephus' interesting information, we might safely assume that Alexander did know of the prophecy. Being that he believed Daniel's words were about him, he spared the city of destruction and even, per Josephus, gave the Jews gifts.

But knowing Alexander's untimely death, it's possible that they didn't read Daniel's word in its entirety *or* the words were not interpreted correctly to Alexander. Perhaps, Alexander's pride may have kept him from reading beyond the victory in conquering Medo-Persia, stopping short before his predicted death. The pride that Alexander possessed was embedded at childhood and promoted through divination and through cunning words offered by The Moon Goddess. Alexander considered himself a god much like Nebuchadnezzar of Babylon. The blood moon may have pointed to a blood-won battle against the Persians but it also

---

[82] William Whiston, *Of the Thundering Legion* (London: 1726), 47-63; c.f. Josephus, *Ant.* 11.304–12.0.

pointed to Alexander's own fate; a fate he could not or would not accept thanks to the distortion of prophecy by The Moon Goddess.

Before the event at the temple of the Jews, Alexander was in other temples. While there is little information about Alexander knowing the prophecy of Daniel, there is plenty of historical information containing Alexander's wide acceptance of paganistic practices and religious rites. Alexander's egotistical nature stemmed from his mother, Olympias, who herself was passionate and imperious, believing that she was a descendent of Achilles, the demigod who fought and died at Troy.[83] She was also, per Plutarch's *Lives*, a worshiper of Dionysus, the god of snakes. Alexa Mutch writes:

> "A few nights after their wedding, Philip witnessed Olympias sleeping with snakes, presumably due to her being a devoted worshiper to a snake cult for Dionysus. Regardless, after this incident Philip lost affection for her. Plutarch notes that Philip did not sleep with her after that 'because he feared that some spells and enchantments might be practiced upon him by her, or because he shrank for her embraces in the conviction that she was the partner of a superior being' (Plutarch, *Lives*, 464, John Dryden)."[84]

In addition to her claim of divinity, Alexander's father, Philip II, also believed he was a descendent of Zeus. Both Alexander's mother and father claimed to have had supernatural encounters with the gods prior to his birth.

One legend purports that the Greek goddess of the hunt Artemis (a.k.a. The Moon Goddess) attended his birth. Philip also had night vision that he was sealing his wife Olympias' womb with the emblem of a lion. Of the most influential stories surrounding Alexander's "divinity" was when his mother informed him of an

---

[83] Plutarch, *Lives (Dryden Trans. Vol 1)*, Edited by A.H Clough, Translated by John Dryden, https://oll.libertyfund.org/titles/clough-plutarch-s-lives-dryden-trans-vol-1;

[84] Alexa Mutch, "Olympias," *Women in Antiquity Blog*, 2 Apr. 2017, https://womeninantiquity.wordpress.com/2017/04/02/olympias/

event that occurred before her wedding night with Philip when a lightning bolt from Zeus struck her womb. These stories stuck with Alexander and with each passing day and passing victory in battle he would grow fonder of the gods of Olympus. While Alexander used acceptance of other religions as a way to win the favor of his captives, he still held firmly to the belief that he was the son of Zeus, who was in his opinion, the father of all gods. This belief was solidified for him by both the temple priestess at Siwa (the Egyptian-Libyan temple of Zeus-Ammon) and Pythia at the Oracles of Delphi. Both claimed him to be the son of Zeus, not Philip II. In fact, legend holds that Alexander was warned not to go to Siwa but he disregarded the warning and went anyway, being led by snakes to help him through the Libyan desert.[85] Though Alexander did make it and received the prophecy he longed to hear, he did disregard warning, a trait that was passed down and would eventually kill him. The false prophets who tickled his ears with false hope only sealed the image of the lioness, The Moon Goddess herself, on his doomed destiny.

The Moon Goddess, through the working of Greek deities and even Alexander's earthly mother and father, convinced Alexander that he was divine, invincible, and king of the world. The impact Zeus and Artemis worship had on the young man led to his family's death. Like Daniel had prophesied, no successor of Alexander would follow him. Conceiving idolatrous practice and disregarding the warning truly affected the womb.

But Alexander died thousands of years ago and his throne has been diminished, so what does he represent exactly in The Blood Moon Prophecy? A brief historical study of the events that played out *after* the death of Alexander shows the connection between Old Testament prophecy and New Testament prophecy.

As Alexander's kingdom was divided to different leaders following his sudden death, the "evils were multiplied in the earth" (1 Maccabees 1:9). Hellenistic influence spread thanks to Alexander's establishment of Greek god worship in all the places

---

[85] Donald L. Wasson, "Alexander the Great as a God," World History Encyclopedia, 28 Jul. 2016, https://www.worldhistory.org/article/925/alexander-the-great-as-a-god/

he conquered. Upon his death, the Seleucid Empire came to control Israel and Jerusalem and it was within this empire that Antiochus IV who called himself Antiochus Epiphanes ("god manifest") ruled. In 167 B.C., Antiochus committed an "abomination of desolation" when he set up an altar to Zeus inside the Jewish temple, sacrificing a pig on it. He demanded that Jewish families do the same. He imposed Hellenism and Greek culture, outlawing Jewish sacrifices, the practice of circumcision, Sabbath observance, and the possession of the Torah.[86] Jewish Mattathias, a priest in Modein, and his sons refused to sacrifice, killed the Syrian officer who demanded they do so, and then fled to the remote hills with his sons. Others joined them, catalyzing the well-known Maccabean Revolt.

Israel soon regained its freedom and was ruled by Mattathias' descendants for a set time called the Maccabean or Hasmonean period. The Jewish festival of Hanukkah celebrates this reestablishment of Jewish traditions. This time of peace lasted until 63 B.C. before Roman general Pompey asserted control at the request of two feuding Hasmonean brothers. It was from Pompey that Antipater would appoint his sons Herod the Great (who attempted to kill Jesus at birth) over Galilee and Phaseal over Judea. Herod's son, Herod Antipas, would be the one in charge at the time of Jesus' crucifixion. The earthly kings to follow Alexander would eventually be dominated by the King of the world, *Jesus* who was both the son of man and the son of God. It would be Jesus' life, death, and resurrection that would evoke Daniel 2:44,

> "In the days of those kings, the God of the heavens will set up a kingdom that will never be destroyed, and this kingdom will not be left to another people. It will crush all these kingdoms and bring them to an end, but will itself endure forever."

The influence of Alexander, and not so much him as a person but more so his death and his assertion of Hellenism, would leave a lasting impression on the world and, like Nebuchadnezzar,

---

[86] Keith F. Nickel, *The Synoptic Gospels: An Introduction* (Louisville, KY: Westminster John Knox Press, 2001), 48.

function in bringing about judgment and restoration of God to the people of Israel. The prophecies of Daniel surrounding Alexander the Great contain as much historical weight as they do futuristic weight. Chapter 12, the conclusion of The Book of Daniel, exhibits this futuristic weight.

The conclusion of Daniel is actually the beginning to an unfulfilled prophecy regarding the end times, that is, the time just before, during, and after The Rapture. In Chapter 12 a prophetic picture is painted for the reader, for the one who reads the prophecy in its *entirety*, not limiting it to the past or stopping short of its futuristic implications:

> "Then I heard the man dressed in linen, who was above the water of the river. He raised both his hands toward heaven and swore by him who lives eternally that it would be for a time, times, and half a time. When the power of the holy people is shattered, all these things will be completed.'
>
> I heard but did not understand. So I asked, 'My lord, what will be the outcome of these things?'
>
> He said, 'Go on your way, Daniel, for the words are secret and sealed until the time of the end. Many will be purified, cleansed, and refined, but the wicked will act wickedly; none of the wicked will understand, but those who have insight will understand. From the time the daily sacrifice is abolished and the abomination of desolation is set up, there will be 1,290 days. Happy is the one who waits for and reaches 1,335 days. But as for you, go on your way to the end; you will rest, and then you will rise to receive your allotted inheritance at the end of days' (Daniel 12:7-13, HCSB)."

In Daniel's last recorded vision, he describes a heavenly figure, the one above the river, who informs him that time would pass before the end of the age but that in the meantime, Jesus would come to earth as the ultimate sacrifice.

We know from both Daniel's message and Paul's letter to the Thessalonians, that there will be a time at the end when there will be a great divide. This divide began at Christ's sacrifice and will continue until the time when the Antichrist, prototyped by

Alexander of Macedon, establishes his temporary throne (the set up of the abomination of desolation, v. 11). Hope will not be totally lost as the prophecy states many will be "purified, cleansed, and refined" –a great end time harvest– but the prophecy also states that many wicked will act wickedly–thus, a great divide between light and dark will appear. This divide will grow more apparent and more defined leading up to the revealing of the unholy trinity: the Antichrist, the False Prophet, and Satan as detailed in Revelation 12 and 13.

   I will expound upon "the abomination of desolation" in Part III. But for now I want to show how Alexander the Great's witty and forceful military foreshadows the Antichrist military nature; again, connecting Old Testament prophecy to New Testament prophecy. Like Alexander, the Antichrist will seemingly come out of nowhere, possibly the west (I personally believe the Antichrist will come out of Europe which is another book for another day) and will bring with him the false notion that he is a god. He will be young in his beginning using his charm to persuade. Through military strength, religious tolerance, and wealth, he will lure in a following before violently turning on the Jews and the Christians. During the beginning of his reign, life will seem peaceful and successful, but as time progresses he will become forceful and recalcitrant. The false prophet will feed the Antichrist's ego, much like Alexander's mother fed him. The days of the Antichrist will be completely Satanic and the days will be distressed as they have never been before, but his kingship on the earth will be short-lived. And just before his utter destruction, his wine will run dry and so will his mouth as he watches the sun darken before his eyes and the moon turn to blood. Those who have insight will see the signs of the times not as antiquated myths but as a true sign of victory for Christ's followers and the defeat of his enemies.

Isaiah

Isaiah, a prophet of God who lived during the latter half of Israel's kingdom, gave warnings of God's judgment, prophecies of the Babylonian captivity, and messages of restoration to the leaders of Judah and Jerusalem. The entire book ends with an eschatological hope of a new Jerusalem in God's new creation. Chapter 13, written before the captivity, prophesies of Babylon's judgment. Chapters 24-27 are often referred to as "Isaiah's Apocalypse" due to the end time nature of the writing. Isaiah 13 and 24 –the chapters of my focus– *are* eschatological and do exhibit astonishing parallels to The Blood Moon Prophecy.

The 13th chapter of Isaiah introduces the divinely-timed and orchestrated punishment against Babylon. Before Israel's fall, Isaiah speaks a promise of hope to the people of God by informing them that, in God's timing, their captors will be punished and they will return to their homeland. And as history proves, this did happen. The people of God did return to their home country in 538 B.C. and the city of Babylon ceased to exist when it came under total Persian control in 539 B.C. But the prophecy didn't end with the Babylonian empire, as v. 6-10 show us:

> "Wail! For the day of the Lord is near. It will come as destruction from the Almighty. Therefore, everyone's hands will become weak, and every man will lose heart. They will be horrified; pain and agony will seize them; they will be in anguish like a woman in labor. They will look at each other, their faces flushed with fear. Look, the day of the Lord is coming– cruel, with fury and burning anger– to make the earth a desolation and to destroy its sinners. Indeed, the stars of the sky and its constellations will not give their light. The sun will be dark when it rises, and the moon will not shine" (Isaiah 13:6-10, HCSB).

The city of Babylon may have been punished in the natural world when it collapsed as a city-state, but the spiritual powers at work behind the city's culture have yet to be fully judged. When this final judgment begins, the stars of the sky will not shine, the sun will be dark and the moon will not reflect any light. This kind of event has yet to happen, meaning the final judgment of The Moon Goddess has not occurred.

Another "now and not yet" prophecy pertaining to the spiritual captivity of Babylon can be found in Chapter 24. This chapter is the beginning of a section regarding YHWH's sovereignty and his justice. The creator God is the focus and his judgment is the theme of the passage. This judgment involves the earth being "stripped" and "made bare" (v. 1) and is the result of the creation, that is his people, who have stripped themselves of his commandments. Their rebellious nature and hardened hearts have led to the point of judgment. But the message isn't limited by the prophet to the Israelites who were privy to the law or the Noahic covenant, but here Isaiah extends the word to *the nations*. Everyone was created in the image of God and thus everyone will be subject to his judgment. No socio-economic or religious status and no amount of fame can prevent one from being seen or judged by the Lord of Hosts when that day comes.

In this heavy chapter, the prophet releases an interesting word of judgment from YHWH, "In the streets they cry for wine. All joy grows dark; earth's rejoicing goes into exile" (Isa. 24:11). The wine which makes men merry and makes them "marry" the prostitute becoming numb to the consequences of their actions will begin to run dry during the tribulation and be completely lost post Rapture. Though Babylon isn't mentioned in this particular verse, the scripture evokes the Revelation passage which informs us that in the days of judgment on the earth, the wine of God's wrath will be poured out on those that drank from the cup of The Moon Goddess' sexual promiscuity. The imagination can make up for the lost imagery here as the world is rampant with sexual perversion and sin, but one prime example of this type of business is human sex trafficking in which men and women sell or use other human beings for sex. Those drunk on the wine of this immorality will pay the price for their actions.

Beyond this earthly judgment is the cosmological aspect of the end times. The judgment of God will be on *all* those who did what was evil in his sight, including the spirits which persuaded men. Additionally, the physical components of the heavenlies will be subjected to God's destruction. Remember that the cosmology for the Ancient Near Eastern peoples was different than it was for the Israelites. For the pagans, the cosmos was unchanging and the progression of humanity was foreign.[87] Their deities were bound to the cosmos and reflected the nature and happenings of earth; their actions driven by human performance (or lack thereof). So for Isaiah to foretell of a time when the heavens and the celestial bodies would be subject to destruction was incomprehensible to the pagans. Especially those who worshiped the sun, moon, and stars.

> "The moon will be put to shame and the sun disgraced, because the Lord of Armies will reign as king on Mount Zion in Jerusalem, and he will display his glory in the presence of his elders" (Isa. 24:23, HCSB).

For some scholars these verses are merely the prophet's dramatic way of describing God's order and control of the cosmos. He created the sun and the moon and he can do as he pleases with them in the same sovereignty that he can deal with Israel and the surrounding nations. And while I agree that this verse is revealing God's Kingship of the earth and cosmos, I also sense a painful recoil from the prophet's punch. How could a natural piece of the universe be put to shame? Or how could an inanimate object like the sun be "disgraced" if it were not to be implying that such cosmic objects were anthropomorphized, inducing human worship of them. Can the moon or the sun feel shame or be disgraced? Or is that the spirits behind their worship, along with those who paid them tribute, will be put to shame and disgraced? I can only imagine what the idolaters of Isaiah's day made of such a statement.

In years to follow, the temples and the shrines of sun gods and moon goddesses would be destroyed. Modern day ruins of their temples can be found throughout the world. But the spirits behind them are still at work. The "will be" nature of the prophecy alludes to the fact that there will be a specific day when the moon worship and the sun worship will be judged in finality. The eschatological connection between the sun and moon goddess' final judgment is seen in Revelation 19.

---

[87] John N. Oswalt, *The Book of Isaiah Chapters 1-39 (New International Commentary on the Old Testament (NICOT)* (Grand Rapids, MI: Eerdmans Publishing, 1986), section "Text and Commentary on Isaiah 24:1-23), Ebook edition.

"After this I heard something like the loud voice of a
vast multitude in heaven, saying,
         'Hallelujah! Salvation, glory, and power belong
to our God because his judgments are true and
righteous, because he has judged the notorious
prostitute who corrupted the earth with her sexual
immorality; and he has avenged the blood of his
servants that was on her hands.' A second time they
said, 'Hallelujah! Her smoke ascends forever and ever!'
Then the twenty-four elders and the four living
creatures fell down and worshiped God, who is seated
on the throne, saying, 'Amen! Hallelujah!' (Rev. 19: 1-5),
HCSB).

The connecting word between Isaiah 24:23 and Revelation 19:5 is
"elders." Who these elders are is debatable but we do know they
are before the throne of God which is in the highest heaven and
they will observe the judgment of The Moon Goddess and her
worshipers (Rev. 4:4, Rev. 19:5). The timing of the final judgment
no one knows as the timing of Christ's return is only known by
God the Father (Matt. 24:36) but we do know that when the timing
of her judgment has come, it will be swift. According to Rev. 18:10,
as the elders, (possibly The Raptured Church) observes her
imprisonment for God's punishment, the men of the earth who
partook in her ways will also observe her judgment, which will
occur "in a single hour." For all the years The Moon Goddess and
Ba'al destroyed God's people, God will repay it "double according
to her works" in a *single* hour (Rev. 18:6). As for the men on earth,
they too will be punished and not only will they be punished after
she is disgraced, they will be punished before and during her trial.
The following scriptures foretell their doom:

"In the streets they cry for wine. All joy grows dark;
earth's rejoicing goes into exile" (Isa. 24:11).

"On that day the Lord will punish the army of the
heights in the heights and the kings of the ground on the
ground. They will be gathered together like prisoners in
a pit. They will be confined to a dungeon; after many
days they will be punished. The moon will be put to
shame and the sun disgraced…" (Isaiah 24:21-23).

"It has fallen, Babylon the Great has fallen! For all the
nations have drunk the wine of her sexual immorality,
which brings wrath. The kings of the earth committed
sexual immorality with her, and the merchants of the
earth have grown wealthy from her sensuality and
excess…the kings of the earth who have committed
sexual immorality and shared her sensual and excessive
ways will weep and mourn over her when they see the
smoke from her burning…the merchants of the earth
will weep and mourn over her, because no one buys their
cargo any longer" (Rev. 18:2, 3, 9).

Those who sold their souls into her sensual and seductive ways will
feel her judgment. There will be no wine to make them numb, no
money to help them escape, no friend to help them get through it
for they will be gathered together in a pit of punishment without
any hope, awaiting their eternal doom. Her disgrace will be their
disgrace.

Maybe, just maybe, there really is more to Isaiah's
prophecies of old. Maybe there is even something to the very fact
that he details this in chapter twenty-four…The *twenty-four* elders
will watch her plagues come and go in one single hour of one
twenty-four hour day. With these fascinating parallels, could it be that
The Blood Moon Prophecy speaks to a specific time of the
tribulation when the "moon" will be bloodied because the
judgment of the spirit and its worshipers has commenced? Or
could it be speaking prophetically of a specific natural event that

will occur *before* this judgment so as to warn that Christ's hand is at the door and his cup of wine is tipping?

I believe the answer is yes and yes to *both*.

The Minor Prophets

Before I explain why my answer is the same for both of those questions, I want to discuss the minor prophets. While there is a lifetime's worth of study that could be done within the twelve minor prophets of the Bible, I am going to pull verses from a select few that I believe pertain to The Blood Moon Prophecy in order to set the stage for Part II. I will especially focus on the prophet Joel whose blood moon prophecy is repeated by the apostle Peter at the outpouring of The Holy Spirit in the Upper Room of Jerusalem. I will also examine the prophets Amos, Malachi, and Zechariah.

Amos

The book of Amos is packed with sobering words. While little is known about Amos' life, we do know that he and Hosea prophesied to Israel in the 8th century B.C. while Isaiah and Micah prophesied in Judah. Amos' ministry began, per his words, "in the days of King Uzziah of Judah and Jeroboam, son of Johash, king of Israel, two years before the earthquake" (Amos 1:1). While the exact earthquake mentioned here is vague, there are historical records and archeological evidence that suggest an earthquake did occur in 750 B.C.[88] Scholars have also suggested that this earthquake was followed by a solar eclipse on June 15 in 763 B.C., which Amos may be alluding to in Amos 8:7-9.[89] Interestingly, it was an earthquake soon followed by a solar eclipse

---

[88] Britannica, "Amos," *Encyclopedia Britannica*, 20 Apr. 2024, https://www.britannica.com/biography/Amos; Billy K. Smith, & Frank Page, *Amos, Obadiah, Jonah: An Exegetical and Theological Exposition of Holy Scripture (Volume 19) (The New American Commentary)* (Holmon Reference: 1995), Amos, Section 1, Ebook edition.

[89] Smith and Page, *Amos, Obadiah, and Jonah*, Amos, Section 1. "Historical Setting"; c.f. R.L. Cate, *An Introduction to the Old Testament and Its Study* (Nashville: Broadman, 1987), 298.

(a darkening of the sun) that led the prophet to release the word of God's judgment on the nation.

The Book of Amos is full of rhetorical questions, visions, and words of prophecy all of which bear both God's judgment and his restoration. Amos informs the readers that he was first and foremost a servant. He was a shepherd of sheep, a servant to the flock before he became a prophet to the nation of Israel, a servant to God (Amos 7:15). And his prophetic ministry would be spirited. So strong were Amos' words of castigation to the rebellious house of Israel and the pagan environs that King Amaziah furiously rejected him and sent him away (Amos 7:1-13). But just because an earthly king sent God's prophet away didn't stop God's word from coming forth. The gifts and callings of God are irrevocable (Rom. 11:29). The agenda of the spirit of The Moon Goddess to silence the prophets could not and would not prevail over the word of God. Amos courageously prophesied anyway, despite the severe pushback.

Of his prophecies and visions, I want to focus on scriptures that pertain to The Blood Moon Prophecy. As a whole, the book definitely holds strong evidence that the same idolatrous behavior that occurred before the flood was still happening. If I were to pin one theme to the book, it would have to be righteousness and God's love of it. The actions of the leaders within the camps of Judah and Israel had once again forsaken righteousness and pursued the way of the pagans. There is one specific passage that highlights such similar acts to their rebellious ancestors and their moon goddess worship.

In the fifth chapter of Amos, the prophet laments for Israel's punishment, offers a word of advice ("Hate evil and love good; establish justice at the city gate. Perhaps the Lord, the God of Armies, will be gracious to the remnant of Joseph," Amos 5:15), and then prophesies of "The day of the Lord" in verses 18-27. Amos, speaking for God, asks a rhetorical question, "Won't that day of the Lord be darkness rather than light, even gloom without any brightness in it?" (Amos 5:20). The answer is an obvious yes. The day will be dark when the Lord of Armies' righteousness flows like a river, his justice like water (5:24). The word for "darkness" that Amos' uses is חֹשֶׁךְ or *chosek* and is the same word used in

Genesis 1 when God separated the darkness from the light on the *first* day of creation. So this darkness doesn't necessarily refer to the sun and moon (which were created on day four) but more to the darkness associated with evil and the brightness associated with righteousness. Being that the light on day one of creation was Jesus Christ Himself, then we can see the eschatological under laminate of Amos 5. When the true separation occurs at the end of the age, that is, when Christ is about to rapture his church, there will be a clear demarcation between what is good and what is evil. The days of judgment will be gloomy, but Christ's church will shine anyway. So, you might be asking, if this isn't in reference to the physical moon and the worship of it, then how does it relate to The Blood Moon Prophecy? I'm glad you asked.

At the end of chapter five, Amos (or more so YHWH speaking through Amos) caps the message with the reason as to why such terrible judgment will occur in the House of Israel.

> "House of Israel, was it sacrifices and grain offerings that you presented to me during the forty years in the wilderness? But you have taken up Sakkuth your king and Kaiwan your star god, images you have made for yourselves" (Amos 5:25-26, HCSB).

Sukkuth and Kaiwan were both astral deities. They were simply other representations of Ba'al and The Moon Goddess. A Babylonian incantation reveals that Sakkuth and Kaiwan were interchangeable names for the later Roman god Saturn, itself derived from ancient Egypt.[90] But before the association of "Horus the bull" with Saturn was Sakkuth and Kaiwan's origins in Babylon. An extensive historical analysis by scholars Marinus Anthony van der Sluijs and Peter James reveals fascinating connections of Saturn to "The Sun of the Night" in Babylonian

---

[90] "Sakkuth and Kaiwan," Bible Gateway, https://www.biblegateway.com/resources/encyclopedia-of-the-bible/Sakkuth-Kaiwan. See also Gert J. Steyn, "Trajectories of scripture transmission: The case of Amos 5:25–27 in Acts 7:42–43," *HTS Teologiese Studies Theological Studies* 69 (1), 2006.

writings.[91] Per their research, there are a number of Babylonian texts that refer to Saturn as the Sun. See their findings below:[92]

#1	^{d}UDU.IDIM.SAG.UŠ: MUL ^{d}UTU	Saturn = the Sun[3]
#2	^{mul}SAG.UŠ MUL *šá* ^{d}UTU	Saturn = the Sun[4]
#3	mul.gi.gi = MUL *kit-tú u me-šar* = ^{d}SAG.UŠ ^{d}UTU	mul-gi-gi = the star of truth and justice = Saturn / the Sun
	MUL GE$_6$ = AN $^{ša-al-me}$DÙL = MIN	black (*ṣalmu*) star = statue (*ṣalmu*) = ditto[5]
#4	^{mul}UDU.IDIM.SAG.UŠ KIMIN ^{mul}zi-ba-ni-tu$_4$ MUL ^{d}UTU Kayamānu KIMIN Zibānītu kakkab Šamaš	Saturn, also called the Scales (or) star of the Sun[6]
#5	MUL.GE$_6$ = ^{d}Zi-[ba-ni-tum] ^{mul}Zi-ba-ni-tum = ^{d}UTU	the black star = the Sca[les] the Scales = the Sun[7]

Table 1. cuneiform passages associating Saturn with the Sun

Additionally, they note that five omen writings refer to Šamaš as "specifically stationed in the 'halo of the Moon' (ina tarbas Sin)."[93] Though the early observations of the sun, moon, and stars were not always scientifically accurate (i.e. Šamaš must mean Saturn in this omen because lunar halos are only seen after sunset), the fact that these associations occurred in the realm of prophecy is important in understanding how the cosmos played a part in Ancient Near Eastern culture, particularly in the worship connected to such associations.[94] It was this Babylonian belief system and the by-product religious practices that would impact Egypt, Canaan, Phoenicia, Assyria, and beyond. The omens derived from the positioning of the heavenly entities and the physical phenomena of their positioning only solidifies the fact that supernatural qualities were attested to the planets, the sun, the stars, and the moon. Van der Slujs and James note the connection

---

[91] Marinus Anthony van der Sluijs and Peter James, "Saturn as the 'Sun of Night' in Ancient Near Eastern Tradition," Universitat de Barcelona: 2013, 279-282.

[92] MA van der Sluijs and James, "Saturn as the 'Sun of the Night,'" 280.

[93] MA van der Sluijs and James, "Saturn as the 'Sun of the Night,'" 281.

[94] MA van der Sluijs and James, "Saturn as the 'Sun of the Night,'" 281.

between the Babylonian sun-saturn nomenclature with the Romans, Greeks, and Hindus,

> "In the Greek world the planet Saturn was usually associated with the god Kronos, whom the Romans identified with the deity Saturn. However, following the Babylonian tradition, some classical statements identified it as the "star" of Hēlios or Sol, i.e. the Sun…These, together with Hindu passages of similar import and a late Egyptian witness, offer abundant evidence that the surprising association of Saturn with the Sun traveled well outside Mesopotamia, probably during the first millennium B.C."[95]

Whether knowingly or unknowingly, the ancient Babylonians did connect the sun to the planet Saturn and the planet Saturn to the moon. In essence, this mirrors the connection in the spiritual plane: Ba'al/Satan (the sun god) is connected to the Queen of Heaven (The Moon Goddess). Saturn was none other than the ancient gods of Ba'al, Ashteroth, and Moloch. Saturn was often connected to seed and harvest and the observance of the physical planet Saturn played a critical part in timing, particularly of the festival designated to the god, Saturnalia. This festival was perverse, literally, as the roles of citizens were said to be reversed on the feast day, all activities ceased, including court sessions (thus justice could not be administered), and death replaced life. Saturn's consort goddess, Lua Mater "Mother Destruction," demanded the heads of gladiators. The dead gladiators served as offerings to the goddess during or near Saturnalia.[96]

While Kronos was the god of time in the Greek tradition, mind you "a god who devoured his children as an allegory for the passing of generations,"the Roman tradition held Saturn to a similar status among the pantheon in which he was associated with the "sickle or scythe of Father Time."[97] Saturn was later syncretized with other deities and depicted with wings like that of Kairos, "Right Time," thus the prophecy of Amos contains

---

[95] MA van der Sluijs and James, "Saturn as the 'Sun of the Night,'" 281.

[96] Ausonius, *Eclogue* 23 and *De feriis Romanis* 33–7; Thomas E.J. Wiedemann, *Emperors and Gladiators* (Routledge: 1995), 47.

[97] Britannica, The Editors of Encyclopaedia. "Cronus". *Encyclopedia Britannica*, 8 May. 2024, https://www.britannica.com/topic/Cronus.

extreme irony. The astral deities of time are actually bound by the creator YHWH's time and their cultic, festivious time will, in God's divine timing, come to an end as the God of the Harvest, Jesus, collects his remnant.

So noteworthy was Amos' mention of Kaiwan and Sakkuth pagan deities that it was repeated by Stephen in Luke's Book of Acts. Stephen repeats the tantamount proclamation of Amos, "But you have taken up the tent of Moloch and the star of your God Rephan" in Acts 7:43, applying it now to the Jewish leaders who resisted Jesus as Messiah. Repetition in the Bible should *always* be noted. Like Joel's blood moon prophecy, the words of Amos 5:26 are repeated in Stephen's stunning sermon. In the translation from Hebrew to Greek, Rephan (or Saturn) is used in place of Kaiwan but both are interchangeable. Like Amos, Stephen was also rejected for connecting it to the current Jewish state and was stoned for it, becoming the first Christian martyr. As he was dying, Stephen looked into the heavens and saw Jesus the Christ, *standing* (Acts 7:55), not sitting. As the God who stands above the stars, Jesus stood for Stephen.

Stephen's martyrdom again shows that the agenda of The Moon Goddess is to silence the prophets. Her agenda has not changed. Recent research shows that more than thirteen Christians are martyred *daily* because of their faith.[98] This number will only increase as the world nears its end. As the fossil of the Genesis account of the demarcation between darkness and light becomes more evident through the dusting away of deception, so too will the persecution of the saints become more evident. The next time Jesus stands from his throne will be when he is mounting his horse to execute justice on the earth and avenge the blood of his saints (Jer. 23:25, Rev. 19:11-16) and, per Amos, "restore the fortunes" of God's people" (Amos 9:14).

Zechariah

---

[98] "13 Christians A Day Killed for Their Faith," Open Doors US, 30 Jan. 2024, https://www.opendoorsus.org/en-US/stories/13-christians-killed-day-average/#:~:text=On%20average%2C%20more%20than%2013,roughly%205%2C000%20people%20each%20year.

Zechariah also contains sections of apocalyptic literature. The Book of Zechariah and the prophecies in it are a staple piece in God's story. Ezra informs us that Zechariah and Haggai were contemporaries during the post-exilic period (Ezra 5:1) and both preached in Jerusalem, their messages centering on rebuilding the temple and renewal of the worshipers. The objective of Zechariah's ministry was to prophesy, preach, and prepare the people of God for ministry in the rebuilt temple upon its completion. Additionally, he was from the tribe of Levi and was therefore to serve as a priest during his ministry.

Darius I (522-486 B.C.) was king during the time of the prophet Haggai's and Zechariah's preaching; and while the Hebrews had been freed from his rule and returned to their homeland Israel, the trauma of Babylonian captivity was still present. The people were distressed, discouraged, and downtrodden. Upon their return, Haggai's short four month ministry exhorted the Hebrews to rebuild their temple, a task which would reignite their faith. Zechariah complimented Haggai's message, encouraging the people to then repent and renew their relationship with YHWH, preparing their mind, body, and soul for a new and fresh encounter with the living God.

The name Zechariah means "YHWH has remembered" and this message is evident throughout the book. God remembered his people because he remembered his covenant with them. Despite the Jews consistent rebellion and rejection of his statues and his laws, God continued to raise up prophetic voices who would exhort, edify, and comfort. In the form of visions, Zechariah encourages the Jews by promising a future everlasting peace to Israel which will be accompanied with the divine judgment of their adversaries as well as a future return of God to his temple when he will establish an everlasting kingdom in Jerusalem (Zec. 1:7-6:15, 9:8-10, 12:8-9, 14:9-11). Out of Zechariah's messages, I want to focus on Zechariah's seventh vision "The Woman in the Basket" found in Chapter 5 and "The Lord's Triumph and Reign" found in Chapter 14.

Following a prelude call to repentance, Zechariah describes eight night visions (Zech. 1:7-6:15) symbolizing a return of God's people to repentance and salvation. In his seventh vision,

Zechariah saw something peculiar. He watched as an angel presented a measuring basket with a lead lid. Upon lifting the lid, Zechariah peered inside to find a woman sitting in a basket. When he asked the angel who the woman was, the angel replied, "This is Wickedness" (5:8). The angel then pushed her back into the basket and covered her with the lead top. The rest of the vision is very interesting:

> "Then I looked up and saw two women approaching with the wind in their wings. Their wings were like those of a stork, and they lifted up the basket between earth and sky.
>
> So I asked the angel who was speaking with me, 'Where are they taking the basket?'
>
> 'To build a shrine for it in the land of Shinar,' he told me. 'When that is ready, the basket will be placed there on its pedestal'" (Zechariah 5:9-11, HCBS).

There is much to unpack from the vision as it pertains to The Blood Moon Prophecy, but what should stand out most dramatically is *"the land of Shinar."* Recall that lands and regions mentioned in the Bible are important and in this case, the land of Shinar was noteworthy because it was where The Moon Goddess worship began. It was in the land of Shinar that the people built a temple to reach into the heavens in order to communicate with their gods, particularly The Moon Goddess. Knowing their hearts, God crushed their plan and scattered their languages. As the people scattered throughout lands, the goddess took on various names and manifestations but the spirit behind the worship never changed. Zechariah, hundreds of years later, sees the woman responsible for wickedness. Could it be Semiramis who embodied The Moon Goddess herself?

Though it isn't clear which woman is being referred to here (Semiramis or the Babylonian Prostitute, as both are essentially one in the same), I do find it intriguing that the basket is carried to the ancient land of Babylon, the city responsible for the spread of her worship and the eventual destruction of Jerusalem and captivity of Israel. The passage indicates that the "woman of wickedness" contained in the basket is a *specific* entity, a source of evil responsible for the woes, destruction, and rebellion in the earth. So wicked is she that she is shoved back down into the basket before it is covered with a lead top.

Skimming over the details in this short vision would be to miss the devil behind them. There are a few parts in this vision that I want to commentate on: (1) the basket, (2) where the basket is located, (3) the lead covering, (4) how most English translations use the word "iniquities" in v. 6.

1) The King James Bible and the New American Standard Bible all use the word "ephah" instead of basket. The Hebrew word used for "basket" is actually הָאֵיפָה or "ephah" which was used to measure grain.[99] The ephah was a Hebraic dry measure that measured approximately one-half bushel.[100] The word "basket" then may not be the best translation as it doesn't translate the use of such a basket well. The ephah basket was used to measure weight. A cross reference with this type of measuring tool is Lev. 19:36 and Deut. 25:14 which both use the *ephah* in reference to weighing *honestly*. Thus the weight of this wicked woman who operates in deception, whose scales are distorted, will be judged by God with his honest scales of justice. Micah 6:11 states that God cannot excuse wicked scales and Proverbs 11:1 reminds us that, "The Lord detests dishonest scales, but accurate weights find favor with him." She *will* be weighed in God's perfectly balanced scales of justice.

We aren't told how large the ephah was from the passage, but we are given a clue that it is, at least spiritually speaking, large as it contains "all the iniquity in the land" and it has to be carried by two spiritual beings to Shinar. Typically, an ephah would not be able to hold an actual life-sized woman, so if we are to take this vision literally, then perhaps the woman may be a small carved idol of The Moon Goddess. However, knowing that visions themselves are supernatural and our minds cannot always comprehend the relative size

---

[99] Strong, *Strong's Exhaustive Concordance*, H374.

[100] Andrew E. Hill, *Haggai, Zechariah, Malachi: An Introduction and Commentary* (Illinois; IVP Academic, 2012), 166.

of spiritual things, the basket in Zechariah's vision may have been ginormous in scale. Though I am the first to consider any and every possibility in the supernatural, I do find it compelling to consider the latter proposition. If the ephah Zechariah was shown could only hold a man-made idol, then it would appear as if something so small could not be so dangerous, which is exactly the lie The Moon Goddess hides behind. The wicked power behind her worship has far greater consequences than one might first consider. A "small and simple" horoscope reading can actually have severe, long-lasting repercussions. So strong is her power that a lead cap, not used on such an ephah, had to be placed over her to contain her. However, if the basket Zechariah observed was massive, then this may be a hint as to the power and wickedness of this entity. Even more, it would reiterate the utmost power of YHWH who will defeat her in the end.

2) We are told that Ezekiel "looked up" to see the basket (5:5). The basket is therefore lifted into a higher realm. But despite its elevation, Zechariah is able to see inside. Belief in YHWH and devotion to him had placed the prophet in a spiritual plane to peer inside something in a higher dimension. This insight is because he walked with the God who is above every other said to be god. The text also informs us that the winged creatures who carried the basket to the land of Shinar lifted the basket between the earth and sky (5:9). We are not told that the basket descends to hell nor are we told it rises to the dwelling place of God in the highest heaven. No. Instead, the author makes it visible to the reader that this wicked spirit will be visible in the *sky* to all earthbound inhabitants. A sign of judgment in the sky that no man or woman will be able to deny.

3) In verse 7 and 8 Zechariah sees a lead covering on top of the ephah to contain the Wicked Woman. Being that lead lids were not used for such measuring baskets, the sight is odd but symbolic. Upon opening the lead lid for Zechariah, the angel soon has to "ram" or "shove" the Wicked Woman back inside and cover it with the heavy lid, implying that this spirit is trying to escape and is strong in power. The use of lead in the ancient days was for weight, as it was one of the heaviest

metals (second to gold) that the Israelites had access to.[101] Exodus 15:10 speaks of the weight of the lead of justice in the Israelites' song of praise upon their deliverance from the land of Egypt through the Red Sea, "They [the Egyptians] sank like lead in the mighty waters." The power of the Wicked Woman is strong, but the weight of God's deliverance from her is mightier still. No matter how bound a person might be in idolatrous practices, God has all the power and the authority to deliver that person out of bondage. And if that isn't convincing enough to turn from her ways, those who surrender their life to Jesus and depart from such evil practices are given the power and authority of Christ to withstand her evil devices and help others escape them (Lk. 10:19). *And* if that still isn't enough, those who draw near to God will experience the same revelation as Zechariah, being given the opportunity to see with spiritual eyes the truth behind the plots and plans of Satan so as to pray and war more effectively. They will be given end-time warnings! They will *not* miss his return.

4) In the beginning of the vision, the angel informs Zechariah that the measuring basket was "the iniquity in all the land" (v. 6). The word iniquity here is also a debatable translation. Most Hebrew manuscripts read "eye" while one Hebrew manuscript, the Septuagint (LXX), and the Syriac Bible (the Greek Translated into Syriac) uses "their guilt" or "their iniquity."[102] While I can see where the translators use the word iniquity to get the point across that the sins of the people are associated with this vision and with the basket, I do want to examine the most accepted word "eye" in this verse. The "eye" or *ayin* is used throughout the Scriptures for human eyes which were made to see in the natural, spiritual eyes which were made to be opened by God to see in the spirit (Gen. 3:5), and the eyes of idols which cannot see (Ps. 15:5). And while we know that what man views with his eyes can lead him either into righteousness or wickedness (Matt. 5:29) and Zechariah's job was to preach to the post-exilic

---

[101] William Smith, "Entry for 'Lead'," *Smith's Bible Dictionary* (1901), https://www.biblestudytools.com/dictionary/lead/#google_vignette

[102] Hill, *Haggai, Zechariah, Malachi*, 166.

Israelites in his ministry, it is interesting that "eyes in all the land" is used in most Hebrew translations of Zechariah's vision of the Wicked Woman in the basket. It reminds me of the "all-seeing eye" of Horus that was (and still is) prominent in Egyptian religion. This eye, or wedjat eye, was one of the most common "protective" amulets worn in the ancient world.[103] Today, this eye is also seen in the common Hamsa hand jewelry worn worldwide, the signage of Illuminati as well as in the top of the pyramid on the United States dollar bill. Am I implying that this is the correct interpretation of the verse, not at all. But the image of "eyes in all the land" is certainly a thought-provoking way of describing the iniquity of the people.

So here in the fifth chapter of Zechariah's prophetic book, we see the revealing of the "woman" behind the evil in the land. Her evil was exposed and judged in the prophet's day and it will be judged again in the future.

Along with this night vision, I want to draw attention to Chapter 14, the final chapter of Zechariah, in which the prophet describes the Lord's triumph and final reign in Jerusalem. In this passage, the promise is declared that God will one day return with "all of his holy ones" (Zech 14:5, Matt. 24:3, Rev. 19:11-21) to battle the nations who have resisted him. Verse six is captivating. The Holman Christian Standard Bible (HCSB) reads:

> "On that day there will be no light; the sunlight and moonlight will diminish. It will be a unique day known only to the Lord, without day or night, but there will be light at evening" (Zechariah 14:6, HCSB).

At this point in the book, the supernatural switch flip of the heavenly lights should be an obvious recurring sign to Biblical readers signaling the end of the age is at hand, or in other words, the presence of Christ has returned. This unique day known only to the Lord will reverse the natural order of the cosmos. This

---

[103] Carol Andrews, *Amulets of Ancient Egypt* (Austin, Texas: University of Texas Press, 1994), https://archive.org/details/amuletsofancient00andr

cosmic cataclysmic event will be a disturbance of what has always been. The sun will not shine and the moon's light will diminish. As previously stated, there will be some who interpret the signs correctly and others who do not.

While I certainly do not want to attribute my own thoughts or assumptions into the text, I do want to go "behind" the text to uncover any mystery that may be concealed in peculiar symbolism, vivid metaphors, and intriguing imagery. To read the Old Testament prophecies, especially the eschatological ones, in black and white is to possibly miss the colorful, spiritual mysteries behind the text and, more dangerously, miss the signs of the times in the day we are living. By relying too heavily on the natural order, perceiving these apocalyptic visions to solely mean the sun, moon, and stars will not shine, is to, I believe, miss the spiritual significance behind such an event. Ironically, it is the very natural order that God will disrupt when the sun, moon, and stars cease their shining in his day of judgment. And while yes, the sun, moon, and stars will literally stop shining at the end of the age, sending the world into confusion, I believe there is a spiritual aspect to this phenomena that can be discerned from the text. Just as the River Nile was a physical river in Egypt, the river represents something more in the spirit (Ezekiel 29:3 and Ezekiel 30:12-13). The apocalyptic imagery reveals that there is more occurring in the spirit world and there is more to "light" and "dark" than we think.

Returning to Zechariah 14:6-7, this special day in which the cosmic lights cease to shine is a future picture of the time of judgment on the earth followed by the new Heaven and new Earth. "It will be a unique day known only to the Lord, without day or night, *but there will be light at evening*" (v. 7, emphasis added). As that day of earthly judgment draws to an end, the light of Christ will take the place of the sun, moon, and stars forever. There will be no need for them because *He will be the light* (John 8:12, Heb. 1:3, Rev. 21:23) and all will worship *him*.

Malachi

There is scholarly debate about who wrote the Book of Malachi, some believing Malachi was a title for a messenger, possibly Ezra;

others believing Malachi was an actual prophet, as he is listed among the 12 prophets (2 Esdras 1:40). The name Malachi means "my messenger" and so it is understandable that there is a divide in authorship. But such arguments are not the point of this book, rather the point is the message of the messenger.

Malachi preached to the Jews in the Yehud as well as the descendants of the Hebrews who survived the Babylonian siege of Jerusalem but were not deported to Babylon. He wrote to this group of Jews during the reign of Darius I.[104] At this point in the Israelites' post-exilic history, the temple had been rebuilt, though it was nothing compared to the grandeur of Solomon's Temple; and while the Jews did worship God again at the temple, the worship was subpar. Dishonest scales for tithes and offerings were present and the priesthood was infiltrated with sin.

The writings of Malachi broadcast a message of God's love, his covenant, his mercy, and his desire for true worship. Mirroring the messages of other prophets, Malachi also warns and corrects against idolatry, encouraging repentance while promoting righteousness. Though the underlying theme of God's goodness is present, the end of Malachi is tart in taste. He gives a final warning to the house of Israel to keep God's statutes and ordinances or he will curse the land and send a consuming fire on the wicked (Mal. 4:1-2). But like sweet and tart candy, the messenger of God prophesies of a soon coming prophet who will walk in the mantle like that of Elijah before "the great and terrible day of the Lord comes" and who will restore hearts of the children to the fathers and the hearts of fathers to the children (Mal. 4:4-6). This person would be John the Baptist who would prepare the way for Jesus. Malachi's book thus concludes the Old Testament. The next word of God to show up on the scene would be roughly 400 years later and would be the word of God himself–Jesus.

Since Malachi is such a dense book, I want to focus on two specific verses in the final chapter.

> "'But for you who fear my name, the sun of
> righteousness will rise with healing in its wings, and you

---

[104] Hill, *Haggai, Zechariah, Malachi*, 278.

will go out and playfully jump like calves from the stall. You will trample the wicked, for they will be ashes under the soles of your feet on the day I am preparing,' says the Lord of Armies" (Mal. 4:2-3, HCSB).

If not already detected at this point in the book, I want to make it more obvious that as I draw closer to Part II, the connection between the events in the Old Testament surrounding God's judgment will mirror the events surrounding his return to judge the world. But in the warning, I also hope to make it apparent that God is a God of *mercy*. He is patient, not wanting anyone to perish but all to come to repentance (2 Pet. 3:9). He does not delight in the death of the wicked (Ezk. 33:11). That is why he sent his one and only Son to make a way of redemption for humanity, to break the curses of sin and death, and to equip people to prepare for his return. Malachi reminds us that God's people *will* go out rejoicing.

So before moving into the final section of Part I, the discussion of Joel, I want to make it clear that God is still saving, still redeeming, still healing. While the world is growing darker and the love of many is waxing cold, the love of God has not changed and never will. God is love (1 John 4:8). His love knows no bounds and he is able to save all who are bound. For all those who worship Satan, who have drunk from the Babylonian spirit's cup and who have martyred and persecuted the prophets and the saints of God, judgment *will* happen. But I believe the final wrath of God will be preceded by a great harvest, miraculous wonders, and terrifying sights in the sky. Hardship will still be present, but Malachi offers a ray of hope, a precious promise to all of God's people which will help suffering saints endure the wonderful yet turbulent days ahead.

In the days of tribulation, there will be trouble, hardship, and persecution but for those who fear the name of God, "the sun of righteousness will rise with healing in its wings" (Mal. 4:2). Interestingly, the Son of God is likened to the sun here. Why? Some might interpret this verse as a solar epithet for YHWH, who is the creator of the sun and light. Others might suggest it is figurative for the dawning of a new day of righteousness.[105] I believe it is both and more.

The day of the Lord will be one of glorious light for those who fear his name and a day of darkness for those who do not. His righteousness will eradicate false worship and sin once and for all and will bear with it healing and joy for those who have accepted Jesus as Lord and Savior. Looking at the Ancient Near Eastern iconography and the time in which the messenger Malachi wrote, we also know that the sun deity was worshiped. So in a double entendre, the messenger could be saying that on the day of the Lord, Jesus will rise like the sun because he is the Son who created the sun and he is the one true God who rose from the grave. In his rising, the sun deity falls. God *is* righteousness, and in *his* wings he will give strength to the weary, joy to the downtrodden, protection from the wicked, and healing to the sick (Isa. 40:31, Ps. 91). Righteousness is often connected with light in the scriptures, so it is the righteousness of God, his Son, who will bring everlasting light to the earth (Ps. 37:6). And in all of this, Jesus' rising from his throne to mount his horse will initiate the falling of the sun, moon, and stars as we know it, a sign that the final fall of Satan, Ba'al, and The Moon Goddess is near.

The light from God's appearance will be his glory, his righteousness, and his fire. For those who revere the name of Satan and serve the son of perdition (the Antichrist), they will be incinerated in God's holy fire like the prophets of Ba'al in Elijah's day. But those who set their eyes on Jesus will see this jealous fire in his eyes as he returns to collect his remnant and rain out his righteousness. The wicked will "be like ashes under the soles of God's peoples' feet" (Mal. 4:3). The destruction of evil will be sure and swift, as fast as *The Rapture.*

Joel

The holy fire of God is where I will begin my discussion of Joel–the dividing fire that also has the power to unify. It may seem paradoxical, but this concept of God's fire was nothing new to the

---

[105] Hill, *Haggai, Zechariah, Malachi*, 358-359.

house of Israel. Fire signified God's presence to Moses on Mount Sinai and to the Israelites in the wilderness while it also signified God's judgment as it rained down on the sin-ridden Sodom and Gomorrah. Fire was used to purge and refine, to extract pure gold from alloy, provide light, and burn up unfruitful chaff. Fire, like the wine allegory, has both positive and negative–balanced if you will–purposes. For now I want to excavate the prophecy found in Joel 2:28-32 for it is this foundation that will set the stage for its dramatic repetition in Acts 2. A drama of *fire*.

But first, we need to answer some fundamental questions: who was the prophet Joel, who was he writing to, what was his message?

Little is known about the life of the author of this book other than he was Joel the son of Pethuel who received the word of the Lord (Joel 1:1). The prophetic words Joel received were directed toward the House of Israel but the date in which he wrote the book is unknown. Scholars are divided; some believe his ministry was pre-exilic, others post-exilic. Regardless, we do know that Joel was addressing the Jewish people in a similar fashion as other prophets. He writes about God's judgment and God's restoration. For the sake of this book, I do not believe the date should be explored. Instead, I want to focus on the overall message of Joel and his unique prophecy.

Leading up to this vivid and exciting prophecy, Joel reiterates the need for repentance (Joel 2:12-17). Forgiveness of sins *always* precedes revival; it is the oxygen the fire needs. To be forgiven by Christ and then reborn in him is to breathe a new air as a new creation. This new air ignites a spiritual flame in a believer who becomes a great light for all to see (Matt. 5:14). The fire to be discussed in Acts 2, which plays on Joel's prophecy, is the same spiritual fire of God's presence that all believers receive upon conversion just a different color and form–a blue fire versus a red fire for lack of a better analogy. But in the beginning, upon conversion, every believer receives the light of Christ. The baptism of the Holy Ghost in Acts 2 is the *fire of power* for service. But before any baptism, the forgiveness of sins is a must.

So as Joel addresses the nation of Israel and their sins, calling them to fasting and prayer and to repentance, he then releases one of the most cardinal prophecies, the prophecy of the gift of The Holy Spirit. In the Old Testament, The Holy Spirit did not indwell the Israelites but rather would "come upon" men and women at certain times to enable them for services: prophecy (king Saul), healing (Elisha), raising the dead (Elijah), strength in battle (Gideon), wisdom (King Solomon), dance (King David), artistic ability (the artisans who made Aaron's garments), childbearing (Hannah), this list goes on. The Holy Spirit would, as Joel notes, descend on the people of God in a new way years after his ministry, upon a people who would live on the other side of the cross. This visitation would not be temporary but everlasting and it would not be limited but *all consuming* (Heb. 12:29).

Joel makes it clear that following a cleansing of sin, whether personally or corporately, restoration comes. Joel 2:25 and 27 reveal, "I will repay you for the years that the swarming locust ate...My people will never again be put to shame." Even better would be the downpayment of the gift of The Holy Spirit through the fulfilled covenant in Christ. And after this promised recompense, the prophet releases the precious promise of God's Spirit being available for *all* people.

> "After this
> I will pour out my Spirit on all humanity;
> then your sons
> and your daughters
> will prophesy,
> your old men will have dreams,
> and your young men will see visions.
> I will even pour out my Spirit on the male and female slaves
> in those days.
> I will display wonders
> in the heavens and on the earth:
> blood, fire, and columns
> of smoke.
> The sun will be turned to darkness
> and the moon to blood
> before the great and terrible day of the Lord comes.
> Then everyone who calls on the name of the Lord will be saved,
> for there will be an escape for those on Mount Zion and in
> Jerusalem,

as the Lord promised,
among the survivors
the Lord calls" (Acts 2:28-32, HCSB).

The purpose of this future outpouring of The Holy Spirit in Joel's prophecy would not be to cleanse the people, for this type of rain would come in the shower of Christ's atoning blood; rather it would be dispersed to endue believers *with power* for service and to make witnesses of God to all nations, tribes, and tongues. This was a new concept to the Israelites in Joel's day where men (not women), the elderly (not the younger), the selected priests (not the layman), the elite (not the slaves) were the ones to receive divine revelation from God. More impactful than the undoing of cosmic order would be the undoing of hierarchy and class when God's Spirit was given to whomever God willed. A true paradigm shift was on the horizon. This boggling prophecy of Joel wouldn't be fully understood until the first outpouring upon the Jews in Acts 2 and then, to make things even more fascinating, the outpouring on the Gentiles in Acts 10. Still then, not every Jew or Gentile would see it nor care to.

Not only would the gifts that were promised to those who received this "separate" baptism (not the baptism by water) be mocked and denied, but so would even the most elaborate or bold acts of faith, miracles, signs, and wonders in the heavenlies and in the earth be doubted and dismissed as being real. The fire of The Holy Spirit would be, as stated before, dividing and uniting. On the one hand, the division would be the marked difference between those who were consumed by faith in Jesus and those who were not; and on the other hand, it would be the eschatological judgment of fire that will one day literally separate the righteous from the wicked as God's wrath consumes the earth. But the promised Holy Spirit was not meant to cause division among men in the form of division as we understand it. Rather, it was meant to divide light from dark so that in that division those in the dark might more clearly see those with the light, become curious, and pursue that same light. Additionally, the separation for believers *from* the world and *into* The Holy Spirit would unite all children of God: Jew and Gentile, male and female, slave and free (Gal. 3:28).

The outpouring of which Joel prophesied spoke from the beginning of time, when God separated light from dark, and to the end of time, when a unified church *will* go out in power as the enemy descends into flames.

The prophets before Joel also spoke to a similar future age when The Holy Spirit would be ever present and all consuming. Ezekiel prophesied of an age when God's Spirit would enable them to obey God from the heart (Ezek. 35:26-27) and Isaiah prophesied of an age when God would pour out The Holy Spirit to recreate a new people (Isa. 32:14-18, 44:3-5). Joel's message has commonalities with these prophecies but with a distinct addition: those who were infilled with The Holy Spirit– regardless of race, ethnicity, gender or socio-economic status–would one day prophesy, dream dreams, and see visions.[106] The signs would be a witness not only to the unbeliever and the lukewarm Christian but also a sign in itself that the Messianic era had begun and the end of the world was near.

Following the distribution of the gifts of the Spirit would be terrifying signs in the heavens and the earth. The "fire and columns of smoke," –traditional theophanic images through the Bible– described in Joel point to a physical event. The mention of blood echoes the blood of the Nile, while also alluding to the apocalyptic, foreboding picture of blood being hurled to the earth in Revelation 8:7. There are both physical and spiritual components in Joel's end-time prophecy that will affect both believers and nonbelievers.

We must remember that the outpouring of The Holy Spirit on his remnant will be followed by the outpouring of God's wrath on the ones who do not fear him, have hardened their hearts against him, and have committed abominations in the name of other gods. And while no one knows the exact day on which that cup of wrath will be turned, the text holds clues as to when the cup of God's wrath is at its maximum tilt.

---

[106] Duane A. Garret and Paul Ferris, *Hosea, Joel: An Exegetical and Theological Exposition of Holy Scripture* (Nashville: Holman Reference, 1997), Section 1. "Gift of the Spirit (2:28-29)" Ebook edition.

"The sun will be turned to darkness and the moon to blood before the great and terrible day of the Lord comes. *Then*, everyone who calls on the name of the Lord will be saved, for there will be *escape* for those on Mount Zion and in Jerusalem, *as the Lord promised among the survivors the Lord calls*" (Joel 2:28-32 HCSB, emphasis added).

The return of chaos to the earth as the natural cosmos unravel is evident from the text as a precursor to the moment when, I believe, The Church will be raptured. Will the bride of Christ see some of the tribulation? Will she see some of the stars fall and the sun darken? Yes, I believe she will; however, as I will discuss through the remainder of the book, she will not see *all* of the tribulation.

Joel's prophecy informs us that the sun will be darkened and that the moon will be turned to *blood*. The sun "being darkened" isn't too difficult to imagine. Solar eclipses happen often. We can see the sun dim during these events and so we could safely assume something similar will happen to the sun before the Lord returns, right? Some readers might say that Joel was using dramatic imagery for a natural phenomena. But here's the problem with shrugging the event off as solely symbolism or humanistically trying to reason with the description: the prophet describes the moon as turning to blood at the end of the prophecy. Why on earth would the prophet use such imagery to describe the moon? Moons don't bleed nor do they turn into anything. And why would *this* be the end of prophecy? This part of Joel's foretelling is more difficult to envision, that is unless one reads with spiritual lenses.

The word Joel uses for blood is דָּם or *dam* and it means what we would expect it to mean– literal blood, the life source of living beings. The prophet uses the anatomical liquid, the life source of living beings, to describe the moon before the Lord returns. Some might say this is because the sun will be eclipsed, causing the moon to give off a crimson hue like the lunar eclipse in Alexander and Darius' day. But that cannot be because Joel tells us that the sun will be "darkened." Remember that the moon is only a luminary meaning it can only reflect the sun's rays. So if the sun is darkened, or "obscure" as some translations read, then the moon would not be able to illuminate nor would it be visible. There is a reason the prophet uses such a detailed image to *conclude* the prophecy and it is because God *intentionally* plans to make the moon visible even in the sun's obscurity and because he *intentionally* plans to turn it into blood at the *end of the age*. So why the anthropomorphic description by the prophet? Because there is a message in the moon. And more than a message, a person!

As the sun is darkened and Ba'al is exposed as a false god who has no control, The Moon Goddess will be turned to blood, a sign to her followers that the Queen of Heaven is not the queen, she is a scummy harlot who will be cast down from her tower to be licked by fire for all eternity. This event will be more real than a 4D movie experience. For those who wear her entertainment glasses, they will tremble in fear, ash between their knocked-knees, as they watch the events unfold. This cosmic event will occur "before the great and terrible day of the Lord comes" that is, before the final bowls of God's wrath are poured out upon the earth as detailed in the book of Revelation.

Following the signs in the sky, those who have Jesus in their heart will be delivered from the final destruction. The deliverance will be for the *remnant*. In Joel's day, under the old covenant, this message was relayed to the Jewish people, however in Peter's day, under the renewed covenant, the message was extended *from* the House of Israel *to* the nations. This extension was only made possible through the bloodshed of Jesus Christ who is the one and only deliverer, the Son of Man *and* the Son of God. The remnant who remain faithful to God in the midst of tribulation *will be* raptured! Praise God!

> "And the ransomed of the Lord shall return and come to Zion with singing; everlasting joy shall be upon their heads; they shall obtain gladness and joy, and sorrow and sighing shall flee away" (Isa. 35:10).

> "As you come to him, the living Stone—rejected by humans but chosen by God and precious to him—you also, like living stones, are being built into a spiritual house to be a holy priesthood, offering spiritual sacrifices

acceptable to God through Jesus Christ. For in Scripture it says:

> 'See, I lay a stone in Zion,
> a chosen and precious cornerstone,
> and the one who trusts in him
> will never be put to shame'" (1 Pet. 2:4-6; c.f. Isa. 28:16).

Jesus Christ is the stone of Zion, the cornerstone by which all things hold together and the water shaft by which believers will escape the wrath of God (Joel 2:32). Any builder knows that you cannot have a house without a proper cornerstone. For the person whose house is built upon the rock and cornerstone of Christ will return to him with singing and joy and will never be put to shame, a reminder of Joel 2:26.

The Old and New Testament prophecies are woven together with Christ as the weaver. All threads of prophecy are colorful, unique, woven intricately and delicately, and when fully complete will cover the bride of Christ from shame once and for all. And God loves people so much that he will give a final sign in a *specific* event to signal the grace period is about to end.

Now having set the foundation for Part II, I'd like to repeat a question from the beginning of this chapter. Could it be that The Blood Moon Prophecy speaks to a specific time of the tribulation when the moon will be bloodied because the judgment upon The Moon Goddess spirit and her followers has commenced? Or could the blood moon be speaking prophetically of a specific natural event that will occur *before* her judgment so as to warn that Christ's hand is at the door and his cup of wine is tipping? In simpler terms, is the blood moon prophecy spiritual or natural and does it occur before or after The Rapture?

Again, I believe the answer is yes to both: yes it is a spiritual *and* natural event; yes it is before *and* after The Rapture.

136

PART II:
The Prophecy that Is

Chapter 7

The Moonies

If anyone tells you then, "See, here is the Messiah!" or "Over here!" do not believe it.
For false messiahs and false prophets will arise and perform great signs and wonders to
lead astray, if possible, even the elect… Immediately after the distress of those days, the
sun will be darkened and the moon will not shed its light; the stars will fall from the
sky, and the powers of the heavens will be shaken. Then the sign of the Son of Man
will appear in the sky, and then all the peoples of the earth will mourn; and they will
see the Son of Man coming on the clouds of heaven with great power and glory. He
will send out his angels with a loud trumpet, and they will gather his elect from the
four winds, from one end of the sky to the other.

Matthew 24:23-31, HCSB

The radiant light of dawn pierced through the cypress and Sakura leaves on the early morning of July 8, 2022, reawakening the sleeping life through Nara, Japan. The priests in the pagodas and Shintō shrines began their morning prayers, offering up whispers of veneration to the *kami*, or mystical spirits that they believe indwell any animate or inanimate object. As the sun rose above the primordial forest that morning, it cast a radiance upon the ornate and oldest Shintō shrine in the Nara Prefecture, the Kasuga-taish. Illuminated by the dance of the sunlight's rays, the shimmer of the shrine's vermillion walls and yellow ochre adornments seemed to flicker in sync with the literal hundreds of deer that pranced from acre to acre and munched on dew-glistened silver pampas grass in Nara Park. This quiet park right outside the hustle of the city was calm, an eerie calm, a *brooding* calm before a soon-coming storm.

One of over 80,000 shrines in Japan, the Kasuga-taisha is a popular tourist and local attraction. It is known for its deep tradition and its Tokae Lantern Festival held yearly in August to celebrate Obon, the Japanese season for honoring the dead. The morning of July 8th began like any other ordinary day as the devout Shintō devotees arose from their slumber to assist in temple upkeep and service. They were likely preparing for the upcoming Tokae Festival in their daily services. As the Tokae lanterns waited for their fall flight, something darker was brewing and had been brewing for years. Something was about to fall. Just fifteen minutes away, steam was boiling near the Yamato-Saidaiji train station.

Outside the railway around 11 o'clock in the morning, 67 year old Shinzo Abe, Japan's former prime minister, arrived to deliver a campaign speech to endorse a lawmaker running for reelection to the National Diet, Japan's Parliament. Abe had been retired for over two years with a clout resume of a lifetime of political power. As he mounted the small platform, his ebony hair smoothed back to reveal cedar colored eyes cornered by the carvings of years of political work, he took the microphone to begin his speech. The crunch of a deer stepping on a fallen twig in Nara Park was stifled as the crack of two gunshots pierced the air and Abe. Abe collapsed, shot in the neck and chest. He was rushed to the hospital where he was pronounced dead by physicians. They couldn't stop the bleeding.

The assailant, 41 year old Tetsuya Yamagami, a local of Nara, was detained and arrested at the scene. His heartless act, as it would turn out, was in fact motivated from the heart, a heart ridden with resentment. But why such resentment toward the former prime minister? As the sun set that day, the deer nestled down under the moonlight oblivious to the cries, concerns, and criticisms throughout the nation and the nations of the world. Of the critics was the murderer Yamagami himself, though he was criticizing for a different reason.

Before I explain how the previous and relatively recent news story applies to The Blood Moon Prophecy in our world today, I want to tell you how this book began. I wasn't searching for such a prophecy. It found me.

In March of 2024, the year of this writing, I was preparing for graduation. I was going to be receiving my Masters of Arts in Biblical Theology in May and my thesis had to be submitted by the end of April. I was finalizing my thesis on Paul's true intent behind 1 Corinthians 11:2-16, arguing that women can prophesy and preach in The Church today. As I buttoned up the paper mid-March, I then asked God, "*Lord, what am I going to do after graduation?*" He didn't answer me for a few weeks and I was antsy to know. I had, I reminded Him, given up a lot to pursue higher education.

Two years prior, The Holy Spirit had asked me to set active ministry on the altar and further my studies of the Scriptures. Before working on my masters, I was leading a prophetic evangelistic ministry, preaching at tent revivals, serving in my local church, writing for a magazine. But when I was pregnant with my third baby, God gently asked me to lay my ministry down and take a season to learn. So I obliged. Two years later I felt accomplished but lost, too. I didn't know what to do with the degree and I was feeling as if I was coming to a dead end. But God always answers sacrifice with fire. Shortly after I prayed that prayer in early March, I packed my bags and headed to Los Angeles with a friend to visit my sister and pray at the Azusa Street Mission Prayer Tower. That's when he answered me and placed a fire in my bones to write the book you are reading now.

Before boarding the plane to LA, I downloaded the new Netflix series, "Alexander: The Making of God." While watching the show during the flight, a particular scene grabbed my attention. It is the scene which shows the blood moon before the famous Battle at Gaugamela. The moon struck me. Though I didn't know what it meant other than what the documentary revealed to me in that moment, I knew in my spirit that there was something God wanted to expound upon in that scene. The words of Peter echoed in my mind, *"And then the moon shall be turned to blood…"*

I finished the episode, arrived in LA, and had a wonderful, eventful time visiting with my sister. We went to the Azusa Street Tower on Azusa Street which is considered the birthplace of Pentecostalism. It was here that a mighty revival in April of 1906 led by William Seymour would lead to a charismatic wave of awakening that would flow into all parts of the world. To date there are an estimated 305 million Charismatic Christians in the world today. Pentecostalism is the fastest growing church in the world with 35,000 members being added daily according to the Pulitzer Center.[107] What leader William Seymour and his friends accomplished at Azusa would have a worldwide impact that they could have never imagined. Though the revival and mission is no longer at Azusa, the feel of renewal and fresh beginnings is still present. The Japanese cherry trees behind the building represent the rebirth that would expand outside the four walls and to the four corners of the earth.

As we waited to enter for our time of prayer, we noticed the beautiful Japanese garden behind the building. Quiet and tucked away, the garden was teeming with birds and exotic plants. It felt as if we had stepped out of the U.S.A. and into Japan. Captivated, we decided to pray there for a moment, interceding for the U.S. and for the country of Japan. It was there that The Holy Spirit reminded me of a dream that he had given me nearly five years ago. A dream I had forgotten. A dream which would be another puzzle piece to the prophecy.

---

[107] Richard Vijgen and Bregtje van der Haak, "Pentecostalism: Massive Global Growth Under the Radar," Pulitzer Center, 9 Mar. 2015, https://pulitzercenter.org/stories/pentecostalism-massive-global-growth-under-radar

Following LA, I returned to Georgia, submitted my thesis and prepared for graduation. I asked God again, *"Lord, why did you have me go through all of this schooling?"* That's when the title *The Blood Moon Prophecy* rushed into my spirit. *"That's why,"* he answered. Without even realizing, I already had a seed to my future. It had been planted in me before birth and grown with time, experience, and maturity. So I began *The Blood Moon Prophecy*, partly inspired by the scene from the Alexander documentary, but, as I would soon find out, also by the Japanese garden at Azusa. I began writing in April though I didn't know what the book really looked like or how it would end.

In May I boarded a flight to Minneapolis, Minnesota for my graduation ceremony. As I waited for an Uber to arrive and take my husband and I to the school, I continued working on the book. As I reminisced on the trip in LA, the garden, and the Netflix series, a news article suddenly flashed before my spiritual eyes. In the blink of an eye, I was reminded of a CNN news article title I had caught a glimpse of in 2022. I knew it had something to do with Japan's prime minister. I couldn't recall the details, so I did a quick Google search and the article appeared: "Shinzo Abe, former Japanese prime minister, assassinated during a campaign speech." Reading through those tragic days' events, I was struck by the moon again but this time the moon was *a person*. Just before the Uber arrived, I found an interesting article describing the reasoning, albeit deranged reasoning, of Yamagami's assault and was stunned.

Per his testimony, Yamagami was rageful at Abe for his ties to a cult, a cult I had *never* heard of but, according to Cornell University, has 3 million members worldwide.[108] The cult is the Unification Church and to my amazement, its cultists are called

[108] "Cults" Cornell University, Section 6 "Sun Myung Moon's Unification Church, https://www.cs.cornell.edu/info/people/kreitz/Christian/Cults/6.moon.pdf

The Moonies. Feeling more confused and yet somehow more on track with my book, I pocketed the ruby of knowledge and headed to the Uber. Needless to say, I fidgeted with that ruby through the entire three hour ceremony.

Now, at the end of May 2024 as I write this book, God has been faithful to show me each day how the parts and pieces, ancient and modern, come to fit together into an intricately woven yet misunderstood Blood Moon Prophecy. The Moonies are yet another piece and the Unification Church is like a bright vermillion blood moon, a sign in the sky that we are truly in the last days.

The Unification Church and Signs of the Times

What happened on July 8, 2022 shook the nation of Japan like an earthquake, a shaking that would be felt throughout the world. There had not been an assassination of a Japanese prime minister since Saitō Makoto's unexpected death on February 26, 1936. His assassination would shift the entire nation and the world. The unrest that followed Makoto's murder only amplified the worldwide unrest during the 20's and 30's with World War I just on the horizon and World War II following shortly after. The latter would end with the most tragic shaking seen in Japan to date, the dropping of the atomic bomb on Hiroshima and Nagasaki on August 5th and 6th, killing an *estimated* 110,000 civilians.[109]

The vacuum to follow the horrendous Nazi regime and mass executions of the Jewish people during the Holocaust, the senseless deaths of boys on the crimson shores of Normandy, the explosion of the bombs on Japanese soil (only to skim the surface of the horrors of the world's wars), created a spiritual void. People

---

[109] Amanda Onion, Missy Sullivan, Matt Mullen and Christian Zapata (eds.), "Bombing of Hiroshima and Nagasaki," History.com, https://www.history.com/topics/world-war-ii/bombing-of-hiroshima-and-nagasaki

of the world were desperate and open to any form of life source they could cling to. The morale of countrymen was failing, their hearts doubting if not hardened to the idea of hope after death. When the world wars were over, Satan was not finished with his war on the world. Taking advantage of the condition of man's wounded soul of the aftermath of such traumatic events, the enemy played upon the mentally exhausted minds of mankind. His maneuver to pit man against man was evident in the wars, and now he would do it again but even more cunningly and more tragically. He would put the name of Jesus on his ploy, skewing the Gospel, fueling apostasy, increasing humanism, mixing the holy with the profane, and turning people away from church.

As World War II fizzled to a faint memory of what felt like a nightmare, the post-trauma of the war was extremely real and still very much forefront, even if people didn't realize it. The events had really happened, the world was truly lost, and people needed a sense of belonging again. Brotherhood and sisterhood had disappeared, or so it would seem; but in reality, the human body is wired for connection and humanity had not ended with the war. Mankind endured and adapted. Man moved forward. So as the wires of such connectivity seemed frayed and frazzled, the SOS signal of humanity was still beeping through the world. Such signals would be caught by many pure-hearted organizations, churches, ministries, and families who would pour their lives into aiding the lost, the broken, the traumatized, the widow and the orphan. But then there would be those who would catch the suffering signal and use it for self-promotion, feeding on the helpless to fatten their egos and their beliefs. Of those people would be Sun Myung Moon.

Let me preface the next section with these words: I do not believe those who are vexed by Satan, those who eventually sell their soul to his control and forever damn themselves to hell, begin that way. It's a slow process from childhood where the heart of a

143

man or woman has galvanized beyond repair. Though we are all born in iniquity (Ps. 51:5), Jesus gives to every man and woman a measure of faith to hear him and choose him (Rom. 12:3). Sadly, many people do not choose Christ and even more upsetting, some think they follow Jesus but actually do not. Moon is a prime example.

Sun Myung Moon was born on February 25, 1920 in the North P'yŏng'an Province of Korea when it was under Japanese rule. He came from a long line of practicing Confucianists until his parents converted to Christianity and joined a Presbyterian church in the 1930's. Moon became familiar with the Bible, attending Sunday school throughout his childhood.[110] He eventually attended the Israel Monastery near Seoul, South Korea with his wife Choi Sun-Kil to learn from the teachings of *The Fundamental Principles of Christianity* written by Kim Baek-moon in 1958.

Following World War II, the Japanese control of Korea ended and Moon began preaching. His messages of hope and peace pacified a mourning people. On May 1, 1954, he and his wife founded the Holy Spirit Association for the Unification of World Christianity (HSA-UWC) in Seoul. The association exploded, amassed thousands of members and established thirty centers nationwide by 1955.[111] Those who joined were called "Moonies." The HSA-UWC expanded worldwide and by the 1970's, the association had reached the western hemisphere. On its 40th anniversary (May 1, 1994), Moon ended the HSA-UWC and inaugurated The Family Federation for World Peace and Unification (FFWPU) which would include HSA-UWC members

---

[110] "Unification Church: Mass Moonie Marriage in the US," BBC News, 29 Nov. 1997, http://news.bbc.co.uk/2/hi/special_report/1997/ unification_church/34821.stm

[111] Eileen Barker, "My Take: Moon's death marks the end of an era," *The CNN Belief Blog*, 3 September 2012, https://web.archive.org/web/20190829065856/ http://religion.blogs.cnn.com/2012/09/03/my-take-moons-death-marks-end-of-an-era/

as well as other religious organizations working toward the goal of sexual morality and reconciliation between different cultures and religions.[112] Moon was also connected with political leaders and the association would even start a political party in South Korea in 2003. By the sky high numbers, the abundant missionary work, and the peaceful gatherings of hundreds of thousands to hear Moon preach, the association seemed to be founded upon true Christian principles, highly favored by God Himself. But don't judge a book by its cover.

The theology of the association was and is extremely twisted and as the organization grew, so did the investigators and the critics. Moon also wrote his own book, *The Divine Principle*, in which he claimed the "principles" were revealed to him over the course of nine years. These principles were, per Moon, downloaded to him after Jesus appeared to him on Easter Sunday in 1936 on the mountainside and "asked him to continue the work that he could not finish while on earth, due to the 'tragedy' of his crucifixion."[113] Moon took this visitation to be a supernatural clarion call for him. From that day forward, he was the messiah and his book with its hypnotizing theology to follow would support his claim.

For the Moonies *The Divine Principle* is just as authoritative as The Holy Scriptures. A read of the first part of the book might not raise much concern. Per Moon, God is creator and He created the world, man and woman, and commanded them to marry and populate. God had a vision of the family being one of peace and love and the ultimate goal of mankind is to be in relationship with

[112] Marc Fisher and Jeff Leen, "Stymied in U.S., Moon's Church Sounds a Retreat," WashingtonPost.com, 24 Nov. 1997, https://www.washingtonpost.com/wp-srv/national/longterm/cult/unification/part2.htm

[113] Britannica, "Sun Myung Moon," *Encyclopedia Britannica*, 27 Mar. 2024, https://www.britannica.com/biography/Sun-Myung-Moon.

God.[114] All true, but the fall of man is when his book really takes a turn.

According to the teaching of the "church," there was no fulfillment of God's plan for the ideal family as Eve had a sexual relationship with Satan. It was this sexual relation that caused the fall of man and placed Satan in the center of the world. Satan's lineage, then, courses through the human race and families are thus created in evil and the children produced from parents are evil. God attempted to correct the evil by sending Noah and then Jesus, but both were unsuccessful. Per Moon, Jesus' mission was cut short by his unfortunate crucifixion; however, upon Christ's second coming, he will be successful. Therefore Moon believed he was created as a messiah to help finish the work that Christ could not. Being that the work of Christ is unfinished, the "earning salvation through work" concept and the uncertainty of life after death is also prominent through the church with followers believing a person's final destination after death is dependent upon the amount of work one does in correspondence with Moon's teachings. Eventually, they believe, everyone will receive salvation.[115]

For a born again Christian, these principles and teachings are outlandish and completely ludicrous. The Scriptures are clear in that Eve was tempted by Satan but had *no* sexual relationship with him (Gen. 3), God does not have to "attempt" anything as he is in complete control (Ps. 135:6, Prov. 16:33,21:30), God sent forth his one and only Son that whosoever believes Him will never perish but have everlasting life (Jn. 3:16), Christ *finished* the work on Calvary and sat down at the right hand of the Father (Jn. 19:30, Heb. 10:12-13), mankind does *not* earn his way to salvation but is saved by grace through faith (Eph. 2:1-10), and Christ will return

---

[114] Dušan Lužný and David Václavík, "Církev sjednocení [Unification Church]" Czech, 1997.

[115] Freddy Davis, "The Unification Church/Moonies," Marketfaith.org, http://www.marketfaith.org/2014/11/the-unification-churchmoonies/

not to deal with sin but to gather his elect before he administers final justice on Satan and his followers (Matt. 24:31, Heb. 9:28, Rev. 22:12). Moon's ideologies and beliefs ought to be extreme red flags and huge deterrents. But for the Moonie cult, the sacrilegious, heretical, bitter teachings were and are coated with a sugar. The sugar being "belonging."

To just belong in this world seems impossible, especially considering the hate and strife that dominates our culture, but for the FFWPU, one could accept their evil lineage and work their way to a perfect, peaceful family unit by belonging to a perfect, peaceful band of brothers. The appeal of such peace and belonging stemmed from the aftermath of the war followed by the 1950's and 60's when rapid religious expansion dominated Japan. As the war torn country recovered and grew economically, so did migration from farms to cities. Far from home, the SOS signal of loneliness was emitted. While many paid tribute to shrines and participated in ancient Shintō and Buddhist practices, many Japanese citizens did not consider themselves belonging to a religion.[116] In such a time, the Unification Church and other religious movements were a way to connect. The Unification Church targeted university campuses, "where the radical leftwing movements of the 1960s left a large number of students alienated."[117] The churches' leaders groomed students to fundraise. The success of receiving money in the name of a good cause only increased the glue of belonging between the young adults and the cult. But what the followers didn't and still do not realize is that when one truly gives their life to Jesus Christ and relinquishes all control to the One who holds their fate in his hands, when they apply the finished work of the

---

[116] Sakurai Yoshihide, "The Unification Church and Its Japanese Victims: The Need for "Religious Literacy," Nippon.com, 28 Oct. 2022, https://www.nippon.com/en/in-depth/d00845/

[117] Yoshihide, "The Unification Church," https://www.nippon.com/en/in-depth/d00845/

blood of the sacrificial lamb to the doorposts of their soul, they *immediately* are adopted into an eternal family (1 Pet. 2:23, Eph. 1:5). Believers *belong* to the Kingdom of God, a kingdom not founded upon faulty foundations, money, or strenuous labor, but a Kingdom founded on truth–unshakable, unwavering truth; a truth that will set a person *free*; a truth that calls a child of God, "Beloved." A truth that *saves*.

So how could such a corrupt doctrine of demons flood the minds of millions? How could a dark and demented organization seem so harmless? Civil restlessness and economic turmoil are two atmospheres in which cults thrive. Such cults that have blasphemed Jesus' name and his earthly ministry have arisen and fallen since the time of Jesus' resurrection. One of the earliest was that of the Gnostics in Paul's day. Jesus himself warned of such false messiahs and twisted teachings in Matthew 24:23-30. In fact, Jesus said it would be the rise of such lunacy that would signal the end was near. Today, the Unification Church has 100,000 members in the USA and over 3 million members worldwide.[118] And with that amount of members, money is not scarce. According to South Korean media, the Unification Church owns 46.2 million square meters of land in South Korea and has a total assets worth 2 trillion won (about 200 billion yen or 1.4 billion US dollars).[119] What is the driving force behind the rise of such a group? The answer goes back to the spirits at work behind the scenes: Satan and his apprentices Ba'al and The Moon Goddess.

So is it coincidence that the Unification Church was founded by a man whose last name was Moon? If one believes in

---

[118] "Cults," Cornell University, https://www.cs.cornell.edu/info/people/kreitz/Christian/Cults/6.moon.pdf

[119] The Ashi Shimbun, "After failures in South Korea, 'heretical' church turned to Japan," Asahi.com, 16 Sept. 2022, https://www.asahi.com/ajw/articles/14720357#:~:text=According%20to%20South%20Korean%20media,billion%20yen%20or%20%241.4%20billion

coincidence, then sure. But could it be that Moon and his cult could be used by God, despite their not knowing God, to point those with eyes to see and ears to hear to Jesus' promised second coming? Is the Unification Church a part of an unfolding mystery of the false messiahs who Christ Himself prophesied about, those who would preface the return of the Lord and the judgment upon The Moon Goddess? I believe so.

While the truth behind the cult was surfacing long before the assassination of Abe in 2022, the money and power by its leaders and cultists masked the voices of concern. It wasn't until the assassination of a prominent power figure, Abe, that officially removed the veil that was shrouding the truth. According to police, Yamagami murdered Abe because of Abe's connections to the Unification Church. Yamagami was enraged, his fury boiling for years, because of his mother's ties to the church. He claims that the church brainwashed his mother who gave hundreds of thousands of dollars to the group, bankrupting their family, and causing him to live a poor and miserable life.[120]

The enemy always exposes himself because darkness always comes to light and so the assassination of Abe, as horrendous as it was, actually highlighted a hidden cult that had been building for years. It had been expanding so rapidly, in fact, that many had missed its ludicrous doctrine and brainwashing schemes. But following Abe's death, their false doctrine preached from their stages was now front and center stage on the world's platform. Additionally, the spotlight on Japan only increased. The spiritual warfare taking place over the territory of Japan has been and still is significant and while Satan has tried to destroy the nation and its people for millennia, Jesus isn't finished with this country yet. In

[120] Isabel Reynolds, "Japan Seeks to Dissolve Unification Church Connected to Shinzo Abe's Assassination," TIME.com, 12 Oct. 2023, https://time.com/6322931/japan-unification-church-disbandment-shinzo-abe/

fact he is just getting started. Exposing the Moonie cult was only the beginning.

Shintoism

Japan, around the size of California, may seem insignificant in comparison to the larger countries but that is far from true. The nation's vibrant culture, beautiful people, and awe-inspiring detail in their craftsmanship has made them stand out among the nations for ages. This only skims the surface of the magnitude of Japan's influence in the world. Their amazing inventions, wisdom writings, love for family, and brave adventures into the realms of the unknown scientific world in addition to their stamina in battle and expertise in maritime trade give them the reputation of being a mighty people of faith and fortitude. Like the Sakura's full, rich blossoms, so are the people of Japan. Japan is truly heavenly and has so much to offer.

It is of no surprise then that Satan, Ba'al, and The Moon Goddess have ruled the territory since its first pilgrims arrived thousands of years ago. Shintoism, Japan's indigenous religion, has persisted since Japan's inhabitation and is a polytheistic and animalistic religion in which *kami* or supernatural entities are in all things and all forces of nature. Thus anything and everything can be claimed as a god and worshiped as supernatural. Pastor Hideo Oshita describes the religion in this way,

> The term *Shintō* is of Chinese origin. *Shin* is the Japanized pronunciation of *Shen,* which means 'good spirits,' *to* is the same as *tao,* the 'way,' in Taoism. The Japanese descriptive term for *Shintō* is *Kami no Michi. Kami* means the 'deities,' or 'gods,' *no* is the possessive, and

Michi means the 'way' or 'road.' Therefore it signifies as a whole, the 'way of the gods.'"[121]

The gods govern the country. Literally. The emperors have long believed themselves to be direct descendants of the gods.

In the 20th chapter of Exodus, Moses reveals the Ten Commandments to the newly freed Israelites who dwelt among many thought to be gods. The first two commandments that were to be inscribed upon the hearts of YHWH's followers were crystal clear:

> "I am the Lord your God, who brought you out of the land of Egypt, out of the place of slavery.
> Do not have any other gods besides me. Do not make an idol for yourself, whether in the shape of anything in the heavens above or in the earth below or in the waters under the earth. Do not bow in worship to them, and do not serve them; for I, the Lord your God, am a jealous God, bringing the consequences of the father's iniquity on the children to the third and fourth generations of those who hate me, but showing faithful love to a thousand generations of those who love me and keep my commands (Exod. 20:1-6)."

These first two commands were critical to the survival of the Israelites. Their continual backsliding and rebellion in taking on the practices of pagans which brought with it violence eventually led them back into slavery. When Jesus arrived on the scene as the final deliverer, he did not abolish the commandments, but confirmed them. He, a *living, breathing, hearing, talking, healing*

---

[121] Hideo Oshita, "Shinto, the 'Way of the Gods': What is Shintoism?" MinistryMagazine.org, March 1949, https://www.ministrymagazine.org/archive/1949/03/shinto-the-way-of-the-gods

Emmanuel ("God with us") walked among his creation and showed humanity the one true God. Moses, the prototype of Jesus, was the only one who could talk to God and reveal His instructions to the people (Deut. 5:5) in the Old Testament, but in the New Testament, Jesus could talk directly to his people. When asked what the greatest commandment was in Matthew 22, Jesus replied:

> "Love the Lord your God with all your heart and with all your soul and with all your mind. This is the first and greatest commandment. And the second is like it: Love your neighbor like yourself. All the Law and the Prophets hang on these two commandments" (Matt. 22:36-40, NIV).

To center one's heart, soul, and mind around God was to abandon any other deity and pursue wholeheartedly Jesus Christ. The second command was to love oneself and others. All the Law and the Prophets hung on those two commandments. As Jesus "hung" on the cross, he fulfilled the Law and the Prophets and made himself known and in doing so made an open spectacle of the disarmed powers and authorities (Col. 2:15). The Creator hung on his creation to redeem his creation. The sight was visible and real; the message was true. To place one's trust in other gods or to worship graven images was a violation and still is a violation of The Greatest Commandment.

While many in modern society will roll their eyes at the notion that consequences for following other gods still exist, Jesus didn't abolish the law, *He fulfilled it* (Matt. 5:17-20). In other words, Jesus made it known once and for all who the true God is, so to follow or worship anything other than him will result in a sure judgment as well as a judgment upon the *next* generation. God's word does not pass away which also brings a joyous hope: if one turns from idols and serves YHWH, God will bless them and their offspring for a thousand generations. This promise, thanks to Jesus, is now for all people, including Shintoists.

Right now, Shintoism is the most acknowledged and practiced form of religion in the country with an estimated 80,000 shrines in the land. Despite its antiquated, indigenous history, The Moon Goddess worship is still extremely present in it. In fact she is the core of Shintoism. In Japan her manifestation is reversed: she is behind the sun and Ba'al the moon. But remember that these are spirits and have no gender. Regardless of what planetary, solar, or lunar form, it's their tactics, schemes, rituals of worship, and spiritual maneuvers that characterize and differentiate them.

The Moon Goddess, revered as the sun goddess in Japan, is called Amaterasu Ōmikami. Amaterasu translates as "Great Divinity Illuminating Heaven" in Japanese. The name presents a similar picture as The Moon Goddess' other name, Queen of Heaven, used by Jeremiah. Per the mythology, Amaterasu married her brother, Susanoo, the storm god (a.k.a. Ba'al in Canaanite religion), and the two produce children. Their incestruous, twisted marriage is unstable and produces a mess of conflict. One day, Amaterasu is rude to her brother who then becomes rageful and destructive. Amaterasu flees to a cave and darkness falls on the world. It takes a myriad of 800 gods plus the goddess Amenouzume's provocative dance which rouses the gods to a loud laughter to bring a curious Amaterasu out of the cave. Once she emerges outside, the kami perform a ritual outside the cave to keep her from going back into it. The story is certainly provocative and has been told for thousands of years. Like the Phoenician, Canaanite, and Babylonian stories, the goddess is unstable, bipolar, fearful, and demands control. She is empowered (or released if you will) through seducing and sensuality. The spirit of the goddess is worshiped in shrines all throughout the country, some of which have been passed down through families for generations. The largest shrine dedicated to her is the Grand Ise Shrine in Ise, Mie Prefecture of Japan.

Her veneration is so prominent that the Japanese emperors have made it a point to honor her upon their succession to the throne. Emperors are considered close to the divine, the word literally meaning "heavenly emperor."[122] Japanese emperors are personally immune from prosecution and as head of the Imperial House, are deemed the head of Shintō religion which holds the emperor to be a direct descendant of Amaterasu. The current emperor, Naruhito, performed the centuries-old Shintō thanksgiving ceremony known as the Daijosai. It is a controversial ceremony due to its state funded rituals and secrets behind closed chambers that are not disclosed to the public.[123] Not only is secretiveness a common theme in The Moon Goddess worship, but the secretive ritual of the Daijosai that really stamps the ceremony with her signature is the final act the emperor performs. The emperor spends the night in these hidden chambers, dedicating special time and sacrifice to the goddess for national peace, harvest, and prosperity. The final sacrifice is not known. Are sexual acts or blood sacrifices performed in those areas, too? Though these theories have been dispelled by the Japanese Imperial Household Agency, it cannot be totally dismissed since similar practices have been reported in other types of secret ceremonial worship through the ages and since the truth still remains concealed behind curtained walls from the public.

Despite these hidings, the worship of The Moon Goddess is so open and forward throughout the country that it leads me to almost claim it as the leader of moon goddess reverence in the

---

[122] Britannica, "tennō," *Encyclopedia Britannica*, https://www.britannica.com/topic/tenno.

[123] Kyodo News, "Japanese emperor performs overnight Shinto ceremony to mark succession," KyodoNews.net, 19 Nov. 2019, https://english.kyodonews.net/news/2019/11/f1decd0aa0e3-japans-emperor-to-perform-thanksgiving-ceremony-as-key-succession-rite.html

world. One of the most widely broadcasted forms of the goddess that reveal her inner workings can be found in a famous Japanese heroine, a black cat, and a silver crystal.

Sailor Moon

Moon goddess worship is just as prevalent today and if not more so thanks to modern technology and the worldwide web. It is seen in every culture, every nation, and every religion. Yes, even some sects of Christianity (like the Israelites) have turned from their first love and "tolerated that woman Jezebel" (Rev. 2:20). As the world continues to spin, so does this principality, weaving her web of deception, attempting to catch any soul she can before her final day.

But praise be to God that Jesus has overcome the world!

For believers nothing will be impossible. So the task of exposing her, rejecting her, and canceling her plot can and should be done. Nonetheless, her powers are still at work until she is judged once and for all. Just as with the Unification Church, The Moon Goddess works through ties, *soul ties*, where she connects emotionally and spiritually two people who are vulnerable and miserable to increase her width of control and her depth of influence. Another way in which this principality maneuvers mankind to do her job is through money and sex. She dangles gold and pleasure in front of men and women with lustful eyes. Some bite the bait and then, once hooked, they are drug deeper down into her murky waters. But one of her most manipulative ploys is through fantasy. As the goddess behind witchcraft and sorcery, divination and fortune telling, it is no wonder then that she spellbinds through fanatical tales, myths, folklores, and legends. Really, what she does, is she uses the creative arts for darkness.

As an artist and dreamer myself, I cherish the creative arts and the giftedness God has put inside me and others to brighten this world, enliven this world, and change this world. God himself is the ultimate creator, the best storyteller, the best dreamer, and the most captivating and extraordinary entertainer! A day at the beach or a visit to a fine dining experience will reveal his creation and his artistry. He uses the senses, the colors, the visible and the invisible realm to reveal himself in and through us daily. A world without the creative arts would be like an ocean without water–dry, mute, barren, and dull.

Satan, an adorned leader of worship himself before his downfall (Ez. 28:13-19, Isa. 14:9-18), knows the power of creativity and art. He has, since his eviction from heaven, tried to worm his way into worship, into the entertainment industry, and into literature so as to receive worship for himself and take the focus off of YHWH. Through dark tactics, he will use mankind's senses, color (i.e. the pride flag), along with music and media to distort, corrupt, and brainwash. The Moon Goddess is no different.

Take for example the extremely world famous Japanese manga series *Sailor Moon* written and illustrated by Naoko Takeuchi. The series ran from 1991 to 1997 in the magazine *Nakayoshi*. It was soon adapted into an anime series which ran from 1992-1997. The show was unlike most cartoons of its time, captivating audiences worldwide, especially teens and young adults. The synopsis is seemingly simple: 14-year-old Usagi Tsukino meets a magical talking black cat named Luna who enables Tsukino with the power of transformation, changing her into a magical alter ego–Sailor Moon–who then takes on the task of locating the moon princess and battling the Dark Kingdom. But the series is anything short of simple. The story grows more detailed, the characters more complex, and, like any well done series, draws the audience into the fiction and into an emotional tie with the characters. The ending *must* be known. The show was incredibly successful. It sold over 35 million copies in printed form and generated $13 billion dollars in merchandise tie-ins.[124] Takeuchi, Sailor Moon's creator, really is a talented artist and dreamer. Her creativity is larger than life. But whether knowingly or unknowingly, her *Sailor Moon* story is filled with moon goddess messages.

While I don't think it is necessary to go through all 200 episodes or discuss all of the characters in depth, I do think pointing out some of the messages through the series is important in showing just how present The Moon Goddess is in modern day media. Additionally, let me make this clear: I do not cast judgment upon those who supported, created, produced, or watched the series. My job is not to shame mankind but to shame The Moon Goddess and her magic.

Magic, in fact, begins *Sailor Moon*. The cat's name, Luna, is that of the Roman moon goddess and this cat gives the 14 year-old-girl the ability to become something greater than herself–a super hero among the stars–through mystical powers. Not a bad message per say, especially for girls who are so mistreated and undervalued in today's world, but the use of magic creates this idea that strength can come from a source outside of God. When we are transformed in Christ, we all become supercharged to change the world. Magic does not accomplish this radical transformation, The Holy Spirit does it by his power. Additionally, the work of God's Spirit does not produce alter-egos, but strips ego. He brings forth the true identity of a man or woman in Christ and it is from this true identity–as a beloved son or daughter–that we then flex *his* strength, not our own.

This magical beginning of *Sailor Moon* immediately sucked viewers and readers into another world. Those who watched the show subconsciously knew (at least for the most part) that the show

[124] Cary O'Dell, "In Search of 'Sailor Moon'" Library of Congress Bloggs, 31 Aug. 2022, https://blogs.loc.gov/now-see-hear/2022/08/in-search-of-sailor-moon/#:~:text=On%20a%20global%20scale%2C%20%E2%80%9CSailor,been%20put%20on%20the%20market.

was fiction. This is where The Moon Goddess used her power. If the show wasn't real, then the characters and their messages weren't real, right? The show could allow one to enter and exit the fantasy as they willed, making viewers feel in control. But what they didn't realize was that the subliminal messages were seeds being planted in their minds. The spirits at work behind the series are real, their messages and agendas masked behind unique, eye-catching dramas.

Throughout the show many characters either have Greek or Roman deity names (i.e. Artemis, Luna, Diana) or possess similar traits and abilities of ancient deities (i.e. fortune-telling). The series was censored in many countries, including the U.S., for near-nudity, violence, and kissing cousins familiar to the incestuous worship of Amaterasu. In Japan the raw parts were released and rewarded. Other images, particularly of the protagonist, Sailor Moon, are brimming with peculiar drawings. For instance, her hair is longer than her body, wisping in all directions like that of tentacles. Similar long, wispy locks are in Amaterasu paintings. The scepter the character wields is also interesting. A Vogue Japan feature released in January 2024, years after the end of Sailor Moon's airing, reveals Naoko Takeuchi's latest rendition of Sailor Moon. Sailor still sports the long, classic, golden pigtails, the enveloping red and indigo cape, and her scepter which dazzles against a galactic background. But in the recent rendering, a crescent moon closely resembling the one associated with Islam tops what looks like a Celtic cross and is adorned with a small crystal ball. Other scepters and wands throughout the series flaunted a spiral heart and crescent moon, the heart eerily resembling the sacred heart of Catholicism. Intentional or not, there is a clear mixture of religions and beliefs in the scepter wand. The magic behind the pictures was and still is at work and one of the messages being planted in viewers' minds is that all religions lead to God, or even worse, that all religions, including Christianity, are fantasy.

But how does The Moon Goddess's tight grip on the throat of Japan play into The Blood Moon Prophecy of the Bible? To my surprise, it plays a very critical role.

A very, very critical role.

Chapter 8

Mirrors and Mimicry

Do not be deceived: God cannot be mocked. A man reaps what he sows.

Galatians 6:7, NIV

The heart of Shintoism is not what most would deem the sacred part of the religion. It's really not a heart at all. Rather the heart of Shintoism is a mirror, a reflection of the sacred tale of the goddess Amaterasu. The treasured bronze mirror is believed to have been crafted by the deity Ishikoridome, the kami of mirrors. It was this mirror which was hung on a tree to lure Amaterasu, the sun goddess, out of the cave amid the laughter of the other gods. This reemergence, per the legend, brought light back to the world. The mirror was then passed down to Ninigi-no-Mikoto, Amaterasu's grandson. This grandson is believed to be the great-grandfather of Emperor Jimmu, Japan's first emperor. Ninigi-no-Mikoto is also believed to have married Konohanasakuya-hime, the goddess of Mount Fuji. The mirror (Yata no Kagami) along with a sword (Kusanagi no Tsurugi), and a special jewel (Yasakani no Magatama) make up the three sacred treasures of the imperial regalia of Japan. The exact location of the objects is only known by the Japanese royals.

Being that Shintoism has no founder, no sacred scriptures, and no fixed dogmas, the treasured mirror, sword, and jewel are the core of the mystic religion and the protective shell guiding Shintō beliefs through the ages. As long as those items remain, the heart of the gods remain. The mirror, in particular, is a charm that holds the core belief of the religion. It is this mirror that brought light back to a dark and dead nation. But the mirror is only mimicry. Jesus is the light source of the world. Not only is he the

160

light that is separated from the darkness, but he is also the creator of the sun, moon, and stars which serve as physical light upon the earth–light to grow, light to heal, light to reveal. The mirror of Amaterasu, whose name literally translates as "Queen of Heaven," is counterfeit. Her mirror is one of magic and her trick is to make followers believe she is the source of life and light.

For the Shintō adherent, the mirror is a reflection of more than just light that restored the world, it's also a story of *how* that light was released. The light emerged from a goddess who was hiding in a cave and *in fear*. Those who follow Jesus know that there is no fear in him. John summed up fear in this way,

> "There is no fear in love. But perfect love drives out fear, because fear has to do with punishment. The one who fears is not made perfect in love" (1 Jn. 4:18).

While the stories behind Shintoism are intriguing and colorful, the core of them is dark. The truth can be seen when one chooses to look into the mirror with spiritual eyes. The Yata no Kagami actually displays fear.

The legend of the goddess Amaterasu begins with fear. The Moon Goddess, who manifests as the "sun" goddess in Japan, was born from fear, induces fear, and promotes fear. Though a Shintō devotee might not admit to being afraid of anything, the emotion permeates everyday life and drives decisions. Fear of the unknown or fear of not appeasing the gods is still present. The concept of the afterlife is not explicit in Shintoism. Yomi, the land of darkness, is limited in its description in ancient texts as well as in modern practice or study. It is believed that the afterlife of a deceased individual is when the spirit continues living apart from the body in the form of kami. These spirits can still feel, eat, and drink after death. The kami spirit is also eternal and can assist those on earth who are still alive. Additionally, punishment and reward in the afterlife is absent in their theology.[125] The unknown of the afterlife only increases fear, thus the goddess' ending is also one of fear.

Being that Shintoism is focused on the "here and now" rather than the afterlife, the decisions or effects of one's actions while living can affect the kami who can then affect the world. In other words, if the natural order of things is disturbed or rituals are not properly followed, then bad things may happen. Also, ironically, the main deity behind the religion is Amaterasu who was a female deity, but in Shintō practice and Japanese culture, the female is typically subordinate to the male. Humans are also thought to be fundamentally good and so evil is caused by evil spirits. Purification rituals, offerings, and prayers to the kami help keep such evil spirits away.[126] With the amount of loose ends and unknowns in the religion, the spurious picture in its mirror is fuzzy.

Clear though are the similarities and differences between it and other monotheistic religions, especially Judaism and Christianity. Recall the section where I talked about Satan, The Moon Goddess and her cohort Ba'al all counterfeiting the biblical stories. Some of the most apparent pirated copies can be found in Shintoism's purification rituals and liturgical practices.

Mirroring Judaism

While the Bible isn't detailed in which modern day peoples came from the three sons of Noah, many scholars believe the Japanese descended from Japheth. If this is the case, then it may be that some of the similar practices were due to the early influence of Hebraic tradition. Some might say the similarities are just

---

[125] Mark Cartwright, "Yomi," World History Encyclopedia, 15 May 2017, https://www.worldhistory.org/Yomi/#
[126] Japan-Guide, "Shinto," in section Religion, Japan-Guide.com, https://www.japan-guide.com/e/e2056.html#:~:text=In%20contrast%20to%20many%20monotheistic,be%20caused%20by%20evil%20spirits.

coincidence, but with the interconnection of all mankind and humanity's connection to the divine, I find nothing coincidental. There is simply too much evidence to write these patterns and prophecies off as myth or lore.

There are many similarities between Judaism and Shintoism, and of course, many differences. I have listed some noteworthy similarities between Jewish and Shintō worship below:

1. Shintō shrines have two chambers like the Holy Place and the Holy of Holies in the Jewish tabernacle, and only the assigned Japanese priest may enter the inner room of the shrine, like the high priest of the Israelite priesthood.
2. The loci for worship is the Ise for Japan like Jerusalem is for Judaism.
3. There is a carriage called the Mikosni which is carried by two poles on men's shoulders during special festivals, resembling the Ark of the Covenant.
4. Purification must take place before entering the shrine. Like those who had to wash in the brazen laver before entering the Tabernacle of Moses, the Shintō worshipers must wash their hands and mouth in a laver known as the rni tarashi.
5. The Day of Atonement in Shintō is known as the Ohoharahi and occurs twice a year "to absolve the offenses against the gods." After purification, the offerings of sacrifice were thrown into a river or a sea, taking with them the sins of the people, a practice similar to the scapegoat of Israel on the Day of Atonement.[127]

---

[127] Oshita, "Shinto, the 'Way of the Gods': What is Shintoism?" https://www.ministrymagazine.org/archive/1949/03/shinto-the-way-of-the-gods

The similarities are striking and the differences are obvious. In Shintoism the gods can die, can be good or bad, and are not omnipotent; while in Judaism and Christianity, YHWH lives forever, is good all the time, and is omnipotent. The target audience for Shintoism is Japan while Christianity is for all mankind. In Shintoism humans are born neither good nor bad, while in Christianity humans are born in iniquity and therefore must be purified by the blood of Jesus. Salvation for Shintoism is not discussed but for Christians, salvation comes by grace through faith in Jesus. The afterlife in Shintoism is limited in detail and has no reward or punishment. But for Christians, heaven and hell are real, described in great detail, and one can only get to the Father through Jesus. Rewards are given to those who faithfully served Christ while on earth and hell is a place of punishment originally created for Satan and the fallen angels. It is a place of torment and eternal, permanent separation from God for anyone who did not accept Jesus as Lord. Shintō worship is therefore centered around making the gods happy for fear of angering them while worship for Jesus is done in and for love without fear.

The similarities between Shintoism and Judaism are fascinating and open many doors of thought as to how the ways of the Jews could have been influenced to Japan thousands of years ago. One theory has been proposed that Japan is one of the Ten Lost Tribes of Israel. Prehistoric Pangea is another. However it happened, there are intriguing similarities between the two religions but it is the foundational differences that really shine light on the counterfeit ability of The Moon Goddess and her demons.

Of her accomplices and more copies of herself are the gods and goddesses found in the nation's other main religions— Buddhism and Hinduism.

The Moon Goddess in Buddhism and Hinduism

164

Buddhism and Hinduism, along with Judaism, Christianity, and Islam, are considered the major religions of the world. Buddhism, in particular, is considered one of the two main religions of Japan, the other being Shintoism. The two religions are separate now but were very much intertwined in Shintō's infancy. Buddhism, coming originally from India, arrived in Japan in A.D. 552 as recorded in the *Nihon Shoki* (*The Chronicles of Japan*). The religion was well received and for many years dominated in influence and practice. Many shrines dedicated to kami at one point were Buddhist temples and kami were understood as avatars of buddhas, bodhisattvas, and other Buddhist divinities.

Buddhism does not acknowledge a god but is centered on many scripts and lessons from Buddha who was a spiritual leader, philosopher, and teacher.[128] There is no profession of faith nor is there mention of the afterlife. Buddhism seeks transcendence above the cosmos. In contrast, Shintoism has over 80,000 deities and seeks the here and now. Both are inherently different, but due to the innate adaptable nature of Buddhism, it blended well into Shintoism. And when empress Suiko, an ardent Buddhist, rose to power, the religion mushroomed.[129] So much of Buddhist culture and practices intermingled with early Shintoism that it was hard to note the differences. Japanese saw Buddha as kami, while some Shintos believed kami could achieve transcendence and enlightenment.[130]

It wasn't until the *Kami and Buddhas Separation Order* (神仏判然令, *Shinbutsu Hanzenrei*) of 1868 that the two were separated

---

[128] Krista Tamilla, "The Syncretism of Shinto and Buddhism in Japan," Stear Think Tank, 4 Aug. 2021,
https://www.stearthinktank.com/post/japan-syncretism-of-shinto-and-buddhism

[129] Japan Wonder Travel Blog, "An Overview of Shintoism and Buddhism in Japan– Differences and History," 22 Oct. 2020,
https://blog.japanwondertravel.com/an-overview-of-shintoism-and-buddhism-in-japan-differences-and-history-20672

[130] Tamilla, "The Syncretism of Shinto," https://www.stearthinktank.com/post/japan-syncretism-of-shinto-and-buddhism; c.f. B. Larsen, "A Brief History of Shinto and Buddhism in Japan," The Culture Trip, 21 Apr. 2018, https://theculturetrip.com/asia/japan/articles/a-brief-history-of-shinto-and-buddhism-in-japan/

nationally. Kamis could not be Buddhas and Buddhist temples could not be used for Shintō rituals. Yet despite the separation, the influence of Buddhism on Shintoism is important in understanding how The Moon Goddess made her way via different names and manifestations into the position of the revered sun goddess of Japan, Amaterasu. A brief history of Buddhism reveals that the religion is deeply involved with the goddess of Babylon, even though they do not acknowledge such deity.

Buddhism was founded by Siddhartha Gautama known as "the Buddha" (meaning "enlightened") around 2,500 years ago in India. It now has 500 million to one billion followers making it a major world religion.[131] Buddhists also believe in reincarnation and karma, or the law of cause and effect. Buddhism spread and eventually seeped into Japan by way of the Korean kingdom of Baekje. Despite Buddhism claiming to be a non-theistic faith, The Moon Goddess is still present, her hand extending into Buddhism from the many arms of Hinduism, the main religion of India.

With its birthplace in India, Buddhism shares many commonalities with Hinduism. They both agree on karma, dharma, moksha, and reincarnation. They differ in that "Buddhism rejects priests of Hinduism, formal rituals, and the caste system."[132] But while some consider Buddhism an atheistic religion, there are many recognized deities in the form of devas and tantric deities in esoteric practices. Some Buddhists believe in Amitabha Buddha who will bring them rebirth in the Pure Land.[133] Most Buddhists would claim that they don't worship these entities nor give them thought because they are merely symbols or distant entities that have no purpose on earth. But that isn't the

[131] History.com Editors, "Buddhism," 5 Apr. 2024, https://www.history.com/topics/religion/buddhism

[132] Paul, "Hinduism and Buddhism," AP World History Bartlett High School, University of Missouri–Saint Louis, https://www.umsl.edu/~naumannj/world%20religions%20page/hinduism%20&%20buddhism.ppt#:~:text=Buddhism%20and%20Hinduism%20agree%20on,to%20seek%20enlightenment%20through%20meditation

[133] Barbara O'Brien, "The Role of the Gods and Deities in Buddhism," Learn Religions, 7 Apr. 2018, https://www.learnreligions.com/gods-in-buddhism-449762

case because to acknowledge any being outside of Jesus Christ as aiding in power, transferring wisdom, affecting nature, or protecting people on earth is to acknowledge those spirits and attach faith to them. It's idolatrous.

So what about The Moon Goddess? There are two Buddhist deities from India, *Mahākāla* and *Sarasvatī*, that influence Shintoism. Mahākāla (Sanskrit for "The Great Black One") is the Buddhist version of the Hindu deity *Shiva* and is known as *Daikokuten* in Shintoism, the deity of fortune and wealth. Sarasvatī, known as Saraswati in Buddhism and at times depicted with four arms, is the "Hindu goddess of knowledge, healing, protection, speech, and texts. She also became known as the consort of Manjushri, the bodhisattva of wisdom (prajña)."[134] She is the most recorded deity in Hinduism and is also known as "inciter of all pleasant songs, inspirer of all gracious thought, and best mother, best rivers, *best of goddesses.*"[135] In Shintoism, Sarasvatī is known as Benten and her temples are often found near bodies of water. She has often been identified with *Itsukushima-Hime*, who in ancient Shintō scripts was one of the trinity water goddesses, all of whom were formed from the sun goddess.[136]

Benten is also known as *Uka-no-Kami* in Japan and as the Dragon God in China. She is worshiped as the water goddess, "who is the womb of all things in the universe."[137] She is associated with dragons and snakes, particularly white snakes. Benten can also be seen with eight arms holding a sword, a dharma wheel, and other Hindu iconographic items. Her ability to influence the arts has found her a special seat in Japanese entertainment. To conclude, Sarasvatī, or Benten, is considered a water goddess, best of goddesses, the originator of music and the arts, and *a snake*! Benten and Sarasvatī *are* The Moon Goddess, the marine born

---

[134] Sunil Sehgal, *Encyclopaedia of Hinduism* (Sarup & Sons: 1999), 1214.

[135] Richard Thornhill, "Sarasvati in Japan," Hinduism Today, 1 Oct. 2002, https://www.hinduismtoday.com/magazine/october-november-december-2002/2002-10-sarasvati-in-japan/

[136] Thornhill, "Sarasvati," https://www.hinduismtoday.com/magazine/october-november-december-2002/2002-10-sarasvati-in-japan/

[137] Thornhill, "Sarasvati," https://www.hinduismtoday.com/magazine/october-november-december-2002/2002-10-sarasvati-in-japan/

spirit of Shinar, the Babylonian spirit of Revelation, the Egyptian snake goddess of the River Nile, and, ultimately, the principality under Satan himself who was once a prominent figure in heavenly worship.

By now it should be apparent, the perverse principality behind The Moon Goddess is the same perverse principality behind other paganistic, even non-theistic religions. This is the same spirit which has lied to the world in that she can bring prosperity, giftedness, fertility, protection, knowledge, wisdom, and healing. The same spirit who, with Satan, has hidden behind the sun and moon. But, in the words of Jesus as recorded in Luke 2:12, "For there is nothing covered, that shall not be revealed; neither hid, that shall not be known."

If the subtle messages of Sailor Moon or the rituals in the temples are not enough to catch the attention of skeptics, then the nation's flag ought to do so. The eye-catching flag of Japan is an open display of the goddesses' talons on the nation. The flag is of Amaterasu. It is white with a single red circle in its center, representing the sun goddess. While the flag comes across as simple, it actually possesses a deep spiritual history in its folds. But the flag of Japan is not the only flag that bears the image of the goddess and contains a hidden mystery. There is another flag that also waves in the wind of her worship, causing turmoil in the spirit; another crater she hides in, another religion that she has yoked herself to. Actually, this religion's emblem depicts her original form— a crescent moon.

Chapter 9

The Black Stone of the Sickle Moon

For we wrestle not against flesh and blood, but against principalities, against powers, against the rulers of the darkness of this world, against spiritual wickedness in high places.

Ephesians 6:12 , KJV

Islam, the second largest religion in the world with 1.8 billion members, means "surrender." Those who have surrendered to Allah, the god who they claim to be the same God of Judaism and Christianity, call themselves Muslims. Islam's roots are deep and its shade vast, reaching to nearly every nation. Within the Islamic faith is a vibrant, colorful culture rich with tradition, profound teachings, and faithful servants. Muslims are incredibly devout. They fast during Ramadan, the 9th and holy month on the Islamic lunar calendar, and they pray five times a day facing Mecca, Saudi Arabia. They are required to make a pilgrimage, if financially and physically possible, to Mecca, specifically to the Kaaba ("The Holy Place of Allah") at least once in their lifetime. They're sacrifice and prayer is incredible and many Muslims pray more times a day than a Christian prays in his or her lifetime! They truly are an enduring, obedient people.

Their history is ancient, going back to the days of Abraham (Ibrahim to Muslims), Hagar, and Ishmael. Many stories in the Qur'an (their sacred scripture) revolve around Abraham setting up a new dwelling place with Hagar and his son Ishmael.[138] Their belief system originally began with the biblical account of Abraham, Hagar, and Ishmael as recorded in Genesis 16; however, Islam became its own religion in A.D. 622 under the leadership of Muhammad. For Muslims, Abraham and Ishmael are the forefathers, while Muhammad was a direct descendent of Ishmael. The sacred Kaaba was built by Abraham and Ishmael as the

---

[138] Dr. Mona Siddiqui, "Ibrahim - the Muslim view of Abraham," BBC.co.uk, 4 Sept. 2009, https://www.bbc.co.uk/religion/religions/islam/history/ibrahim.shtml

original place of worship to Allah. In Islam, Ishmael (Abraham's son with Hagar who was Sarah's slave) is the "true son of promise" not Isaac (Abraham's son with Sarah) recorded in Genesis 22. Though Ishmael is mentioned little in the Qur'an, it is widely accepted that he aided in the building of the Kaaba and was the progenitor of the prophet Muhammad, who would officially form the religion known today as Islam.

Muhammad of Islam

Muhammad was born A.D. 570 in Mecca. His parents died when he was around six years old, leaving him an orphan. He was then raised by his grandfather and uncle. Legends report that the orphaned Muhammad visited a nearby cave named Hira for solitude, serenity, and sacred prayer. In his prayer time, he reflected on world suffering, discrimination, and social unrest, something he was a witness of and to. His young heart was to see a nation healed but his beginning was one of sorrow and vulnerability. Muhammad was open to hearing and seeing in other realms because of his broken heart and he was willing to accept any vision as truth because of his orphan spirit. Light and dark came through the cracks, and his broken heart and isolation would eventually produce a broken, isolated religion.

At the age of 40, he reported being visited by the angel Gabriel in Hira one night during Ramadan and around A.D. 613, he began publicly preaching his revelations. Of those revelations was that submission (*islām*) to Allah is the right way of life (*dīn*) and that he was a prophet sent by Allah to steer people to Allah.[139] But the events that transpired in the cave and jump started the Islamic revival were shaky to say the least. Muhammad claimed that the angel Gabriel (God's messenger angel) squeezed him in the cave and commanded him to read. Muhammad answered, "I am unable to read" (Qur'an, 96:1-5). He then received writings on his heart and ran to his first wife Khadija (he had many wives, one as young as seven years old) in fear. To console him she unveiled her

---

[139] Anis Ahmad, "Dīn" in John L. Esposito (ed.), *The Oxford Encyclopedia of the Islamic World* (Oxford: Oxford University Press, 2009).

genitalia to Muhammad, concluding that the angel he saw, despite her absence in the event, could not be Satan because angels of God do not watch exposure of men and women.[140] But that wasn't enough to quell Muhammad's fear. So he and Khadija went to her elderly paternal first cousin, Waraqa, to get his opinion. After hearing Muhammad's story, Waraqa concluded that the angel was the same Gabriel that appeared to Moses. Afraid of retaliation to his revelations, Muhammad tells Waraqa to support him. Waraqa vows to support him all of his life. Khadija, a polytheist, and Waraqa, a "Christian" (see the footnotes for more on this), both embraced Muhammad and his revelations, accepting the ways of Islam.[141] Waraqa promised to support him all the days of his life, however his promise was cut short as he died a few days later. His death left Muhammad suicidal with reports claiming that Muhammad attempted to kill himself on many occasions. It should be obvious by now that there were *many* cracks and confusion in Islam's beginning.

In the Bible Gabriel did not appear to Moses. He only appeared to Daniel, Zechariah, and Mary. Furthermore, when Gabriel did appear to special people in the Bible, he did not appear to instill fear but to bring a word of peace from God. In fact his first words to mankind were, "Do not fear!" Fear is what drove Muhammad to his wife who then fearful herself needed confirmation from a second source. Fear gripped Muhammad who became suicidal at the lack of promised support. Later, this same fear would be admitted by Muhammad himself when he mentioned he feared he was possessed by demons (pfanoter

---

[140] Sahih al-Bukhari 4953

[141] Aisha, one of Muhammad's wives, states that Waraqa was a Christian who read the Gospel in Arabic. The oldest evidence of an Arabic Translated New Testament was discovered in the 19th century at Saint Catherine's Monastery. The manuscript is called the Mt. Sinai Arabic Codex 151 and was created in AD 867 in Damascus by Bishr Ibn Al Sirri. Waraqa is said to have died in 610 AD. This would have been *many* years before the first Arabic Bible. Some scholars state that Waraqa was a Nestorian Christian. Nestorianism was a Christian sect that arose out of Asia Minor and Syria whose heretical doctrine held that Jesus was a "God-inspired man" but not a "God made man."; See John N.D. Kelly, "Nestorius" in *Encyclopedia Britannica*, https://www.britannica.com/biography/Nestorius for more information.

1910:345). According to Ahmad b. Hanbal, "He became distressed, foaming at the mouth and closing his eyes. At times he snorted like a young camel" (Ahmad b. Hanbal I, 34, 464, vi.163). These manifestations were not holy but were typical signs of demon possession. The hadiths record that later Muhmmad was under an evil spell, too.[142]Another major contradiction is that 600 hundred years prior to the event at Hira, Gabriel had appeared to Mary, the mother of Jesus, and told her that *she* would conceive the savior of the world (Lk. 1:30).

The fearful unrest instilled in Muhammad's life followed into the afterlife theology of Islam. Most Muslims believe that when a person dies, their soul enters a state of waiting until the Day of Judgment. After dying the person's soul is questioned by angels. If a person answers correctly, his or her soul is "good" and is permitted to keep sleeping in the waiting place, but if a person answers incorrectly, the "bad" soul is tormented by angels.[143] This sounds similar to the belief of the ancient Egyptians, who believed a person's heart was weighed against the feather of Maat, the goddess of truth and justice. If the scales were balanced, then the person was good enough to live forever in paradise with Osiris but the bad person was eaten by Amenti, "the gobbler," a monster who eradicated the soul entirely.[144] The uncertainty of the afterlife followed a person in life *and* death. A Muslim can be devout, fast, pray, and do many good deeds during their entire life and still have to face uncertainty after death. The soul is not at rest in life nor does it find rest after life.

Despite all of the concerns and contradictions, the religion had a spellbinding effect. The religion grew in following and today

---

[142] *Bukhari* Vol.4, Book 53, Chapter 34 and Vol.4, No. 400, 267; Hadith is a collection of traditions containing sayings of the prophet Muhammad which, with accounts of his daily practice (the Sunna), constitute the major source of guidance for Muslims apart from the Koran.

[143] "Life after death," BBC.co.uk, https://www.bbc.co.uk/bitesize/guides/zdxdqhv/revision/5#:~:text=The%20afterlife,to%20question%20the%20waiting%20soul.

[144] Joshua J. Mark, "The Egyptian Afterlife & The Feather of Truth," *World History Encyclopedia*. 30 Mar. 2018, https://www.worldhistory.org/article/42/the-egyptian-afterlife--the-feather-of-truth/

is fast approaching Christianity in numbers. There seems to be a spiritual race taking place over the soul and at a faster pace. While much study can be done on the Islamic faith, I want to focus on The Moon Goddess and her assigned role in the religion.

The Black Stone at Mecca

A quick look inside an Islamic wedding ceremony will reveal a colorful, vivid religion, or better yet, *people*. While the culture and traditions of Islam are colorful, the heart of the religion is a dark stone called the Kaaba. It is a shrine located near the Great Mosque in Mecca, Saudi Arabia. Muslims orient themselves in the direction of the Kaaba each time they pray, bury their dead in its direction, and are expected to visit the stone at least once in their lifetime. The word *ka'bah* means "cube" in Arabic and the Kaaba worshiped in Islam is roughly 50 feet high and 35-40 feet long. It is constructed of gray stone and marble and is oriented so that its corners correspond to the points of a compass. Its interior contains a few hanging lamps and three pillars. During most of the year, the Kaaba is covered with an enormous black brocade. But it is the special black stone that draws pilgrims from the four corners of the world.

    The stone that is positioned in the eastern corner of the Kaaba is not Islamic in origin. The stone, which most believe to be a stony meteorite, was worshiped prior to its amalgamation with the Islamic faith. Pre-Islamic, Arabic deities of the region included Al-Ilāt or Allāt ("the Goddess"), the daughter or consort of al-Lāh or Allāh ("the God"), Lord of the Kaaba in Mecca. Al-Ilāt was considered the equivalent of Aphrodite and Venus. For the Greeks a similar stone was worshiped under the principality's form of Cybele, who was believed to have taken the form of an unshaped stone of black meteoric iron.[145] Thus the worship of such meteoric stones is paganistic in origin and was a common idol in ancient times.

---

[145] Eugene N. Lane, *Cybele, Attis, and Related Cults: Essays in Memory of M.J. Vermaseren Religions in the Graeco-Roman World* (Brill Academic Publishing, 1996), ISBN: 978-90-04-10196-8.

Muslims believe that the pre-Islamic stone was purged of pagan idols upon Muhammad's return to Mecca in A.D. 629/30. It was then that the shrine became the focal point of Islam. Islamic tradition teaches that Abraham and Ishmael constructed the foundations of the Kaaba as a place to worship Allah. One popular Islamic legend is that the stone was given to Adam after his fall from paradise and was originally dazzling white but has become black as it has absorbed the sins of thousands of pilgrims who have touched and kissed it through the years.[146] Touching and/or kissing the stone is believed to transcend one into a higher spiritual realm as well as be a public display of submitting to Allah and paying respect to Muhammad. Ultimately, it is an intimate exchange between The Moon Goddess and her worshiper.

The black stone from space is a well known symbol of Islam. Another well known sign is its flag.

The Sickle Moon

The Islamic flag is one of the most recognizable flags in the world. Though the colors can vary from green to red to white, the Islamic flag is most commonly identified by its sharp crescent moon enveloping a star. But how did the crescent moon and star come to be associated with Islam? The origins of the flag go back to ancient Greece and Rome and, unsurprisingly, to the gods of those days.

The Roman goddess Diana and the Greek version, Artemis, was, as I have already mentioned, another form of The Moon Goddess. She was revered as the deity of wisdom, the hunt, and the moon and was the patron goddess of the city Byzantium. Her main symbol was a sickle-shaped moon cupping a star and could be found on coins, sculptures, and pottery throughout the empire. Even before Diana, the symbol of a crescent moon with a star can be dated back to early Palestine in the 13th century B.C. as a reference to Venus and the moon god, Sin.[147] During the reign of Emperor Constantine from A.D. 324-337, the Roman Empire

---

[146] Saying of the Prophet, Collection of Tirmizi, VII, 49

[147] "Crescent Moon and Star," Education.com, https://www.education.com/activity/article/crescent-moon-and-star/

moved their capital from Rome to the site of Byzantium and renamed the capital Constantinople. This city would become the heart of the Roman Empire for nearly 1,000 years and it would serve as a major influence in the heart of Islam.

Upon the establishment of Constantinople, the moon and star symbol transitioned from a pagan symbol to the symbol of the city. Coins, jewelry, and buildings within the empire were stamped with the crescent moon and star. Ironically, Constantinople would become the Christian capital of the world until the Ottomans captured it in 1453 by Sultan Mehmed II, officially making it a Muslim empire.[148] Mehemed adopted the moon and star as the sign of his new Islamic Empire and the image remains to this day.

The star featured on the Muslim flag is different from the star of David. The star of David is a hexagram, two equilateral triangles compounded, while the star of Islam is a five pointed star. The star of David and the star of Islam became identifying signs in the 17th and 18th centuries, respectively. Some Muslims today do not associate the moon or star with Islam but rather the early Arabic writings or the Kaaba. But still, functioning as a worldwide nametag, the crescent moon and star are a sign of Islam. And while their direct religious associations are relatively new in worldwide history, their roots are ancient in origin, similar to the rising sun on the Japanese flag. The sun, moon, and stars are at the core of all religions. As God created them to do, they serve as signs whether in the heavens or in the earth. The Christian flag, however, features no sun, moon, or star, only a cross. The sign *is* the cross.

The Muslim flag interestingly features a sickle moon, which is not uncommon to the Jews. The Jewish people had long known that the crescent of the new moon represented the beginning of a new month. The visibility of this crescent moon from Jerusalem marked Rosh Chodesh ("head of the new month") and signaled to the Jews that it was time to bring an offering to the Lord. At the silver crescent's first appearance, the news was presented to the Sanhedrin who would either confirm or deny the new month's

[148] Myles Hundson, "Fall of Constantinople," *Encyclopedia Britannica*, https://www.britannica.com/event/Fall-of-Constantinople-1453.

beginning. If it was confirmed, fires were lit on the Mount of Olives and other hills to inform the people. A meal was also prepared and enjoyed as the crescent of the new moon represented the sickle used for the harvest. The sickle new moon was also the beginning of the *Festival of Trumpets*.[149]

In Islam the crescent of the new moon is to represent "progress" while the star represents "light of knowledge."[150] The sighting of the crescent moon signals the beginning and end of the observance of Ramadan. Some believe the five points correlate to the five pillars of Islam, though this is just conjecture. However, most Muslims would agree that the star represents the light of knowledge. This is interesting considering the Genesis account of the tree of knowledge and good and evil, a tree that God forbid Adam and Eve to eat from; the same tree that opened the door, like Pandora's box, to knowing about evil entities such as The Moon Goddess. Knowledge is not bad, in fact the Bible tells us to have knowledge, but knowledge is found in the reverential fear of YHWH (Prov. 1:7) and wisdom is found in Christ and Christ alone (1 Cor. 1:24). Jesus is the Spirit of God who came in the flesh to redeem the world, thus Jesus *is* God (Jn. 1:14), so it is Jesus that represents the light of knowledge, not Allah or Muhammed.

The significance of a sickle shaped moon and star as it relates to Islam is, like a flag flying in the sky, another sign lifted up for those who have spiritual eyes to see. The fact that the sickle of the new moon also signaled the beginning of a new year known as the Feast of Trumpets (Rosh Hashanah) in the Jewish tradition is not a coincidence. Now that Christ has fulfilled the observance of such festivals–which were a shadow of things to come (Col. 2:16-17) –the signs represent the new beginning found in Jesus, his ultimate sacrifice so that the law might be fulfilled, his sickle for harvest, his return in the sound of a trumpet, and his wine of

---

[149] Deuteronomy 16:9, Jeremiah 50:16, Joel 3:13

[150] "10 Religions in Stained Glass," Brandon University, https:// www.brandonu.ca/religion/labyrinth-of-peace/10-religious-symbols-in-stained-glass/ #:~:text=Crescent%20and%20Star%3A%20The%20faith,the%20extended%2 0meaning%20of%20peace.

wrath against Satan and his minions: The Moon Goddess, Ba'al, and all of their worshipers.

> "I looked, and there before me was a white cloud, and seated on the cloud was one like the son of man with a crown of gold on his head and a sharp sickle in his hand. Then another angel came out of the temple and called in a loud voice to him who was sitting on the cloud, 'Take your sickle and reap, because the time to reap has come, for the harvest of the earth is ripe.' So he who was seated on the cloud swung his sickle over the earth, and the earth was harvested.
>
> Another angel came out of the temple in heaven, and he too had a sharp sickle. Still another angel, who had charge of the fire, came from the altar and called in a loud voice to him who had the sharp sickle, 'Take your sharp sickle and gather the clusters of grapes from the earth's vine, because its grapes are ripe.' The angel swung his sickle on the earth, gathered its grapes, and threw them into the great winepress of God's wrath" (Rev. 14:14-19, NIV).

The "Sickle Moon" is what modern day scientists call the "Waxing Crescent." This phase of the moon occurs once a month. *Waxing* means "increasing" and *Crescent* is the area of the moon that is illuminated during this phase. The shape of a crescent moon resembles that of a sickle sword, an agricultural tool which featured a curved blade and was used for harvesting in the ancient world. From these early hook-like swords came the *khopesh* swords. These elongated and curved swords were a popular military weapon in ancient Egypt.[151] The khopesh would develop over time and make its way throughout the world. The Vikings used the *ulfbert* swords, the ancient Japanese used *samarai* swords, the ancient Islamic warriors used *scimitars* or *sabers*.[152] The sickle sword that was used to

---

[151] Evan Andrews, "9 Blades that Forged History," History.org, 23 Apr. 2018, https://www.history.com/news/knives-that-changed-history

[152] Department of Arms and Armor, "Islamic Arms and Armor," in *Heilbrunn Timeline of Art History* (New York: The Metropolitan Museum of Art, 2000), http://www.metmuseum.org/toah/hd/isaa/hd_isaa.htm

harvest eventually traveled beyond the farm. In the hands of men, these swords would eventually be used to damage and kill. In the Lord's army, the sickles his angels carry are used to gather the elect of Christ while also cutting off the rotten fruit, symbolism for salvation of the believers and the death of the wicked. God's sword is sharper than any man-made sword because it holds the power of death *and* life, because it is *his word* (Heb. 4:12).

In our sin ridden world, swords being utilized to kill animals and other human beings is nothing new. One gruesome use of the sword is decapitation, or the removal of a person's head from his or her body either by murder or execution. This practice was common throughout much of the world's history. Beheading was regarded as an honorable means of death by the Romans and Greeks but as a dishonorable and contemptuous means by other civilizations and nations (i.e. the Japanese soldiers in World War II were known to behead prisoners of war[153]). Since the conclusion of the second world war, the practice of beheading has waned and is now associated with terrorism. There are only two countries that openly admit to and allow the act of decapitation as a means of execution: Saudi Arabia and Yemen. The official religion of both countries is Islam.

The spirit behind such a grisly act of terrorism has reared its ugly head for millennia. In the Old Testament, Jezebel–the woman who manifested The Moon Goddess–was fond of killing anyone who would threaten her power, particularly YHWH prophets. Though 1 Kings 18 does not explicitly say *how* Jezebel killed the prophets, we can gain a hint through an intertextual comparison between Jezebel's story and Herodias, the woman responsible for beheading John the Baptist. According to the gospels of Matthew and Mark, John the Baptist, a prophet and cousin of Jesus, was executed by King Herod Antipas at the request of Herodias. John had been imprisoned because he condemned Antipas for unlawfully divorcing his wife and marrying his brother's wife, Herodias. John's rebuke resonated as resentment in Herodias' heart (Mk. 6:17-20) and her hatred festered with time. On Antipas'

---

[153] Cliff Roberson and Dilip K. Das, *An Introduction to Comparative Legal Models of Criminal Justice* (FL: CRC Press, 2008), 172.

birthday, Herodias' daughter danced before him and his guests. Pleased with her, Antipas promised that he would give her whatever she wanted. She asked her mother, Herodias, what they should ask for and Herodias asked for the head of the prophet, John the Baptist. Antipas reluctantly agreed (Mk. 6:14-29; Matt. 14:1-12).

Herodias' evil plot, her scheming for John's death, her manipulation and control over her husband and her daughter, her seducing Antipas with sexual insinuations using her daughter to do so, and her desire to see a prophet of God dead all mirror Jezebel's behavior and characteristics. Jezebel, too, executed an evil plot to harm Elijah and the prophets of God, she schemed Naboth's death to take over his vineyard, and she manipulated and controlled her husband Ahab through promiscuous and seducing means. Comparing the two reveals that the spirit at work in Jezebel was the same spirit at work in Herodias. And while some may disagree with me, I believe Jezebel beheaded the prophets and I believe it is the spirit of Jezebel at work behind modern beheadings seen in Saudi Arabia and Yemen. Interestingly, the Saudi Arabian flag is green and features two scimitars. The Yemen flag is red, white, and black. The four horses of the Apocalypse are green, red, white, and black (Rev. 6). There may be no connection between the flags and the four horses but then again, what if there is?

But let me be clear that in all of the darkness that coats Islam, Muslims are still children of God. Muslims are some of the most dedicated, faithful, smartest, loyal, and generous people in the world. I have friends who are Muslim and they are beautiful inside and outside and have taught me how to love, how to give, and how to be proud in what I believe. Many Muslims do not understand the roots of the fruit they consume. Studies show that 99% of Muslims condemn the decapitation performed in terrorism and are extremely opposed to terrorist organizations such as ISIS,

179

HAMAS, and Hezbollah to name a few.[154] To be in the Islamic religion does *not* mean that a person has the spirit of Jezebel or Herodias. But terrorists *do* and terrorists can be from any religion and any nation. To be a murdering terrorist, *especially* in the name of a false religion, is to be a blatant puppet in the hand of Satan, Ba'al, The Moon Goddess and their demons.

Perhaps the crescent moon of the Islamic flag has two sides: on one side, it is a beautiful sign of hope for Muslims in the last days who surrender to Jesus and will be gathered by God in the final harvest; while on the other side, it is a sign to the followers of The Moon Goddess that the crescent moon they defend will actually be their downfall. The crescent moon may very well represent, in the words of Buzz Aldrin, beauty *and* destruction.

---

[154] Jacob Poushter, "In nations with significant Muslim populations, much disdain for ISIS," Pew Research Center, 17 Nov. 2015, https://www.pewresearch.org/short-reads/2015/11/17/in-nations-with-significant-muslim-populations-much-disdain-for-isis/#:~:text=Distaste%20toward%20ISIS%20was%20shared,Shia%20Muslims%20and%20Lebanese%20Christians.

Chapter 10

The Blood Moon Prophecy

I will display wonders in the heaven above and signs on the earth below: blood and fire and cloud
of smoke. The sun will be turned to darkness and the moon to blood before the great
and terrible day of the Lord comes. Then everyone who calls on the name of the Lord
will be saved.

Acts 2:14-21, HCSB

Pentecost of the New Testament is considered the birthplace of the early church. It was in this perfectly orchestrated event that the precious baptism of The Holy Spirit would be sent from heaven to endue believers with power. In the second chapter of Acts, written by Luke, the followers of Jesus were gathered in an upper room of a building, praying and waiting on God and likely hiding from persecution. In their gathering under heaven and yieldedness to God, The Holy Spirit descended not like a dove this time, as he had in their water baptisms, but in fire. This fire would fall to consume the altar of mankind's heart, igniting a flame which would shine in the darkness and branding Jesus' followers with undeniable, unexplainable gifts. Of the distributed gifts the most intriguing was that of *tongues*, or glossolalia.

As the sound of wind swept through the room early in the morning, another sound emerged. The Jews who had gathered in the name of Jesus, their strong tower, began speaking in different tongues "as the Spirit enabled them" (Acts 2:4, Prov. 18:10). Suddenly, the languages filled the room and united those listening. Onlookers who had traveled near and far for the Jewish festival of Pentecost, who also spoke different languages, could suddenly understand the Messianic Jews. The scattering of languages in the lands of Shinar was now mute.

The charismatic gift of tongues, or glossolalia, was distributed by The Holy Spirit in flames of fire upon the heads of the Jews gathered in the upper room in Acts 2 and was then given again to the Gentiles in Acts 10. The unification of the brethren in one apostolic faith, bearing witness to one name–Jesus–the son of the One and Only God–YHWH– mended the gap between cultures, ethnicities, and religious backgrounds. The language of love is universal; the work of Christ restorative.

Not only did Joel prophesy of such a day when The Holy Spirit would fall upon men, women, the young and the old, the Jew and the Gentile, but Jesus also promised the same in John 14:15-17. The Old Testament prophecy of Joel was fulfilled in Christ and now Christ had fulfilled the promise for both Jew and Gentile, male and female, slave and free. While the pagans had unified themselves under The Moon Goddess and Ba'al at the Tower of Babel bringing division and curses upon themselves, those who had surrendered their life to Jesus could now be united to Him, empowered by Him, and equipped by Him to share the Gospel of Peace.

Peter, realizing the prophetic magnitude of the event, repeats the prophecy of Joel under the unction of The Holy Spirit. Peter and Joel's prophecies are almost identical, the difference lying in the last verse: "Then everyone who calls on the name of the Lord will be saved" (Acts 2:21). Recall in Ezekiel 8:18, Ezekiel is shown via a supernatural vision the vile practices of the priests in God's temple. As he peered into the inner chambers of the temple and witnessed the priests and servants of YHWH secretly worshiping the pagan gods, God spoke a sobering word to the prophet, "Though they will call loudly in my hearing, I will not listen to them" (Ezekiel 8:18). The consequential judgment of God muting the prayers of the Jewish people because of their idolatry of Ba'al and The Moon Goddess was repealed through Jesus who would come as God in the flesh to bear the sins of the world. In Jesus' life, burial, and resurrection, the truth was evident for all to see and hear. As the Holy Spirit was then sent to ignite fire in the inner chambers of peoples' hearts, the dire consequence of God not hearing His people was placed upon Jesus as he cried out on the cross. As Jesus was resurrected, so was the hope for mankind. Peter, recognizing this, makes it known that, through Jesus, God *will* hear and save *all* those who call upon Him, regardless of their background, language, status, sin, or religion!

This difference in the prophecies is critical in understanding the living word behind the ancient prophecy. Though Jesus finished his work of salvation, he is still not finished in his judgment. The now and not yet of Joel's prophecy repeated by Peter under the finished work of Christ has been a debated topic among scholars and theologians since Peter spoke. While the events that were occurring during Peter's homily were present then, the open ended part of the prophecy remains a mystery:

> "I will display wonders in the heaven above and signs on the earth below: blood and fire and a cloud of smoke. The sun will be turned to darkness and the moon to blood before the great and glorious day of the Lord comes. Then everyone who calls on the name of the Lord will be saved" (Acts 2:19-21).

That the "sun will be turned to darkness and the moon to blood before the great and glorious day of the Lord comes" did not happen during Pentecost means that a part of this prophecy is pending. Due to this, the verse paradoxically divides, much like that of the blood moon in the days of Alexander. For Cessationists the miracle of tongues and healing ceased at the end of the apostolic age as did the prophecy. For some Christians, the mention of the heavenlies being altered is symbolic. But for me, the event is literal, and I believe this for two reasons.

First, the heavenlies being shaken before Christ's second coming is found in both the Old and New Testament. In Matthew's Gospel, Jesus gives a detailed prophecy concerning the end of the age quoting Isaiah 13 and 24 as well as Ezekiel 32:

> "Immediately after the distress of those days, the sun will be darkened, and the moon will not shed its light; the stars will fall from the sky, and the powers of the heavens will be shaken. Then the sign of the Son of Man will appear in the sky, and then all the peoples of the earth will mourn; and they will see the Son of Man coming on the clouds of heaven with power and great glory. He will send out his angels with a loud trumpet, and they will

183

gather his elect from the four winds, from one end of the sky to the other" (Matt. 24:29-31, HCSB).

Jesus' words are then seen in a present yet future visionary revelation by John on the isle of Patmos which John details in Revelation 6-20. The event is repeated too many times to write it off as symbolic. Those with spiritual eyes to see the layers of this prophecy will see the natural and supernatural components of it as well.

Second, the verse about the moon turning to blood is unique. Why say that the moon will turn to blood? The anthropomorphic depiction is quite peculiar. The Greek word used in this verse is αἷμα, or *haima*, and it means blood as in the life-giving liquid found in humans and other living beings (the same blood of the Hebrew *dam* in Joel's writing). The verbiage is interesting considering that the Hebrews and the Jews of Peter's day knew that the sun, moon, and stars were created on the fourth day of creation as *objects* to guide time and seasons. That was and is their only purpose. To worship them as power-giving entities was idolatry. To attach a deity to them was a crime in the courts of heaven. Thus, the concept of a "heavenly" structure bleeding was likely bizarre to those who would have read or heard the prophecy. For the moon to turn to blood could only be a miracle just like the River Nile turning to blood. And so the moon turning to blood will also be a miracle. Both were signs of a subliminal message to the gods of Egypt and to their worshipers, a cut to the throat of the land's voiceless idols. In the same fashion, the sun being darkened and the moon turning to blood will be a sign that Ba'al and The Moon Goddess have met Judgment. But who exactly will see the sign? And when will the event occur?

The answers to these questions are found within the prophecy.

Chapter 11

A Midnight Deliverance

For the Lord himself will descend from heaven with a shout, with the archangel's voice,
and with the trumpet of God, and the dead in Christ will rise first. Then we who are
still alive, who are left, will be caught up together with them in the clouds to meet the
Lord in the air, and so we will always be with the Lord. Therefore encourage one
another with these words.

1 Thessalonians 4:16-18, HCSB

The prophecy of Acts 2 which marked the birth of The Church as well as the birth of the last days contains within it a timeline for the moments before the great and terrible day of the Lord. It is a mystery that wields warning and wisdom. If one pays attention to the signs and reads the words with faith, he or she will find great encouragement in the prophecy, even in its mysteriousness.

When Will Such Things Take Place?

On the day of Jesus' ascension to heaven and only a few days before the world was turned upside down by the outpouring of The Holy Spirit at Pentecost, Jesus was questioned by his followers about the end of the world. Feeling the enemy breathing down their necks and having witnessed Christ's incredible ministry, the early Christian converts were feeling the pressure from the angry Jews and the pagan Romans while clinging to the signs and wonders they could not deny. The main sign was the resurrected Jesus standing in their midst. What would happen to them if he left again? In their anxiety, they believed the final days were at hand and Jesus would not leave them for long. He would return quickly for his people.

"While he [Jesus] was with them, he commanded them not to leave Jerusalem, but to wait for the Father's promise. 'Which,' he said, 'you have heard me speak about; for John baptized with water, but you will be baptized with The Holy Spirit in a few days.'

So when they had come together, they asked him, 'Lord, are you restoring the kingdom to Israel at this time?'

He said to them, 'It is not for you to know the times or periods that the Father has set by his own authority. But you will receive power when The Holy Spirit has come on you, and you will be my witnesses in Jerusalem, in all Judea and Samaria, and to the ends of the earth'" (Acts 1:4-8, HCSB).

And while the last days had in fact begun, the tarry for The Holy Spirit in the Upper Room was a sign for the church that as they came together again under heaven, there would be a tarry for the bride. As Jesus had promised, The Holy Spirit was sent to the Upper Room in Jerusalem, but the full restoration of all things did not occur at Pentecost, meaning one thing–there is still time before the bride of Christ will join her bridegroom in the air as Paul described. We are in a Pentecost tarry. But this tarry isn't one of huddling but of hustling.

Jesus made it clear in Acts 1 there was still work to do. Souls needed to be won. The temptation and the trial, the mockery and persecution would inevitably accompany the miracles, signs, and wonders, but Jesus encouraged his seekers that power would be their portion. They would survive and thrive through the tribulations with the gift of The Holy Spirit. His Holy Spirit would empower them to go forth into all the nations and share the Good News. We have the same power and assignment as the early followers: we are to occupy in power while we wait.

But just as the promised Holy Spirit came suddenly, so will the second coming of Jesus Christ. The exact day of His return is not known and Jesus made it clear that we are not to be so consumed with the future that we neglect the present assignment— to win souls for the Kingdom. *But,* Jesus *did* prophesy while on the earth concerning the days just prior and the days right after his return. The in-between of these days will happen in a twinkle of an eye. The in-between is *The Rapture.*

The Jail and The Rapture

I will address rapture theology as it pertains to The Blood Moon Prophecy in greater detail in Part III. But for now, I want to introduce the term "rapture."

The word *rapture* has two meanings. It can mean "an intense feeling of pleasure or joy" or "the transport from earth to heaven in the Second Coming of Christ" or, I suppose, both.[155] The etymology of the word is derived from the Medieval Latin *raptura* meaning "seizure, kidnapping" a derivation from the Latin *raptus* meaning "a carrying off." The word *rapture* is not actually found in the Bible but was connected to the Second Coming of Jesus described by Paul in his letter to the Thessalonians when it was translated from the Koine Greek into the Latin Vulgate. In 1 Thessalonians 4:17, the Koine Greek word used is ἁρπαγησόμεθα or *harpagēsometha* meaning "we shall be caught up." Strong's Concordance defines the Greek verb of "to snatch" or "catch up" as ἁρπάζω or *harpazō*.[156] As the Bible was translated into Latin and then into English from Latin, the word *rapture* became associated with the imagery of the believers in Christ being caught up with Jesus and snatched out of the tribulation.

---

[155] Oxford Dictionary, "Rapture," https://www.oxfordlearnersdictionaries.com/us/definition/english/rapture

[156] Strong, *Strong's Exhaustive Concordance,* G726.

To further illustrate The Rapture using the Holy Scriptures, I want to examine a famous story which is also found in The Book of Acts. This story involves none other than The Moon Goddess herself and is therefore an ideal starting place for connecting the end-time rapture and The Moon Goddess' rapidly approaching punishment.

Acts 16: Paul and Silas Delivered

In Acts 16 Luke gives an account of a miraculous intervention in Paul and Silas' evangelistic ministry. The men had been traveling through Europe evangelizing and preaching The Gospel. Many were joining The Way (or Christianity) daily and The Church was growing in faith (v. 5). One day as Paul, Timothy, Luke, and Silas were making their way to the house of prayer, a slave girl of a nearby Greek temple in Macedonia began following them. Luke informs the reader that the girl was used for fortune-telling (v.16) which brought in large sums of money for the temple. As she followed them for many days, she called out, "These men, who are proclaiming to you a way of salvation are the servants of the Most High God." Finally, annoyed by the spirit operating through the girl, Paul turns to the spirit and commands it to come out. With the girl spiritually free and unwilling to work for the temple, the temple owners became enraged, stirred up the crowds, had Paul and Silas flogged and thrown into the inner prison with their feet bound in stocks (v. 18-24). But their setback was just a setup for a comeback.

Before I move into the jail scene of this story, I want to pause and connect some pieces for you. Recall that in ancient Greece there was a Pythia priestess of Apollo in Delphi who was sought out by many for her ability to predict the future. Alexander the Great is one of many historical leaders who is believed to have visited the temple in Delphi. For Alexander it was a Pythia priestess who declared him invisible. The specific priestess Alexander visited was called a "Pythia" but for years before and after his reign, the Pythia role was passed to gifted and selected priestesses and there could be as many as three Pythias working at the same time.[157] On a specific day, the chosen Pythia would give oracles from a tripod which straddled a crack in the earth. It was Greek legend that the cracks upon which the priestess sat and gained revelation were caused from an earthquake.[158] The vapors that entranced the priestess were said to have arisen out of the crack, enabling the priestess with the future-predicting gift.[159] The Oracle at Delphi thus became the hub of fortune-telling, along with many other perverse activities.

Many years after Alexander, the temple of Apollo was still in operation and Pythias were still operating throughout Greek temples. Paul and his team exposed the unclean spiritual entities at work behind the Greek pantheon. The Greek word that Luke chose in his recount for the spirit of divination working in the slave girl was Πύθωνα, puthón or *python*. Thus Luke saw the connection of Satan and the Greek deities. The temple Pythia were operating out of a serpent spirit, a Python spirit, and they were using deception to lure in captives. The means by which these priestesses and "prophetesses" prophesied was through a dark realm, a realm managed by Satan, the evil serpent himself. They were enslaved to Satan in the name of Apollo and his counterpart Artemis. Apollo was, per Greek mythology, the sun god and the twin brother of Artemis, the goddess of the hunt and the moon. The slave girl was truly the one in jail.

---

[157] Plutarch, *On the Fortunes of Rome*, Translated by F.C. Babbitt, Vol. IV Loeb Classical Library Edition, 1936.

[158] William J. Broad, *The Oracle: Ancient Delphi and the Science Behind Its Lost Secrets* (New York: Penguin Press, 2007), 155-157.

[159] Science Adviser, "The Prophet of Gases," Science.org, 2 Oct. 2006, https://www.science.org/content/article/prophet-gases#:~:text=The%20officiant%20at%20the%20oracle,the%20wisdom%20of%20the%20gods.

As she followed the men and cried out repeatedly, "These men, who are proclaiming to you a way of salvation, are the servants of the Most High God" (v.17), she did so with a harmful motive. The word she used for "servants" is *doúlos*, meaning "slaves." In other words, she was shouting among a curious crowd that the Christian men were slaves to her master, Apollo, in an attempt to enslave the minds of those listening. To lose the crowd would be detrimental to the temple funds. Paul was patient with the girl who followed the men for days, but his discernment and his frustration was intensifying with each step. To claim them as "slaves" to Christ in the sense of her slavery to Apollo and Artemis, not to mention putting YHWH and Apollo in the same boat, was blasphemous. So while the unclean spirit tried to expose Paul and Silas as rioters and bigots to the crowd, Paul actually exposed it. Eventually, Paul had enough and cast the spirit out of the girl. This exposure landed Paul and Silas a position in jail...but not for long.

> "About midnight Paul and Silas were praying and singing hymns to God, and the prisoners were listening to them. Suddenly there was such a violent earthquake that the foundations of the jail were shaken, and immediately all the doors were opened, and everyone's chains came loose" (Acts 16:25-26).

While in jail, Paul and Silas began praising God, singing psalms and spiritual hymns. Then, in a most brilliantly orchestrated deliverance by God, Paul and Silas are snatched out of a terrible situation by a powerful earthquake. The esteemed earthquake that supposedly caused the crack for the vaporous fumes to bewitch the Pythia was shamed as the true God of creation, YHWH, shook the jail by an earthquake, not binding the prisoners but *loosing* them!

The praises of Paul and Silas prophesied a future hope. And God, who inhabits the praises of his people, delivered them because justice cannot be jailed (Ps. 22:3). As Paul and Silas stood from the stocks free, the fear of God gripped the prisoners and the jailer and, per Luke's story, the jailer's *entire* household became believers of Jesus Christ (v. 29-034). The sign was undeniable. The truth was out. Artemis and Apollo were not gods.

How does this victorious story illustrate The Rapture?

In the midnight hour, God rescued Paul and Silas. God rescued the believing men by an earthquake which would serve as a sign of freedom in Christ to the unbelieving jailer. Following this earthquake, the opportunity was presented for the jailer and his family to repent and call upon the name of Jesus. In the same way, it will be at the midnight hour when God will rapture all those who call on his name from the despair of the world. And as I continue this book, I will tell you why I believe The Rapture will occur shortly after a particular earthly event, much like that of the earthquake in Acts 16.

The Answer in the The First and Second Blood

Who will see the "moon" turn to blood and when will they see it?

The answers to these questions are found in the prophecy of Joel itself. The first *haima*, or "blood," mentioned in the prophecy, which was again released by Peter in Jerusalem on Pentecost morning, was a direction as to where on the timeline The Rapture occurs. Many are divided on when The Rapture occurs and some believe it will not happen, but in my research and revelation concerning Joel's prophecy, I believe there is an important clue in the blood as to the placing of The Rapture on the world's timeline.

In Acts 2:19 Peter reiterates that there will be wonders in the heavens and signs on the earth. Of those signs is "blood and fire and a cloud of smoke." The Greek word *haima* is used first in verse 19 which describes the natural events that will precede Christ's return. It is then used again in verse 20 which describes the moon turning to blood before the great and terrible day of the Lord. The first blood accompanies signs on the earth. The second blood involves a heavenly sign. While "fire and a cloud of smoke" can allude to the glory of God and I believe they do, they may also allude to the earth manifesting and contracting in labor pains.

The "labor pains" metaphor that Jesus used to describe the days leading up to The Rapture involve many catastrophic natural events such as earthquakes, famines, man-initiated wars, rumors of wars and martyrdom (Matt. 24:3-8). Geological science informs us that earthquakes are also the cause of fires, tsunamis, avalanches, and some volcanic eruptions. Knowing this, I posit that the first blood of the prophecy involves the blood of the saints via martyrdom as well as the blood of animals and humans through war and natural disasters. If this is true, then the second blood sign in the prophecy is a spiritual, heavenly sign. What happens between the two signs is important. This in-between, as I discussed above, is The Rapture. While the exact hour only the Father knows, we are to pay attention to the signs. The first blood will be seen by *all*, believer and non-believer, the second blood however will be seen by *the unbeliever*.

During the tribulation, the specific natural and man-initiated events will serve as a flashing light to the people of God that Christ will very soon come like a flash of light to take his followers. It is also a flashing sign to the believer that Satan and the fallen angels and all that worship him will fall like lightning to their place of eternal torment *very* soon. But The Blood Moon Prophecy is not one of fear but one of hope to the body of Christ. The prophecy does and will serve as a ray of hope that help is on the way. It will also serve to boost the morale of God's enduring and bleeding people, reminding them that, like Alexander's waning men, the victory is *sure* and deliverance will come suddenly at the midnight hour. And who will rescue them? Not an earthly king but the King of Kings, Jesus Himself.

With each passing day since Pentecost, the pressure in the world and in the spirit realm continues to build and it will continue to build until there is an explosion. In fact the ultimate explosion to occur from this pressure will quite literally form a cloud of smoke which will darken the sun. This explosion will occur during the tribulation. And, as I am about to reveal, it is an explosion that will occur in a specific place, at a specific time, and for a specific reason– to initiate the countdown to *The Rapture*.

PART III:
The Prophecy To Come

Chapter 12

The Volcanoes of Venus

Immediately after the distress of those days, the sun will be darkened, and the moon will not shed its light; the stars will fall from the sky, and the powers of the heavens will be shaken. Then the sign of the Son of Man will appear in the sky, and then all the peoples of the earth will mourn; and they will see the Son of Man coming on the clouds of heaven with power and great glory. He will send out his angels with a loud trumpet, and they will gather his elect from the four winds, from one end of the sky to the other.

Matthew 24:29-31, HCSB

J ust as the first part of this book began with a dream– Joseph's dream– I want to begin the final part of this book with a dream. While not all dreams are sent from the Lord, I do wholeheartedly believe that God speaks to his people in dreams, visions, and words of prophecy as Acts 2:17-18, along with countless other scriptures, reveal. I also believe that The Holy Spirit will continue to give dreams and visions until the return of Christ. Most of the time, these dreams will be for the dreamer but occasionally, a dream will contain information about or warning for someone else, a city, a region, the world, the future or–like the one I'm about to tell you–for all of these.

On the morning of April 25, 2019, I awoke from a surreal and sobering dream. It began with me riding in a red pick-up truck on a foreign planet that was a rusty orange color. The landscape was filled with jagged, lifeless mountain peaks. In the passenger seat was an faceless man who was directing me on which way to drive. We drove across the barren planet and then a few other planets like it before stopping on a planet that had emerald-colored vegetation.

The plants revealed to me we had arrived on a planet that God was renewing. Curious, I asked the man next to me, "What are we doing?" He responded, "Wait for it."

I parked the truck on a hillside beside various other cars and waited. An older model white two-door pickup truck was parked in front of me and its tailgate read TOYOTA. Next to me was a red four door sedan. To my surprise, a girl from my high school named Olivia (I will not reveal her last name for privacy reasons) was in the driver seat and, to my astonishment, half naked. The other car next to her was filled with one of my aunts and a few of my cousins. There were unfamiliar people standing around the cars on the hill with us. While still wondering where I was, I heard everyone begin counting down from five. "Five! Four! Three! Two! One!" They shouted in unison. On the final count, there was an explosion, a *massive* one. In the distance I could see an enormous pillar of gray smoke blast into the sky. The entire planet shook as the mountain spewed smoke and bits of ash into the atmosphere. I was shocked that no one around me was jumping in cars and running away. But it was understood in the dream that the pillar of smoke was so high that it would take some time for the effects of it to rain down on the civilians.

Upon realizing this, I watched as people began to, albeit slowly, get into cars and zoom away. After the bystanders were gone, I noticed a woman in the distance. She was the only woman who remained standing, and I sensed a darkness within her. She was in a burgundy, floor length dress and had black, loosely curled waist long hair. Her skin was pallor and her eyes were ebony. She smiled eerily while looking up to the heavens. I asked her, "Why are you not getting into your car and running away?" While still gazing into the cloudy sky, she responded through a broken smile, "I like the feeling before the ash comes." At this response, a piece of ash fell onto the center of her forehead. She then jumped in her car and sped away. After she left the scene, I noticed that the only

195

other car remaining was Olivia's and, because she had been drinking and smoking and engaging in promiscuous activities during the event, she and those with her had missed the volcanic eruption. Once the dark woman sped away is when Olivia quickly dressed herself and followed suit.

Needless to say, I awoke from this dream with a heavy burden. I didn't understand it nor did I know what to do with it. The Holy Spirit (who I now know was the passenger in the truck) instructed me to write the vision down and keep it to myself until an appointed time of release. It wasn't until I began writing this book five years later *to the month* of the dream that The Holy Spirit brought the dream to the forefront of my memory. After gaining revelation about The Moon Goddess and Japan, I gasped in astounding revelation.

TOYOTA!

Suddenly, the dream made sense. The volcano was Mount Fuji, the dark woman was the Babylonian spirit of Revelation, and Olivia was to point me to the Olivet Discourse in which Jesus prophesies of end time events: "the sun will be darkened, and the moon will not shed its light; the stars will fall from the sky, and the powers of the heavens will be shaken" (Matt. 24:29). Olivia and her friends had missed the disaster because they had given into the world's temptations.

The dream was a vision for an appointed time. It was a future prophecy. A time Jesus himself alluded to as being a futuristic event. Yet in his revealing this dream to me, there was an urgency in it. The countdown to *"the countdown"* has begun. For the remainder of this chapter and to set the stage for the conclusion of this book, I will now decode this dream in greater measure.

Mount Fuji, the Tribulation, and The Blood Moon Prophecy

As I stated before, the "first blood," or *haima*, in Joel's prophecy is connected to a *natural* event. Continuing in the vein of labor and delivery imagery, the first blood will be like the spotting of blood which a pregnant woman can experience just before labor. The first blood of the prophecy will point to the second blood, which will be the final delivery of the wrath of God upon The Moon Goddess and her followers as well as the full delivery of God's elect out of the tribulation. The "blood and fire and a cloud of smoke" in Acts 2:19 will be broader in scope. This means that the persecution of God's people, the natural trembling of the earth, and volcanic activity will happen *worldwide* during the tribulation. However it is also a *specific* event, and I draw this conclusion from my dream.

The pick-up truck I was driving with The Holy Spirit in the passenger seat signifies The Holy Spirit led ministry God has gifted to me. In this ministry truck, I will pick-up not only people but also revelations concerning end-time events. The fact that I was driving "out of this world" on other planets informed me that the revelation is not of this world, just as Jesus is not of this world (John 18:36). Additionally, the dream began with a dry and desolate planet, much like Mars, and ended with vegetation. The planet Mars was named after the Roman god of war and it is the fourth planet, the one right after earth; thus this part of the dream speaks to the wars and rumors of wars which will occur during the tribulation, as well as The Battle of Armageddon. But the vegetation on the final planet informs me that God is renewing ancient prophecies while also prophesying a *coming* renewal.

While parked on the planet with vegetation, I noticed the white Toyota pick-up truck in front of me. Being that Toyota is a Japanese car manufacturing company, this informs me that the location of the event is in Japan and this is an ancient yet futuristic prophecy. And, even more amazing, a Google search of the exact model I saw in my dream was a 1993 model, the year I was born! He gifted me this prophetic call and ministry at birth!

Being that Mount Fuji is the most sacred of mountains in Japan and is currently an active volcano, it will be the eruption of this particular mountain and the destruction that follows which will initiate the final countdown to The Rapture. Recall that The Holy Spirit told me to wait for the event. There is a key in this instruction. Just like those who waited for the promised Holy Spirit in the Upper Room, so too the bride must wait for these things to take place. But, the wait isn't much longer as the countdown in my dream reveals.

Upon the countdown, Mount Fuji erupted and did so in such great measure that the sky was darkened by a thick, gray smoke. As this pillar ballooned out over the planet, there was a delay in peoples' responses. Some immediately zoomed away in their cars, signifying some will catch the warning in the sign and respond to it, while others took their time and missed it. In the time between the eruption and the end of the dream was when the Babylonian spirit, the dark woman of Revelation, The Moon Goddess, revealed herself. Per her words, she will enjoy the time she has left before the ash of her fiery doom falls upon her. She will also relish in the short span of time between the eruption and the Second Coming of Christ, when she will use all her might to distract and deceive any who, at this point in the tribulation, have not surrendered to Christ. The "second blood" of The Blood Moon Prophecy is the wrath of God upon *her and her followers*.

Upon the ash hitting her head, she fled the scene. It was then that I noticed Olivia and her friends remaining. They were engaging in the ways of the world (drunkenness, carousing, etc.) and had missed the warning of the event. The name Olivia was to point me to the Olivet Discourse in which Jesus warns of such happenings. Those who miss the signs will miss him (Matt. 24:37, Rev. 21:8). However, there is great hope in this dream. Not only was there green vegetation pointing to the restoration of all things, but there was a time of waiting between the eruption, the ash falling, and the Babylonian spirit's judgment. This time of tarry is a blessing and it highlights a few hopeful takeaways. Below is what composes The Blood Moon Prophecy:

1) There is yet a massive harvest of souls to be won *before* the eruption of Mount Fuji. While Christians will live in at least some of tribulation days and those days will be severe and brutal, God is still saving and rescuing. At the midnight hour, just when the bride feels as if she cannot hang on one more second, Jesus *will* return for her.

2) The time between the eruption of Mount Fuji and the Babylonian spirit's judgment will be just long enough for any straddling the fence of decision about Jesus to make their choice because "everyone who calls upon the name of the Lord shall be saved" (Acts 2:21).

3) There will be an exposure of The Moon Goddess in the days leading up to The Rapture. This exposure will bring hardship but, as my dream shows, Christ's followers have the power to not cower in fear or intimidation because they know who they are and whose they are. Greater is He that is in us than he is in the world (1 Jn. 4:4).

4) When The Rapture occurs (and it will) it will happen at the exact moment the bowls of judgment of God's wrath are released on the world (Rev. 16). Thus those who see the moon turn to blood will be those who worshiped The Moon Goddess. They will watch the judgment of the notorious marine-dwelling prostitute who also "sits on seven mountains." She and Satan's

followers and those who pledged allegiance to the Antichrist, will experience and see the bloody event in the form of God's wine of wrath. Those whose names are not written in the Lamb's book of life will be "astonished when they see the beast that was, and is not, and is to come" (Rev. 17:8).

5) Last and most encouraging: The Rapture is for *all* who bear the name of Jesus and it occurs *before* the seven bowls of judgment. Praise God!

Death of a Planet

One night after writing the previous chapter, I turned on the TV and, having binge watched Star Wars for the previous four days, decided I would remain in the river of space. As I searched documentaries, one caught my eye. It was titled, "Venus: Death of a Planet." Of course I had to watch it, considering I had finished writing the section about Mount Fuji the day before. I began the movie and was amazed at what I learned.

Having always loved space, I grew up reading books and watching shows about the planets. In my childhood Venus was neat to me, but I was, for some reason, always drawn to Saturn and Neptune. Saturn with its many rings and Neptune, the bright blue ball suspended among stars, captured my attention. However, Venus was light years from my interest despite it being Earth's neighbor. While watching the movie, I had forgotten just how beautiful this planet is until the screen flashed incredible modern photographs of the fiery planet and pictures taken by the Soviet Union's Venera of its surface in 1975 and 1982. These pictures revealed a fumy, toxic atmosphere, jagged landscape, and many, many *volcanoes*. As the astrologists began to detail Venus and their findings, I was nodding my head in agreement, but more so from a spiritual standpoint. I was picking up what God was laying down.

The planets were crafted by God, placed in perfect order by his finger, and remain fixed by his power. They're a delight to study, explore, to gaze upon, and to use for imaginative purposes. The planets were a cosmic wonder and mystery to the ancient inhabitants of the earth just as they are to us today. In most ancient civilizations, the planet Venus was called by her association to the mythology of that culture's religion. I knew Venus was the Roman goddess of love and beauty but it was new to me, and yet not new considering my findings from my research, that the Sumerians called the planet Inanna. The Akkadians and Babylonians called it Ishtar. As the historians in the documentary discussed these ancient names, my interest peaked. God had created the planets but man had named them based on gods and goddesses, deities whose origins go back to The Moon Goddess and Ba'al.

Because of the planet's close proximity to the sun, Venus's movements seemed to be discontinuous to ancient observers and was therefore believed to be two separate stars: the morning star and the evening star. The Sumerians and Babylonians knew the two stars to be one but were unable to explain the strange movements so they deemed the two stars as *one* deity— Inanna for the Sumerians, Queen of Heaven for the Babylonians.[160] The dual nature of the planet correlated to the mythology of Inaana. Recall the chapter on mimicking and how Satan uses and twists Biblical stories. The planet Venus' ancient associations to The Moon Goddess cult reveals the mimicry. In an ancient Sumerian tale called *Inaana's Descent into the Underworld*, the dualistic quality of the planet is connected to the goddesses' descent into hell where she is killed and then resurrected in three days, hence the rise and fall of

---

[160] Jeffrey L. Cooley, "Inanna and Šukaletuda: A Sumerian Astral Myth" *KASKAL* 5: 161–172. ISSN:1971-8608; "Ishtar," Brooklyn Museum, https://www.brooklynmuseum.org/eascfa/dinner_party/place_settings/ishtar

the "same" yet "separate" entity in the sky.[161] In classical Latin the planet was called Lucifer.[162] It is of no surprise then that Jesus tells John in Revelation 22:16 upon his defeat of Satan and the Babylonian spirit, "I am the root and descendant of David, the bright and morning star."

While all the other planets are named after gods or goddesses, Earth is the only planet that is not. It is a standalone planet in not just its ability to contain life but in its unique name as well. All the other planets are named after Roman gods and goddesses. Venus is the second planet from the sun and comes just before Earth. The planet's colors from space are yellow and white and its features are obscure to observers from earth due to the thick blanket of smoke masking the toxic planet's active volcanoes. Venus actually has the most volcanoes out of *all* the planets in our solar system with over 1,600 major volcanoes and thousands if not millions of smaller ones.[163] The association between the lava ridden planet and the deity Ishtar/Inanna/Venus is hardly coincidental. These facts solidified my connection between The Moon Goddess and the eruption of Mount Fuji in my dream. The planet which ancient humans named after The Moon Goddess *is* the volcano planet! And, like the title of the movie, Venus is a *deadly* planet.[164]

Amaterasu, The Bamboo Cutter, and Mount Fuji

[161] Joshua J. Mark, "Inanna's Descent: A Sumerian Tale of Injustice," World History Encyclopedia, 23 Feb. 2011, https://www.worldhistory.org/article/215/inannas-descent-a-sumerian-tale-of-injustice/

[162] Christoph Auffarth and Loren T. Stuckenbruck eds., *The Fall of the Angels* (Leiden: Brill, 2004), 62.

[163] "Venus," Oregon State University, https://volcano.oregonstate.edu/venus

[164] Dave Brody and Thomas Lucas, "Death of a Planet," https://www.imdb.com/title/tt15462680/

Mount Fuji is an incredible sight, drawing thousands of locals and tourists yearly who gaze at its magnificence. God truly painted our world with awe and wonder and Mount Fuji is one of his masterpieces. But while the mountain ought to point to the Creator and encourage worship of him, it has for some become an idol. The sacred mountain of Fuji has ancient religious connections to the sun and moon gods like that of the Babylonians to Venus. Remember that The Queen of Heaven is seen throughout all cultures in different manifestations and forms. Though the spirit is often given feminine attributes by mankind, the spirit is a spirit. It has no gender. It is feminine in appearance to counterpart Satan who appears more masculine in appearance and description. But the two are fallen angels working together simultaneously to bring about deception and destruction. Thus in a twist, The Moon Goddess becomes the sun goddess of Shintō religion. The tales of her mythology and the connection to the sacred Fuji reveal the true identity behind the deity.

Mount Fuji's beginning is a matter of legend among the Japanese. While scientists know that the volcano's origin is around that of 8,500 B.C., the myth of the mountain's birth in Japanese folklore dates it to around 86 B.C. This could be because the volcano erupted around 86 B.C. Per one Japanese legend the creation of Mount Fuji occurred in a single day. Remember that in Revelation 18 the Babylonian spirit is defeated "in one day" (v. 8). The legend states that a woodsman named Visu was awoken by what he believed to be an earthquake. He grabbed his family and they ran from out of their home, but as they exited the house they saw that a mountain had appeared out of a dry and desolate land. Enamored, Visu named the mountain "Fuji-yama" meaning "The Never-Dying Mountain."[165]

---

[165] Kurt Jones, "Japan," Volcano Folklore, Oregon State University, https://volcano.oregonstate.edu/
japan-0#:~:text=The%20creation%20of%20Mt.,coming%20from%20under%20the%20Earth.

In the mountains' miraculous appearance, deities were nonetheless connected to it. Of those deities, is the goddess Sengen, known as the Goddess of Fuji, whose temple was once said to reside on the summit of the mountain. One tale claims that those who pilgrimed to the top of the mountain with an unclean heart were thrown down by the goddess.[166] This is yet another mimicry of Psalm 24:1-5:

> "The earth is the Lord's, and everything in it,
>   the world, and all who live in it;
> for he founded it on the seas
>   and established it on the waters.
> *Who may ascend the mountain of the Lord?*
>   *Who may stand in his holy place?*
> *The one who has clean hands and a pure heart,*
>   *who does not trust in an idol*
>   *or swear by a false god.*
> They will receive blessing from the Lord
>   and vindication from God their Savior."

The goddess' seemingly delicate beauty displayed in the mountain's snow-capped tip and blossoming trees at its base is actually violent on the inside. Shrines that were built to worship and appease her in an attempt to keep the volcano from erupting have yet to prove stable with sixteen eruptions recorded since A.D. 781.

The unstable Sengen, also known as Konohanasakuya-hime and Sakuya-hime, may seem different from Amaterasu, the sun goddess who is Shintoism's prime deity, but it is actually the same goddess. The Moon Goddess masquerades herself behind complex mythology. Sengen is, per the Japanese mythology, the wife of Ninigi-no-Mikoto who was the grandson of Amaterasu and believed to be the great-grandfather of Japan's first emperor,

---

[166] Boye Lafayette De Mente, "Japan Encyclopedia," (Chicago, IL: Passport Books, 1995).

Jimmu.[167] An 11th century legend along with a Heian period tale connects the goddess with Mount Fuji. In the 11th century legend known as "Yosoji's Camellia Tree," a young boy by the name of Yosoji becomes desperate to find help for his mother who is dying from smallpox. He visits a local fortune-teller who instructs him to take water from the streams at the base of Mount Fuji. As the boy arrives at the mountain, there are three different paths he can take. Not knowing which one to pursue, Yosoji is suddenly approached by a young girl dressed in white who emerges from the forest and tells him which way to go. After the boy's mother and some other villagers are healed from the river's magic, the boy wants to know the young girl's identity. Upon his inquiry, she tells him that "her identity is not important" before being taken away in a cloud on Mount Fuji. Her disappearance into the mountain could only mean to the boy and his townspeople that Sengen is the goddess of Mount Fuji.[168]

In addition to this tale and slightly older is the "Tale of the Bamboo Cutter" written in the late 9th to early 10th century during the Heian period (A.D. 784-1185). In this story a bamboo harvester named Taketori no Okina stumbles upon a mysterious golden bamboo stalk. When he cuts open the stalk, he finds an infant the size of his thumb inside the bamboo. Having no children of their own, he and his wife decide to raise the infant and name her Nayotake-no-Kaguya-hime, "Shining Princess of the Bamboo." Gold nuggets begin to appear in the stalks following her adoption and the family becomes wealthy. As the girl grows into an attractive woman and her family's wealth builds, suitors begin pursuing her hand in marriage. Five nobles desire her and not wanting to marry any of them, the princess gives them five impossible tasks to complete. Whoever is able to complete them, she says, is worthy of her hand in marriage. The five fail miserably before she is approached by the emperor of

[167] Roy Willis, ed., *World Mythology: The Illustrated Guide* (New York: Oxford University Press, 2006), 114, 116, 120.

[168] Richard Gordon Smith, "Yosoji's Camellia Tree," *Ancient Tales and Folklore of Japan* (Montana: Kessinger Publishing, 2006), 189-196.

Japan who quickly falls in love with her. She does not subject him to an impossible task but does inform him that she is not of his world, her place is with the moon, and therefore she cannot marry him.

Just before her departure by chariot in a feather robe, she instructs an officer of the earth to give the emperor a letter along with a small capsule of elixir of immortality. The officer obeys. The emperor then asks, "Which mountain is the closest to heaven?" to which another officer answers, "The Great Mountain of Surgura." He then orders the men to burn the elixir and letter on this mountain. From this tale, some believe Mount Fuji was named after this magical immortality elixir *(fushi)*. The smoke, per the legend, that ascends from the mountain is the continual burning of this immortality potion.[169]

While these imaginative tales may seem like myths, legends, or folklore, the influence of The Moon Goddess in the culture is undoubtedly real. So important is this spirit behind Fuji that it is connected to the sun goddess Amaterasu, the great light, who is the nation's main Shintō deity and who is believed to be the matriarch of all emperors. This spirit via the form of Sakuya-hime or Amaterasu or Sengen is still worshiped via ceremonies, rituals, and offerings on Mount Fuji and throughout the nation. Japan is as deep in this spirit's stronghold as Mount Fuji is high.

Labor Pains to Delivery

Thankfully, God established a plan of redemption at the birth of the world. In Earth's delivery, God delivered a wonderful, restorative plan. God already knew that Satan would deceive Adam and Eve, Ba'al would lure men and women into horrendous practices, and The Moon Goddess would sexually corrupt the

---

[169] Yai Theodora Ozaki, "The Tale of the Bamboo Cutter and the Moon-Child" in *Japanese Fairytales* Lit2Go Edition (New York: A.L. Burt Company, 1908), https://etc.usf.edu/lit2go/72/japanese-fairy-tales/4834/the-bamboo-cutter-and-the-moon-child/

world. God will not allow The Moon Goddess to have the final word nor shed the final light.

God's plan from the foundation of the world was *His* Word, Jesus Christ. "In the beginning was the Word, and the Word was with God, and the Word was God" (Jn. 1:1). Jesus is the beginning, the middle, and the end, the alpha and omega (Rev. 22:13). He is the author and finisher of our faith (Heb. 12:2) and his story is one of a glorious, joyful ending for *all* of those who call upon his name. Even the most bound of individuals can be loosed at one mighty word–*Jesus*! The living God was at the beginning and he *will* be at the end. While Amaterasu was too fearful to emerge from her cave, Jesus defeated the cave! His beginning and ending is one of love and *not* fear.

Matthew 24 informs us that as Jesus came out of the temple one day, he made a curious comment which hinted at a toppling of the temple. Intrigued by Jesus' comment about one stone not being left upon another, the disciples approached him *privately* as he was sitting on the Mount of Olives (Matt. 24:1-3). It was then that he began his Olivet Discourse, a discourse which would be for his private followers, information found for those *who seek out their answers in him*. Jesus, God's living and breathing Word, informed his disciples in Matthew 24 that there would be trials and tribulations before his return. He forewarned them of many false prophets who will claim themselves to be the Messiah, he prophesied of increased lawlessness and the waxing of love worldwide (v. 11-12). But the prophecy had components. The disciples would witness those trials but so would the Christians after them. Jesus made it clear that The Church will suffer *some* of "The Great Tribulation" before he returns for his elect. The Church will also see some important worldwide events before his return. What else besides the earthquakes, volcanic activity, heavenly shaking, famines, wars, and false prophets will The Church see before The Rapture? The answer to this question was first given by the prophet Daniel.

207

The Abomination of Desolation

> "So when you see the abomination of desolation,
> spoken by the prophet Daniel, standing in the holy place'
> (let the reader understand), 'then those in Judea must flee
> to the mountains. A man on the housetop must not come
> down to get things out of his house, and a man in the
> field must not go back to get his coat. Woe to pregnant
> women and nursing mothers in those days! Pray that
> your escape may not be in winter or on the Sabbath. For
> at that time there will be great distress, the kind that
> hasn't taken place from the beginning of the world until
> now and never will again. **Unless those days were
> cut short, no one would be saved. But those days
> will be cut short because of the elect**" (Matt.
> 24:15-22, HCSB, emphasis added).

The words of Jesus are sharp. There will be days of heartache, confusion, and disbelief leading up to his return. However Jesus reminds us that "immediately after the distress of those days" is when he will come back for his people, for his elect. And although The Rapture will happen suddenly, it will not catch those who know the signs off guard.

Of the most obvious signs will be the "Abomination of Desolation" standing in the holy place. Who or what is this? And why is it mentioned in both the Old Testament and New Testament? And what does it have to do with The Moon Goddess?

The "abomination of desolation" prophesied by Daniel in Daniel 9:27 and 11:31 was repeated by Jesus in Matthew 24:15. Scholars have studied and deciphered these verses for hundreds of years and most agree that there are two major events that fit the description of the wicked desolator who set up abominations. In the Book of Daniel, the prophet foretells of a future event in

208

Israel's story in which an evil man, now thought to be Antiochus IV Epiphanes, would do something terrible in the temple. Though Daniel doesn't name Antiochus IV, it is agreed upon by most scholars that this is likely who Daniel was referring to.

If you'll recall from Part I, after the unexpected death of Alexander the Great, the empire was divided to successors and the kingdom's power began to crack. It was out of this shaky division that the Seleucid Kingdom of Syria was established in the north and the Ptolemaic Egypt in the south. These two kingdoms warred with each other for a century while the Jews remained relatively hidden. But when Antiochus IV, also called "madman," came to power in 170 B.C., the Jewish people were instantly spotted. He hated the Jewish people and the God they served. He, like the ancient Alexander of Macedon and Emperor Jimmu claimed himself a god (Epiphanes, "God manifest"), a reincarnate of Zeus himself. Under his tyrannical rule, he forced the Jewish people by threat of death to take on Hellenistic traits and rituals. In 167 B.C. he captured Jerusalem and desecrated the Temple of YHWH by sacrificing a pig to Zeus in the Holy of Holies, an utter abomination to the Jewish people. He forbade them from worshiping YHWH, burned their texts, stole the temple's treasures, burned their buildings, and killed or enslaved many men, women and children.[170]

Many years later, Jesus would prophesy of a similar abomination of desolation in Jerusalem (Matt. 24:15-22). It is one of the reasons Jesus lamented over Jerusalem as he approached the city recorded in Matt. 23:37-39, because he knew they would deny him and he knew that the city would be desecrated after his death. His weeping was not in vain. Those events did take place under the

---

[170] Josephus, *Ant. XII. 5.4* (Thackery LCL); John Gregory Drummand, "Antiochus Epiphanes–The Bible's Most Notoriously Forgotten Villain," Bible Archeology, 24 Nov. 2023, https://www.biblicalarchaeology.org/daily/ancient-cultures/ancient-israel/antiochus-epiphanes-the-bibles-most-notoriously-forgotten-villain/

Roman general Titus, a villain who also had pagan roots to Ba'al and The Moon Goddess. In April A.D. 70 around the time of Passover, Titus besieged Jerusalem and trapped many pilgrims and locals inside the city walls, depleting them of food, water, and resources. By August, the Romans breached the final defenses and slaughtered any survivors and destroyed the Second Temple. In celebration of Jerusalem's fall, Rome erected the Arch of Titus, an idol to the general and emperor who massacred the Jewish people. The arch's friezes depict his triumphal procession into the city, artifacts from the Jewish temple (trumpets, the Table of Showbread, and the Menorah), the goddess of victory, and Titus' deification. Spoils from the Temple were used to fund the Colosseum, which would be used for bloodsport, sacrificing Jews, Christians, and gladiators to the gods and goddesses. Titus only ruled two years before dying from a fever, others said he was poisoned by his brother.

From Antiochus IV and Titus' harsh resistance to Judaism comes the model through which the Antichrist will operate. Both villains had pagan roots and both brought about horrendous destruction to the people of God. While some believe that the destruction of the temple in Jerusalem in A.D. 70 under Titus was the fulfillment of Jesus' warning in the Olivet Discourse, there still remains a future component, a piece that has yet to be fulfilled. The days of such hardship for God's elect will be cut short, also known as The Rapture (Matt. 24:22). Viewing Jesus' warning with a futuristic lens gives insight as to how the Antichrist and the false prophet will operate: there will be an illusion of peace with Israel that will turn into a deadly siege, there will be an idol of Satanic worship set up in Jerusalem, worship of the Antichrist will be required, and there will be starvation and depletion of resources for followers of Jesus, hence Jesus' caution, "Be always on the watch, and pray that you may be able to escape all that is about to happen, and that you may be able to stand before the Son of

Man," (Lk. 21:36) and again his stern warning in Revelation to not take the mark of the beast (Rev. 13, 19:20).

The Beast of the Sea

While the spirit behind The Moon Goddess was thought to be high in the sky, floating among the stars, her influence was actually earthly, her kingdom marine in nature. The "beast of Revelation" described by John represents two similar entities: the end-time empire and the political figure who is the head of the beastly empire. In Revelation 13, the "beast" is representative of the Antichrist, the son of perdition, who rises out of the sea and is given power by Satan to wage war against God's people which will eventually bring about the terrible wrath of God (Rev. 13:7, Dan. 7:21).

In Revelation 17 the beast is described again while the seven bowls (the final outpouring of the wine of God's wrath) is occurring. John describes this beast as having seven heads, ten horns, covered in blasphemous names (Rev. 17:7). Sitting on top of this beast is The Moon Goddess, or the Babylonian Harlot, "the notorious prostitute who is seated on many waters" (Rev. 17:1). An angel explains to John that the seven heads represent the seven mountains upon which the prostitute is seated and the horns represent governmental leaders and systems who have made alliances (and sold their souls) to the Antichrist. The Moon Goddess/Babylonian whore works in tandem with Satan to bring about political turmoil and worldwide domination. The "waters" from which she will rule from "are peoples, multitudes, nations, and languages" (Rev. 17:15). Her Babylon-like religious influence will become hated by those who serve the Antichrist in the end times and she will eventually be "killed" by the ten kings and the Antichrist. While it isn't entirely clear as to how that "killing" will happen or what it will look like, it is clear that her exposure and her destruction will occur at the hands of those submitted to the Antichrist who works under the hand of Satan. It is hard to draw a final conclusion from the apocalyptic, encrypted text, but what is evident is that her end is *destruction*.

Also obvious is that this occurs during the bowls of judgment, which is the final and most excruciating outpouring of God's wrath upon the earth, and her final destruction is by the hand of God Almighty who commissions an angel to throw a large millstone into the sea–that is, into the belly of her control and the waters upon which she sits–and annihilate her sorcery (Rev. 18:21-24). God will avenge the blood of the prophets and the saints who were murdered under her hand. And as he is pouring his wine of wrath down her throat, the saints in heaven will rejoice as they prepare to drink from the cup of God's mercy at the marriage supper of the lamb.

Chapter 13

The Great Harvest

What has been will be again, what has been done will be done again; there is nothing new under the sun.

Ecclesiastes 1:9, NIV

A ny farmer, hunter, or fishermen knows just how important timing is in harvest. Preparation, patience, and pursuit are key factors in obtaining the harvest. From antiquity until now, harvest times have not stopped. After God cleaned the earth with the flood, he promised Noah and his descendants: "As long as the earth endures, seedtime and harvest, cold and heat, summer and winter, day and night will never cease" (Gen. 8:22). Knowing that the sun and moon were created and suspended in space by God for the purpose of signs, seasons, days and years (Gen. 1:14), then believers can rest assured that as long as those remain then so does the harvest.

The moon as discussed in Chapter 1, played a special role in the festivals of ancient Israel, and when we understand that the spine of the conjoined Old Testament and New Testament is Jesus, then we can study the harvest festivals in a Christological perspective. Jesus, a devout Jewish rabbi, knew how important the harvest was, even referring to God Himself in Matthew 9:38 as "The Lord of the Harvest." Jesus, who was a manifest sign of the fullness of time, told his disciples as he preached on the Kingdom of God in Matthew 9 to pray for laborers who would go out and win souls for the Kingdom (Gal. 4:4, Matt. 28:16-20). So while the feasts and festivals were appointed by the moon's phases, the God of all creation and time came as a sign himself into the timeline of man to reveal the true purpose behind such feasts and festivals. These were celebrations of the harvest and in the eschaton, the marriage supper will be the celebration of the world's final harvest.

213

In the Old Testament, when a Jewish man or woman harvested land, that person was instructed by the Lord through Moses not to glean to the edges but to leave some for the foreigner and the poor (Lev. 23:22). In the New Testament, the harvesters became the servants of Jesus who is the Lord of the Harvest. As born again Christians, we are commissioned now to go out into all the nations preaching this hope, the good news of Jesus while clothing the naked and feeding the poor, baptizing in his name, and teaching his instructions.

King Solomon in his wisdom acknowledged mankind's subjectivity to a higher power upon the building of the first temple, "For we are all aliens and temporary residents in your presence as were all our ancestors. Our days on earth are like a shadow, without hope" (1 Chron. 29:15). In the New Testament, believers in Christ become the sons and daughters of God who, as Peter exclaimed in 1 Peter 1:3, have been given a new birth into a living hope through Christ's resurrection from the dead. Under the renewed covenant, the law has been fulfilled through the atoning blood of Jesus for both Jew and Gentile, slave and free, man and woman (Matt. 5:17, Col. 3:11). The harvest knows no boundaries. Believers are the temple of God, bringing good news to the poor and freedom to the prisoner (1 Cor. 6:19, Lk. 4:18). We were once undeserving in our iniquity of any blessing. *We* were the edge, we were the foreigners, poor in spirit and dead in transgressions, but God—the Lord of the Harvest—sent His son, a lowly servant, to be the one waiting at the field's edge for the foreigner, those at death's door, for the poor and hungry, the mourning and rejected, the persecuted and weary, to bring them out of death and into his marvelous light (1 Peter 2:9)! Praise be to God that he is the Lord of the Harvest!

While the "final harvest" will be The Rapture of both the dead and living in Christ, there is still worldwide harvest that will take place. This harvest will be marked not by the moon phase but by the leading and prompting of The Holy Spirit. As the ecclesia grows and matures from glory to glory, many will be added into the faith until God's glory covers the earth as the waters cover the sea

(Hab. 2:14). At Pentecost Luke claimed that about 3,000 people were added to the Christian faith. From Pentecost forward, the growth of the body of Christ has been exponential. If the prophecy of Joel was fulfilled partially in Acts then we can only imagine what a worldwide outpouring will look like. The latter rain will be better than the former!

Before God gathers the elect from the four corners of the earth in The Rapture, there will be a time of peace. Psalm 72:7 reads, "May the righteous flourish in his days and well-being abound until the moon is no more." Those covered by the blood of Jesus will walk in abundance, joy, and flourish in the land before *and* during troubling times. The unshakable peace of God's people will be everlasting. The wicked will also have a season of "peace" and safety, a time in which the world will seem to be bending according to the enemy's will. But 1 Thessalonians 5:3 informs us that this perceived peace and security will be short lived, "...for sudden destruction will come upon them, as labor pains on a pregnant woman, and they will not escape." The Rapture is not for the unbelieving but for the believing.

Everyone will be given a chance to choose their fate. Jesus will make sure he is known to all nations, tribes, and tongues before he returns (Matt. 24:14). Some Christians call this a worldwide revival, others a great awakening. While revivals are typically localized outpourings of The Holy Spirit evidenced through the display of spiritual charismata, a large number of conversions, miracles, signs, and wonders; awakenings are more of a movement, spreading rapidly through regions. Awakenings produce a change in culture, economics, business, the arts, etc. Both are necessary components to the ushering in of The Messiah. Many outpourings of God's Holy Spirit have happened through the course of history such as The Welsh Revival (1904), The Azusa Street Revival (1906), The Healing Crusades of the mid 1900's just to name a few, and I believe there is still another massive wave that will wash over the earth before Jesus returns. While scholars debate the terms and some even dispute previous revivals and awakenings, the truth is that many *unbelievers* will wake up and rise to the truth and many *believers* will be revived with fresh fire to accomplish their God-given purpose.

Jesus stated in Matthew 24:14, "And this gospel of the kingdom shall be preached in all the world for a witness unto all nations; then shall the end come." New technology, social media, and advanced transportation have made it possible for the Good News to reach many. As the Kingdom of God advances and expands, Jews and Gentiles will be added to the body of Christ, and when the news has reached all people, the groom will suddenly return for his bride. A God-given sign in the sky *will* appear before Jesus reappears in the sky!

> "The sun will be darkened, the moon will not shed its light, the stars will fall, and the powers of heaven will be shaken. *Then the sign of the Son of Man will appear in the sky…*" (Matt. 24:29-30, emphasis added).

Knowing this truth, we must be attentive to the end-time events while also occupying where we wait and praying while we tarry.

The Hidden Day

Just as God spoke a word and the world was created, so a sound will come from heaven that will signal the end of the world. It will be a glorious sound of renewal and restoration, redemption and revival. It will call up and call out. Being that Jesus himself was a Jew, I believe it is important that we pay attention to the Jewish festivals and feasts as signs of his return. While some have been fulfilled, such as the Day of Atonement when Jesus became the sacrificial lamb for us, others have not been. The Feast of Trumpets is one of those feasts. Paying attention to the Jewish holidays and festivals can also illuminate the timing of The Rapture.

As discussed in Part I, the Israelites followed a lunar based calendar. The moon's phase was critical to the beginning of a Jewish day, month, and year. It was also significant in the beginning and end of festivals and feasts, sabbaths and holy convocations. A number of major and semi-major Biblical and Rabbinical holidays and festivals revolve around the full moon. The full moon feasts and holidays include Passover and Sukkot (Feast of Tabernacles), which are two of the three pilgrimage festivals, and Purim, a non-Torah festival.[171] One particular festival that was not observed on a full moon but on a sickle moon was The Feast of Trumpets, also known as "The Hidden Day."

Yom Teruah, or Feast of Trumpets, is a loud holiday, marking the beginning of the new Jewish year known as Rosh Hashanah. Yet despite this feast's loud nature, Yom Teruah is the most shrouded in mystery of all its neighbors. It is observed on the first two days of the seventh Jewish month of Tishri (September-October on the Gregorian calendar).[172] The Feast of Trumpets begins a ten day period known as the "High Holy Days" or "Days of Awe." These ten sacred days include self-reflection and repentance which culminates on the fast of Yom Kippur, or The Day of Atonement which is the holiest day in the Jewish year. As The Feast of Trumpet commences, rams' horns are blown throughout temple services. A ram's horn is blown at least 100 times during a typical Rosh Hashanah service. Everyone knows when The Feast of Trumpets has started.

But *when* the Feast of Trumpets begins depends on the new moon, which, if not observed by the naked eye on the first day, then is delayed to the second day. This variableness in timing is why some call The Feast of Trumpets "The Hidden Day." Its beginning is mysterious in timing and meaning. This feast is only mentioned two times in the Torah and the meaning is not very

---

[171] Passover, or Pesach, is the Jewish holiday which commemorates the Israelites liberation from the Egyptians and occurs from the 15th-21st in the month of Nisan (March-April). Sukkot is a week-long celebration of the fall harvest when the Jewish community remembers God's divine provision for the Israelites after they left Egypt and it occurs the 15th-21st days in the seventh Jewish month known as Tishri (September-October). Purim is the Jewish holiday which celebrates the defeat of Haman's plot to massacre the Jewish people as recorded in the book of Esther and it occurs annually on the 14th of Adar, the 12th Jewish month (February-March).

[172] "On the first day of the seventh month, hold a sacred assembly and do no regular work. It is a day for you to sound the trumpets" (Numbers 29:1).

[24] "Speak to the people of Israel, saying, 'In the seventh month, on the first day of the month, you shall observe a day of solemn rest, a memorial proclaimed with a blast of trumpets, a holy convocation. You shall not do any ordinary work, and you shall present a food offering to the LORD'" (Leviticus 23:23-25).

apparent. Ironically, the Hebrew word for trumpet is not used, but the Hebrew word for "blast" (*teruah*) is used, presupposing a trumpet. From Numbers and Leviticus it appears that a shofar (ram's horn) along with silver trumpets were used in the ceremony. This unique clarion call of the trumpets was used before battles to excite the warriors and terrify the enemy. The loud blast is to awaken and warn and can happen at any moment on the first or second day of Tishri.

Since God is the only one who knows the hour in which Jesus will return, the timing and significance in their fullness may only be known to God, but as Christians we can pay attention to the divinely orchestrated placement of the feasts, festivals, and holidays and their connection to the end times. The Feast of Trumpets is yet another compass to add to our bag of clues concerning The Rapture. The feast's placement in the seventh month is strategic, as is the final hour of the tribulation for the saints. The number seven in the Bible has always represented "wholeness" and "fullness." Thus the placement of the Feast of Trumpets in the seventh month is no coincidence.

We also know from Revelation 11:15 that the *seventh* angel sounds his trumpet just before a multitude of voices in heaven declare, "The kingdom of the world has become the kingdom of our Lord and his Messiah, and he will reign forever and ever." There are *seven* seals to be opened, *seven* trumpets, and there will also be *seven* bowls of judgment poured out onto the earth as the final act of God's wrath, and there are *seven* mountains and *seven* kings connected to The Moon Goddess and the beast (Rev. 17:9-10). Seven is an important number in the beginning of time and the end of time. The picture is clear that seven is a purposeful and significant number to God. So while the sighting of the new moon to begin The Feast of Trumpets may be variable, the placement of the feast is not. It always occurs in the seventh month and begins the Jewish new year.

If we assume that the Feast of Trumpets is connected to The Rapture, then the mysteriousness of "The Hidden Day" hides the exact moment in which Jesus will return. The suddenness of such an event will take mankind as well as Satan and his cohorts by surprise. Paul mentions trumpets in his letters to the church at Thessalonica and Corinth:

> "For the Lord himself will descend from heaven with a shout, with the archangel's voice, and with the trumpet of God, and the dead in Christ will rise first. Then we who are still alive, who are left, will be caught up together with them in the clouds to meet the Lord in the air, and so we will always be with the Lord" (1 Thess. 5:16-17).

> "Listen, I tell you a mystery: We will not all sleep, but we will all be changed— in a flash, in the twinkling of an eye, at the last trumpet. For the trumpet will sound, the dead will be raised imperishable, and we will be changed" (1 Cor. 20:51-52).

Again, these are postulations and we should be alert at *all times*, but the significance of timing and the *sound* of God's return is without debate. There will be a literal day in which Jesus will raise up all of those who have put their trust in him. The sun will not strike them by day, nor the moon by night (Psalm 121:6). This day will occur suddenly, like a thief in the night, in the midst of hardship and earthly contractions. Yet, when it happens, the children of God will be protected as the final judgment upon Satan, The Moon Goddess, the Antichrist, the false prophet, and any of their worshipers begins.

Chapter 14

The Birth of the Final Battle

"Shall I bring to the time of birth, and not cause delivery?" says the LORD. "Shall I who cause delivery shut up the womb?" says your God.

Isaiah 66:9, KJV

A s the final end of this age approaches and The Church grows wider with a pregnant, hopeful anticipation for her Messiah, there is a birth taking place within the heart of heaven. It is a birth that has been, is, and will be. While the earth is confined to a time as set by the sun, moon, and stars; heaven knows no time. God has been, is, and will forever be. The vision of the expectant Mother Mary in Revelation 12, the one I mentioned in Chapter 1, is also a glimpse into the final delivery of God's Messiah to his people. Mary cried out in pain as she was about to give birth to Jesus *and* a war. From the beginning of creation, the final outcome was established.

In this vision Satan was cast out of heaven with ⅓ of the angels who joined his cause. In his attempt to exalt himself above God, he was thrown down by God as quick as lightning (Lk. 10:18, Isa. 14:13). As Satan built himself up in pride, his fall was happening simultaneously. Since his expulsion from heaven, he has made it his mission to kill, steal, and destroy God's creation (Jn. 10:10). Just as the short lived tower of Shinar was built to gain access to a heavenly realm illegally, so too will Satan's kingdom attempt to build itself up before his ultimate destruction. He will rally as many troops as he can to war against believers and, in the final Battle of Armageddon, God himself.

Recall from Revelation 12 that when Mary gave birth to Jesus, neither she nor Jesus were harmed by the dragon. In Matthew 2, Herod ordered a mass execution of all Hebrew boys in order to kill Jesus, functioning like Pharaoh who murdered all the Hebrew boys in Exodus 1. But like Pharaoh, Herod's satanic plan failed. As we know, Jesus lived, grew up, and fulfilled his purpose, which according to 1 John 3:8 was to defeat the work of Satan. If we remember that prophecy is past, present, and future, the birth of Jesus through the apocalyptic lens of Revelation gives The Church the outcome of the battle that will take place against Satan, the Antichrist, the False Prophet and The Moon Goddess. That battle has *already* been won.

> "Then war broke out in heaven. Michael and his angels fought against the dragon, and the dragon and his angels fought back. But he was not strong enough, and they lost their place in heaven. The great dragon was hurled down–that ancient serpent called the devil, or Satan, who leads the whole world astray. He was hurled to the earth, and his angels with him" (Rev. 12:7-9).

Enraged that his plans to kill Mary and the child failed, Satan then pursued the daughters and sons of God with full fury, unleashing the limited power he has to devour mankind (Rev. 12:13-17). His agenda was evidenced in the Roman world following Jesus' resurrection, through the middle ages, the Renaissance period, the Reformation, the Enlightenment, and into today. Modern examples include: the insane amount of abortions performed on the altar of Moloch, sex trafficking as worship to The Moon Goddess; idolatry, greed, envy, bribery as worship to Ba'al, twisting of The Gospel as seen in prosperity driven doctrine of some televangelists and ministries; the increased hostility against Christians in the underground churches of China, North Korea, and Iran; World I and II and the genocide of the Jewish people, the eradication of prayer from U.S. school systems in 1962; the increased tension between races; the "normalizing" of gender confusion where men can be women and women can be men; the rise in new age occultism, paganism, Luciferianism, and witchcraft; the Freemasonry and Illuminati secret societies; biological and chemical warfare. Not to mention the backbiting among believers, slander of authorities, lying in the churches, world pestilence and plagues. The world is crying out in agony for the awakening of the sons and daughters of Christ who will prepare the way for Jesus (Rom. 8:19)! Even an atheist will tell you that something isn't right about all the evil in the world. But God through his prophet Isaiah promised a future delivery, not just for Mary and Jesus but also for the sons and daughters of God who are tormented by Satan. God *will* save his people in his perfect, divine timing. The labor pains do not nullify the delivery, they push for the delivery to occur!

Just like the water breaking before the delivery of a baby, and just like Jesus was baptized into water before the fire at Pentecost fell, and just like Jesus walked on water to rescue a fearful, drowning Peter; so too will a massive wave of revival occur as deliverance breaks out across the nations; so too will many people be baptized by water and then walk in fiery faith; so too will many who are fearful by the chaotic storms, plagues, and natural disasters around them be rescued by God who controls the wind and the waves. To be saved from the troubling waters and the unclean spirits, one must be born of a spiritual water, a water from the womb of Heaven, and filled with The Holy Spirit. A person must give their loyalty to Jesus, who is the one and only King, and be baptized in his refreshing, renewing waters and infilled with his precious, all-knowing Holy Spirit. To be born again is to reign victoriously as a child of God and co-heir with Christ (Rom. 8:17).

To live outside of The Holy Spirit is to be in enemy territory, prey to a lion who roams about looking for anyone that he can devour (1 Peter 5:8). To ignore the signs is to miss the appointment. To deny Jesus is to willingly turn a back on the only one who is able to save. The grace period before the return of Christ does have an expiration and that date is approaching rapidly. As the moment of deliverance approaches, The Church is not to hide in a cave and wait it out, but is to put on the full armor of God (Ephesians 6:10-20) and war from a place of victory in Christ. The battle belongs to the Lord; our job is to preach his name in love without compromise, complacency, or cowardice. The Church will wait and war differently when she knows who she is waiting and warring for—the King of Kings and Lord of Lords.

Chapter 15

The Prophecy to End All Prophecies

Love never ends. As for prophecies, they will pass away; as for tongues, they will cease; as for knowledge, it will pass away.

1 Corinthians 13:8, ESV

The prophecy that the moon will turn to blood is the final prophecy to end all prophecies. It is the wrath upon The Moon Goddess that will bring forth the marriage supper for the saints in heaven and the Rider on the White Horse–Jesus–in the Battle of Armageddon on earth. This battle will be won by the bright and shining One, The Morning Star– *Jesus*. The saints will reign with Christ before and after Satan, the accuser of the brethren who deceived the whole world and the one who meets his doom in the lake of fire. The final sign of the moon turning to blood is a prophecy of a final, end-time event; it is Prophecy, Jesus Himself, ending *all* prophecy.

The testimony of Jesus is the spirit of prophecy (Rev. 19:10), meaning if God defeated Satan at the foundation of the world, he can do it at the end of the world; if God delivered the Israelites out of Egypt in the Old Testament, then he can deliver his people out of the hands of Satan under the renewed covenant in Christ; if Jesus created the heavens and the earth before, then he can create them again. Thus Jesus *Himself* is a testimony of the final victory. *He* will execute the triumphant finale of the prophecy when he slaughters The Moon Goddess and her worshipers and he will do this upon his return; not as an earthly Jewish prophet, not as an earthly king, not as a lowly servant but he will judge in righteousness and wage war as The King of Kings and Lord of Lords. Jesus was a prophet and more than a prophet, he was *The Prophet*. He is prophecy and he is the beginning and the end. And so it will be Jesus' final promise through his prophet Joel as repeated in Acts 2, the promise to eradicate the sun and moon gods and goddesses, that will cease all prophecy. What remains will be faith, hope, and love, and the greatest of these will be *love* (1 Corinthians 13:8-13). There will be no more need for prophecies because the restoration of all things will be complete. There will be no more need for preparation because the bride will have married the groom and sat down at a feast prepared for her in the presence of her enemies. In Isaiah's triumphal words,

> "Then the moon will be confounded and the sun ashamed, for the LORD of hosts reigns on Mount Zion and in Jerusalem, and his glory will be before his elders" (Isaiah 24:23).

Chapter 16

The Light of God

Thy word is a lamp unto my feet, and a light unto my path.

Psalm 119:105, KJV

ach March across the luscious islands of Japan, as the sun rises and the moon sets, something beautiful happens, an event that has occurred since God spoke vegetation to the planet. Amid the gray, winterized forests, seafoam green buds begin to emerge on curvy, lichened branches at the first warm ray of spring sun. In just a few short weeks, the lands are peppered with fluffy bundles of dainty pastel pink petals. The Sakura blossoms form a soft pink blanket that covers the land in a sign of renewal. The snow-capped Mount Fuji peaks its head above the blanket as the locals celebrate the sign of hope.

This picture of renewal through the Sakura is a beautiful sign of our Creator who sent his son, Jesus, to be the passover lamb; to renew the covenant, a covenant of hope. The prophecy of the destruction of The Moon Goddess is followed by the promise of hope for all who believe. Everyone who calls upon the name of the Lord *will* be saved (Acts 2:21). They will be born again into the family of Jesus Christ whereby no darkness, no depth, no angel, no demon, neither death nor life, no thing to come, nor any created power will be able to separate them from the love of God that is in Christ Jesus (Rom. 8:38-39). As God birthed his powerful vision for earth and its inhabitants by a spoken word, he made it possible for us to be born into his presence by *His* own word–*Jesus*. The birth of the world was also the world's death and our death to the world is also our birth.

The goddess' doom was foretold at the beginning of creation. The first spirit to hover over the darkness and the surface of the waters of the earth was *The Holy Spirit*, who brought peace and order to the chaos (Gen. 1:1-2). God's first spoken word was, "Let there be light" (Gen. 1:3). This light was not the sun, moon, or stars but was the light of Jesus Christ, the Messiah, the Anointed One. This light was separated from the darkness and God called the light "day" and the dark "night" (Gen. 1:5). This disassociation happened on day one of creation and will happen on the last day of the world as we know it as YHWH begins his renewal in the heavens and in the earth. In Revelation 21, John is allowed to catch a glimpse into the new heaven, the new earth and into the new Jerusalem.

> "I did not see a temple in it, because the Lord God the
> Almighty and the Lamb are its temple. The city does not
> need the sun or the moon to shine on it, because the
> glory of God illuminates it, and its lamp is the Lamb.
> The nations will walk by its light, and the kings of the
> earth will bring their glory into it. Its gates will never
> close by day because it will never be night there" (Rev.
> 21:22-24, HCSB).

John reveals a stunning truth. On day one of creation, God separated the day and the night, the light from the dark. The divine light source was none other than Jesus Christ himself who in one day separated evil from the earth and in one day judged The Moon Goddess (Rev. 18:8). This one day creation event was the beginning and the end of earth. Prophecy Himself–*Jesus*–had a plan of redemption at earth's conception. His testimony would be the fulfillment of all prophecy, a testimony which begins and ends with justice. The blood of the lamb slain at the foundation of the world, who is the precious Son of God, testifies to a triumphant day when the sun will be darkened once and for all and the moon will turn to blood. The blood of Jesus makes it possible for humanity to be born again out of war and into everlasting peace. And his blood testifies to the beginning of a new heaven and a new earth in which the eternal light of Christ, all that is good and holy, will illuminate creation.

The face of Jesus will be the eternal lamp as it reflects the glory of the Father, his powerful word sustaining all things (Heb. 1:3). Signs for seasons will not be needed because the full and final harvest will have been reaped, the final feast will have been consumed, and the final new moon trumpet will have been blown. The sun, moon, and stars will be under his feet, just as they were in the beginning, and the magnificent Prince of Peace will reign supreme forever and ever while his people go out rejoicing.

The moon truly is a *beautiful, beautiful, magnificent destruction.*

Afterword

Like the moon, this book came about in phases. Each part was woven together by God and the information was revealed to me in his timing. Along the journey, The Holy Spirit would uncover the The Blood Moon Prophecy, taking me one mile deeper with every chapter. On the day that I began writing the first chapter, April 8th, 2024, there was a total solar eclipse which drew worldwide attention. I didn't plan to begin on that significant day and was unaware of the event. It wasn't until my children came home from school wearing funny glasses exclaiming they saw the sun darken that I pieced the events together. From Chapter 1, God was already showing me signs in the spiritual *and* the natural.

Each day following, God would lead me on a path of The Blood Moon Prophecy, guiding me by His Spirit. The deeper I went into the book, the more intense the warfare and the more vivid the confirmations became. Confirmations came through news articles popping up on my phone, signs on trucks or street addresses while driving, or my children randomly telling me something about the moon before bed. They didn't know that I was writing a book about the moon, actually no one did. So with each comment or sign, I smiled to myself knowing that this book was ordained.

The warfare also reassured me. The enemy's resistance to this book release was the most extreme and intense warfare I have *ever* experienced. Leading up to this book, my son had an injury to his eye that could have killed him, sickness hit our house to an unbelievable degree, our marriage took a beating, our physical home began falling apart, our farm animals suddenly became terminally sick, our finances were hacked and money was stolen. In fact, the first day that I released to the public that I was working on this book, I had a severe car wreck *that night*, a wreck which should have taken my life and the other driver's life. My car was totaled but thanks be to God that he preserved us! The pushback only pushed me forward in prayer, confidence, and courage. God watches over his word to perform it, and I can assure you that he has watched over every word of this book, helping me push through to its conclusion. God wants this book in your hands.

And even though this book is over, there is still much to be revealed. The end is just the beginning in the Kingdom of God, and as I began to conclude this book, I sensed another word growing in me; a prophecy involving a fig tree, the pacific ocean, a bridge in Boston, and the return of the *Nephilim*.

Stay tuned...

Bibliography

Ahmad, Anis. "Dīn," John L. Esposito (ed.), *The Oxford Encyclopedia of the Islamic World*. Oxford: Oxford University Press, 2009.

Albright, William Foxwell. *Archaeology and the Religion of Israel* (Louisville, KY: Westminster John Knox Press, 2006.

Alvar, Jaime. Translated by Richard Gordan. *Romanising Oriental Gods: Myth, Salvation, and Ethics in the Cults of Cybele, Isis, and Mithras, Spanish Edition.* Leiden: Brill Academic Publishing, 2008.

Andrews, Evan. "9 Blades that Forged History," History.org, 23 Apr. 2018. https://www.history.com/news/knives-that-changed-history

Ausonius, *Eclogue* 23 and *De feriis Romanis* 33–7.

Assmann, Jan. *The Search for God in Ancient Egypt*, Translated by David Lorton. Ithaca, NY: Cornell University Press, 2001.

Barker, Eileen. "My Take: Moon's death marks the end of an era," *The CNN Belief Blog*, 3 September 2012. https://web.archive.org/web/20190829065856/http://religion.blogs.cnn.com/2012/09/03/my-take-moons-death-marks-end-of-an-era/

Binz, Stephen J. *Jerusalem, the Holy City*. Waterford, Connecticut: Twenty-Third Publications, 2005.

Black, Jeremy and Anthony Green. *Gods, Demons, and Symbols of Ancient Mesopotamia: An illustrated dictionary*. The British Museum Press, 1992.

Boettiger Louis A. "Studies in the social Sciences: Armenian Legends and Festivals," *Studies in the Social Sciences: Armenian Legends and Festivals* 14 (1918): 10-11.

Bowden, Hugh. *Mystery Cults of the Ancient World.*Princeton, NJ: Princeton University Press, 2010.

Bozeman, Adda Bruemmer. *Politics and Culture in International History: From the Ancient Near East to the Opening of the Modern Age*. Piscataway, NJ: Transaction Publishers: 1994.

Brandon, S.G.F. *Dictionary of Comparative Religion*. New York City, NY: Charles Scribner's Son, 1970.

Bremmer, Jan N. *Initiation into the Mysteries of the Ancient World*. Berlin: Walter de Gruyter, 2014.

Broad, William J.*The Oracle: Ancient Delphi and the Science Behind Its Lost Secrets*. New York: Penguin Press, 2007.

Brody, Dave and Thomas Lucas, "Death of a Planet," https://www.imdb.com/title/tt15462680/

Cartwright, Mark. "Coatlicue," 28 Nov. 2013, WorldHistoryEncyclopedia.org, https://www.worldhistory.org/Coatlicue/

Cartwright, Mark. "Yomi," World History Encyclopedia. 15 May 2017. https://www.worldhistory.org/Yomi/#

Cloud, Bill. "The Feasts of Israel: The Mystery of the Seven Feasts of Israel," International School of the Word, https://isow.org/.

Cyrino, Monica S. *Aphrodite (Gods and Heroes of the Ancient World)*. New York and London: Routledge, 2010.

Davis, Freddy. "The Unification Church/Moonies," Marketfaith.org, http://www.marketfaith.org/2014/11/the-unification-churchmoonies/

Denecker, Evelien and Katelijn Vandorpe, "Sealed Amphora Stoppers and Tradesmen in Greco-Roman Egypt," *BABESCH*, 82(1): 115-128, DOI:10.2143/BAB.82.1.2020764

De Mente, Boye Lafayette. "Japan Encyclopedia." Chicago, IL: Passport Books, 1995.

Drummand, John Gregory. "Antiochus Epiphanes–The Bible's Most Notoriously Forgotten Villain," Bible Archeology. 24 Nov. 2023. https://www.biblicalarchaeology.org/daily/ancient-cultures/ancient-israel/antiochus-epiphanes-the-bibles-most-notoriously-forgotten-villain/

Fisher, Marc and Jeff Leen. "Stymied in U.S., Moon's Church Sounds a Retreat," WashingtonPost.com, 24 Nov. 1997. https://www.washingtonpost.com/wp-srv/national/longterm/cult/unification/part2.htm

Flurry, Gerald. "The Incredible Origins of Ancient Jerusalem," January-February 2023, *Let the Bones Speak*, https://armstronginstitute.org/843-the-incredible-origins-of-ancient-jerusalem

Flusser, David and Shua Amorai-Stark. "The Goddess Thermuthis, Moses, and Artapanus," *Jewish Studies Quarterly* 1 (3): 217–33, JSTOR 40753100.

Franci, Massimiliano. "Isis-Thermouthis and the anguiform deities in Egypt: a cultural and semantic evolution," *A Journal of Intercultural and Archeology* (2) 2016: 35-40.

Garret, Duane A. and Paul Ferris. *Hosea, Joel: An Exegetical and Theological Exposition of Holy Scripture*. Nashville: Holman Reference, 1997.

Griffin, Annette. "What Do We Know About Semiramis, Nimrod's Wife?" 22 Jan. 2024, BibleStudyTools.com, https://www.biblestudytools.com/bible-study/topical-studies/who-was-semiramis-the-wife-of-nimrod.html

Hanson, Arthur J. *Metamorphoses (The Golden Ass), Volume II: Books 7–11*. Harvard University Press, 1989.

Hastings, James. *A Dictionary of the Bible Volume II: (Part II:I-Kinsman), Volume 2*. Honolulu, Hawaii: University Press of the Pacific, 2004.

Herodotus. The History of Herodotus,Vol 2. 4 vols. Translated by George Rawlinson. New York: Tandy-Thomas Co., 1909.

Hill, Andrew E. *Haggai, Zechariah, Malachi: An Introduction and Commentary*. Illinois; IVP Academic, 2012.

Hislop, Alexander. *The Two Babylons*. https://archive.org/details/theTwoBabylons.

Homer, *Iliad*, Translated by Samuel Butler, Barnes and Noble, 1995.

Hooke, S.H. *Middle Eastern Mythology*. North Chelmsford, MA: Courier Corporation, 2004.

Hundson, Myles. "Fall of Constantinople," *Encyclopedia Britannica*, https://www.britannica.com/event/Fall-of-Constantinople-145

Jones, Kurt. "Japan," Volcano Folklore, Oregon State University. https://volcano.oregonstate.edu/japan-0#:~:text=The%20creation%20of%20Mt.,coming%20from%20under%20the%20Earth.

Josephus. Translated by William Whiston 10 vols. LCL. Cambridge; Harvard University Press, 1999.

Kilroy-Ewbank, Lauren."Coatlicue," Khan Academy, https://www.khanacademy.org/humanities/art-americas/early-cultures/aztec-

mexica/a/
coatlicue#:~:text=The%20myth%20notes%20that%20several,by%20offeri
ng%20their%20own%20lives.
Lane, Eugene N. *Cybele, Attis, and Related Cults: Essays in Memory of M.J. Vermaseren Religions in the Graeco-Roman World.* Brill Academic Publishing, 1996.
Larsen, B. "A Brief History of Shinto and Buddhism in Japan," The Culture Trip, 21 Apr. 2018. https://theculturetrip.com/asia/japan/articles/a-brief-history-of-shinto-and-buddhism-in-japan/
Leick, Gwendolyn. *Sex and Eroticism in Mesopotamian Literature.* New York, NY: Routledge, 2013.
Livingston, Dave. "The Fall of the Moon City," 2003, http://davelivingston.com/mooncity.htm
Lužný, Dušan and David Václavík. "Církev sjednocení [Unification Church]" Czech, 1997.
Lynch, Mike. "Sky Watch: Orion and Artemis and forbidden love," 14 Feb. 2016, Twin Cities Pioneer Press, https://www.twincities.com/2016/02/14/sky-watch-mike-lynch-orion/
Marini, Paolo. "Renenutet: worship and popular piety at Thebes in the New Kingdom," *Journal of Intercultural and Interdisciplinary Archaeology* (2) 2015, 73-84.
Mark, Joshua J. "Sammu-Ramat and Semiramis: The Inspiration and the Myth," *World History Encyclopedia,* https://www.worldhistory.org/article/743/sammu-ramat-and-semiramis-the-inspiration-and-the/.
Mark, Joshua J. "The Egyptian Afterlife & The Feather of Truth," *World History Encyclopedia.* 30 Mar. 2018, https://www.worldhistory.org/article/42/the-egyptian-afterlife--the-feather-of-truth/
Mark, Joshua J. "Ba'al," WorldHistory.org, 5 Nov. 2021, https://www.worldhistory.org/baal/#google_vignette
Mark, Joshua J. "Inanna's Descent: A Sumerian Tale of Injustice," World History Encyclopedia, 23 Feb. 2011, https://www.worldhistory.org/article/215/inannas-descent-a-sumerian-tale-of-injustice/
Marcellinus, Ammianus. *History, Volume I: Books 14-19.* Translated by J. C. Rolfe. Loeb Classical Library 300. Cambridge, MA: Harvard University Press, 1950.
Merkelbach, Reinhold. "Mystery Religion," *Encyclopedia Britannica,* https://www.britannica.com/topic/mystery-religion
Merrell, Nathan. "Nimrod, Semiramis, and the Mystery Religion of Babylon," https://findinghopeministries.org/nimrod-the-mystery-religion-of-babylon/
Merrill, Steven. *Nimrod: Darkness in the Cradle of Civilization.* Maitland, FL: Xulon Press, 2004.
Mutch, Alexa. "Olympias," *Women in Antiquity Blog,* 2 Apr. 2017, https://womeninantiquity.wordpress.com/2017/04/02/olympias/
Nickel, Keith F. *The Synoptic Gospels: An Introduction.* Louisville, KY: Westminster John Knox Press, 2001.
O'Dell, Cary. "In Search of 'Sailor Moon'" Library of Congress Bloggs, 31 Aug. 2022.https://blogs.loc.gov/now-see-hear/2022/08/in-search-of-sailor-moon/

#:~:text=On%20a%20global%20scale%2C%20%E2%80%9CSailor,been
%20put%20on%20the%20market.

Onion, Amanda and Missy Sullivan et al. (eds.), "Bombing of Hiroshima and
Nagasaki," History.com, https://www.history.com/topics/world-war-ii/
bombing-of-hiroshima-and-nagasaki

Oshita, Hideo. "Shinto, the 'Way of the Gods': What is Shintoism?"
MinistryMagazine.org, March 1949. https://www.ministrymagazine.org/
archive/1949/03/shinto-the-way-of-the-gods

Ozaki, Yai Theodora. "The Tale of the Bamboo Cutter and the Moon-Child"
in *Japanese Fairytales* Lit2Go Edition. New York: A.L. Burt Company, 1908.
https://etc.usf.edu/lit2go/72/japanese-fairy-tales/4834/the-bamboo-
cutter-and-the-moon-child/

Pinch, Geraldine. *Egyptian mythology: a guide to the gods, goddesses, and traditions of
ancient Egypt.* New York: Oxford University Press, 2003.

Plutarch, "De Defectu Oraculorum (Περὶ τῶν Ἐκλελοιπότων Χρηστηρίων),"
Translated by F.C. Babbitt, Vol. V Loeb Classical Library Edition, 1936.

Plutarch, *Lives (Dryden Trans. Vol 1)*, Edited by A.H Clough, Translated by John
Dryden, https://oll.libertyfund.org/titles/clough-plutarch-s-lives-dryden-
trans-vol-1;

Poushter, Jacob. "In nations with significant Muslim populations, much disdain
for ISIS," Pew Research Center, 17 Nov. 2015. https://
www.pewresearch.org/short-reads/2015/11/17/in-nations-with-significant-
muslim-populations-much-disdain-for-isis/
#:~:text=Distaste%20toward%20ISIS%20was%20shared,Shia%20Muslim
s%20and%20Lebanese%20Christians.

Pryke, Louise. "Ishtar," World History Encyclopedia, 10 May 2019, https://
www.worldhistory.org/ishtar/#google_vignette

Pryke, Louise M. *Ishtar.* New York and London: Routledge, 2017.

Reynolds, Isabel. "Japan Seeks to Dissolve Unification Church Connected to
Shinzo Abe's Assassination," TIME.com, 12 Oct. 2023, https://time.com/
6322931/japan-unification-church-disbandment-shinzo-abe/

Roberson, Cliff and Dilip K. Das. *An Introduction to Comparative Legal Models of
Criminal Justice.* FL: CRC Press, 2008.

Roller, Lynn Emrich. *In Search of God the Mother: The Cult of Anatolian Cybele*
Berkeley and Los Angeles, California: University of California Press, 1999.

Roscoe, Will and Stephen Murray. *Islamic Homosexualities: Culture, History, and
Literature.* New York, NY: New York University Press, 1997.

Sahih al-Bukhari 4953.

Sehgal, Sunil. *Encyclopaedia of Hinduism.* Sarup & Sons: 1999.

Siddiqui, Mona. "Ibrahim - the Muslim view of Abraham," BBC.co.uk, 4 Sept.
2009. https://www.bbc.co.uk/religion/religions/islam/history/
ibrahim.shtml

Simkovich, Malka Z. "Pharaoh's Daughter: A Woman Worthy of Raising
Moses," TheTorah.Com, 2002, https://thetorah.com/article/pharaohs-
daughter-a-woman-worthy-of-raising-moses

Smith, Billy K., and Frank Page. *Amos, Obadiah, Jonah: An Exegetical and Theological
Exposition of Holy Scripture (Volume 19) (The New American Commentary)* (Holmon
Reference: 1995), Amos, Section 1, Ebook edition.

Smith, William. "Entry for 'Lead'". *Smith's Bible Dictionary*, 1901. https://
www.biblestudytools.com/dictionary/lead/#google_vignette

Sluijs van der, Marinus Anthony and Peter James. "Saturn as the 'Sun of
Night' in Ancient Near Eastern Tradition," Universitat de Barcelona: 2013.

Spangler, Ann and Lois Tverberg. *Sitting at the Feet of Rabbi Jesus: How the
Jewishness of Jesus Can Transform Your Faith*. Grand Rapids, MI: Zondervan
Academic, 2009.

Strong, James. *Strong's Exhaustive Concordance of the Bible*. Peabody, MA:
Hendrickson Publishing Marketing, LLC, 2007.

Tamilla, Krista. "The Syncretism of Shinto and Buddhism in Japan," Stear
Think Tank, 4 Aug. 2021.
https://www.stearthinktank.com/post/japan-syncretism-of-shinto-and-
buddhism

Thompson, J.Eric S. *Maya History and Religion (Volume 99) (The Civilization of the
American Indian Series)*. University of Oklahoma Press, 1990.

Thornhill, Richard. "Sarasvati in Japan," Hinduism Today, 1 Oct. 2002.
https://www.hinduismtoday.com/magazine/october-november-
december-2002/2002-10-sarasvati-in-japan/

Vijgen, Richard and Bregtje van der Haak. "Pentecostalism: Massive Global
Growth Under the Radar," Pulitzer Center. 9 Mar. 2015. https://
pulitzercenter.org/stories/pentecostalism-massive-global-growth-under-
radar

Wade, Jenny. "The Castrated Gods and their Castration Cults: Revenge,
Punishment, and Spiritual Supremacy," *International Journal of Transpersonal
Studies* 38(1). https://doi.org/10.24972/ijts.2019.38.1.31.

Walton, John H. *Ancient Near Eastern Thought and the Old Testament Second Edition*.
Grand Rapids, MI: Baker Academic, 2018.

Whiston, William. *Of the Thundering Legion*. London, 1726.

Wiener, James. "Egyptian Relations with Canaan," 7 Jul. 2016, https://
etc.worldhistory.org/interviews/egyptian-relations-canaan/

Wiedemann, Thomas E.J. *Emperors and Gladiators*. Routledge: 1995.

Wolkstein, Diane and Samuel Noah Kramer. *Inanna, Queen of Heaven and Earth:
Her stories and hymns from Sumer*. New York City, New York: Harper & Row
Publishers, 1983.

Yoshihide, Sakurai. "The Unification Church and Its Japanese Victims: The
Need for 'Religious Literacy.' Nippon.com, 28 Oct. 2022. https://
www.nippon.com/en/in-depth/d00845/

ZA Blog. "What the Bible Tells Us about the 10 Plagues of Egypt," Zondervan
Academic (2018), https://zondervanacademic.com/blog/what-the-bible-
tells-us-about-the-10-plagues-of-egypt

About the Author

Lauren J. Brown is founder of SOUND Ministries, Testimony Magazine, LJB Prophetic Art and The Elijah Crusade. She holds a B.S. in Biology Pre-Professional from The University of Tennessee Chattanooga and a M.A. in Biblical Theology from Jakes Divinity School. She currently lives in Georgia and is a proud wife to her high-school sweetheart, joyful mother to their three precious children, and grateful servant of Jesus whose heart is to see the knowledge of the glory of the Lord cover the earth as the waters cover the sea.

Concluding Prayer

Our Father, who art in heaven, hallowed be thy name. We extol you! We praise you and we thank you for your redeeming blood! You are glorious, magnificent, and wonderful and your love knows no bounds! We thank you for your awesome power, your sustaining Word, and your infinite wisdom. Forgive us our trespasses as we forgive others who have trespassed against us. Keep us from evil in the days to come, shield us from the darts of doubt and destruction, deliver us from the sorrows of this world, and keep us tuned to Your Holy Spirit; our mind set on things above.

May you place your angels around us as we pursue the mark of the prize of our high calling and as we set our gaze upon Jesus, the author and finisher of our faith.

We pray that Your will would be done in the earth as it is in heaven, that your Church would be purified and your Bride adorned with the crown of wisdom, glory, and power. Give us the joy of strength and grant us stamina to resist the schemes and wiles of the devil. Help us to take up the sword of the Spirit— which is the word of God— to dispel and disarm the enemy.

Empower us, O' Lord, to pull down every evil spirit that has set itself up against the knowledge of who You are, guide our feet by Your light into the paths of righteousness, and equip us with knowledge in this hour.

The victory is Yours, the battle has been won, and we are the servants of The Lord of the Harvest.

Send us, Father, to the field…

In Jesus' name, Amen.

Made in the USA
Columbia, SC
05 January 2025

48929995R00146